The Mysterious Mr. Oliver

EMMA MELBOURNE

One

Mayfair, London
April, 1817

"Mr. Oliver, my lord," Matthews announced. "Here to apply for the position of land agent at Stonecroft."

The Earl of Langley gave his butler a nod, and seconds later a young man strode into his study. Mr. Oliver was a tall man with an athletic build, dressed neatly but simply in a blue waistcoat and dark trousers. Langley put his age at around thirty, although his hazel eyes looked older.

Oliver bowed, and Langley gestured to the chair on the other side of his mahogany desk.

"Have a seat, Oliver," Langley instructed.

"Thank you, my lord."

Langley stood and strolled to a sideboard, giving Oliver the chance to survey his prospective employer. The earl, who was in his early thirties, was casually dressed in buckskin breeches and riding boots. His hair and eyes were dark, and his expression gave no hint of his thoughts.

Langley poured two glasses of brandy from an elegant cut glass decanter and set one in front of Oliver before resuming his seat. "You understand the position is temporary?" he asked.

"Yes, sir."

"Very good," Langley said. "My current land agent, Mr. Pettigrew, is taking a leave because his father is ill, and I've told him I'll hold the position. He expects to be away for three months, possibly four."

Oliver nodded. "I understand. That would suit me very well." He doubted many men would be kind enough to accommodate a leave of absence as Langley was doing for Mr. Pettigrew. Either Langley was a particularly generous employer or Mr. Pettigrew was a particularly capable land agent.

Langley glanced down at some papers on his desk, and Oliver recognized the letter he had written to apply for the position.

"You fought for Wellington?" the earl asked.

Oliver nodded. "Yes, for five years. I was an officer in the Light Dragoons."

"You must find civilian life dull after the excitement of battle."

"I didn't find battle exciting, sir," Oliver said quietly. He fidgeted in his chair and tried not to think about the glass of brandy sitting in front of him. It was excellent brandy and deserved to be savoured, but it was taking all of his willpower to sip it slowly.

Langley steepled his fingers and looked back at the papers in front of him. "You come highly recommended by your commanding officer. He writes that you're a natural leader with great tactical instincts, and he frequently benefited from your advice."

"He is very kind."

"He is, although I'm not sure those skills are relevant. I can't recall when we last ran a military campaign at Stonecroft," Langley said dryly. "What do you know about estate management?"

"My father owns land in Derbyshire, and I helped with the farming while I was growing up. He has all the usual crops and livestock."

Langley nodded. "Stonecroft is my primary seat, and it's a large estate. There's a bailiff to help collect the rents, but the land agent has vast responsibilities."

"I understand, my lord, and I think I am equal to the task."

Langley looked at him thoughtfully, and Oliver decided to take a risk.

"I grew up close to a ducal estate, and I was acquainted with the land agent there," Oliver explained. "I helped him in the summers, and he taught me a great deal."

"I see," Langley replied. Oliver held his breath and waited for the earl to ask for the name of the estate, but he didn't.

"Is there anyone who could speak to your knowledge of farming?" Langley asked.

Oliver shook his head. "I'm afraid not, sir."

The earl raised an eyebrow. "No? What about the land agent with whom you were acquainted?"

Oliver shook his head. "He retired, and we have lost touch."

Langley smiled enigmatically. "I don't suppose there's any point in asking for a reference from the duke?"

"None at all," Oliver admitted.

Langley nodded, and didn't appear surprised. "I understand you went to Cambridge?"

"Yes, sir." Oliver sipped his brandy and noticed that although his glass was almost empty, the earl's was barely touched.

"I was at Oxford, and likely only a few years ahead of you," Langley told him. "I expect we have some acquaintances in common."

"I think it's unlikely, sir," Oliver lied, for he had actually met Langley at a dinner party years before. He wondered if the earl would recognize him, but he thought the odds were in his favour. Since his return to London two months earlier, Oliver had passed several of his former friends in the street, and none had known him. This had surprised him, as he had made it through the war without serious injury, and his features were fundamentally unchanged.

There were other differences, though. Oliver had joined the army as a callow young man, but five years as a soldier had hardened both his body and his attitude. Before he enlisted, he had considered himself a gentleman of fashion, and he was ashamed to remember how much time he had spent getting dressed every day. Now his clothes were practical rather than fashionable, and he could put them on without the help of a valet. Instead of being coaxed into fashionable disorder, his dark blond hair was cropped short, and any disorder was naturally achieved.

Langley leaned back and sipped his brandy. His

expression was inscrutable, but although Oliver found this frustrating, it wasn't a surprise; the earl was known as a man who didn't show his feelings. Six years ago, Langley had been jilted at the altar, and his calm response to the rejection had led the gossips to conclude that he didn't feel emotion. Oliver knew this was ridiculous; he had seen enough of the world to know that all men show emotion with the right provocation.

Langley was also rumoured to be cold, but Oliver wasn't convinced that was true either. The earl had not only given his land agent, Mr. Pettigrew, a leave of absence, he had given Oliver a glass of the finest brandy he had ever tasted. Oliver knew Langley had married the year before, and the union was reportedly a happy one. Perhaps the new countess had softened him.

Oliver hoped his own expression didn't show how desperately he wanted the position, and that he didn't know what he would do if Langley didn't give it to him. He could look for a job as a secretary, or a clerk in a solicitor's office, but he knew that if he spent his days behind a desk he would go mad. The money from the sale of his commission might last several years if he was frugal, but the idea of a frugal life in London held little appeal.

Oliver certainly didn't have the money to rejoin the *ton*, and his pride wouldn't allow him to resume his real name and live in London in a smaller way. Doing so might embarrass his father, which was almost reason enough to do it, but he was mature enough to know it was foolish to make decisions based on spite. He was twenty-seven years old, and he needed to be his own man.

So Oliver knew he had to leave London, which was littered with his relations and former acquaintances, and where it was only a matter of time before he was recognized. A position at Stonecroft seemed like the perfect solution.

"I should tell you about my wife," Langley finally said.

Oliver almost laughed. There was certainly no need for Langley to warn him to stay away from the countess, since he had had no interest in women since he joined the army.

"I assure you, my lord, you have nothing to fear on that score," Oliver said. "I doubt I will ever cross paths with Lady Langley."

The earl smiled. "Oh, she may cross your path. She's interested in farming, and she has some strong opinions on how things should be done. She assisted Pettigrew on occasion."

"I see," Oliver said, trying to hide his surprise.

Langley's expression softened to one of pride. "Lady Langley is with child and expects to be confined this summer."

"Congratulations, my lord."

"Thank you. She has promised not to exert herself, but I fear her definition of exertion differs from mine. If you think she is doing more than is suitable for a lady in her condition, I would like to be informed."

"Of course, sir," Oliver said, with more confidence than he felt. None of the ladies of his acquaintance had been interested in farming, and he wasn't sure what degree of exertion was suitable for a countess who was expecting a child.

"Very good," Langley said abruptly. "When can you start?"

"Are you offering me the position, my lord?"

"Don't look so surprised, Oliver, or I may change my mind," Langley said dryly.

"I can start immediately. I have no other commitments."

"There's a cottage on the estate for the land agent's use. Could you be ready to go to Stonecroft tomorrow?"

"Yes." Oliver had very few belongings to pack, and there was no one in London he wished to see before he left.

"Excellent. Leave your address with the butler, and my coachman will call for you at ten tomorrow morning."

"That won't be necessary, sir," said Oliver, who could hardly believe the earl was proposing to send him to Stonecroft in his carriage. "I can take the mail coach to Kent."

"I don't doubt that you could, but I want you to go in my coach," Langley said. "Pettigrew left last week, so I would like you at Stonecroft as soon as possible."

"I hate to put your coachman to the trouble," Oliver protested.

"It's hardly a kindness, Oliver. In my absence, you will have authority over all of my outdoor staff and my tenants. I'd like to show them that I respect you enough to send you down in my carriage." Langley smiled. "Don't underrate yourself, Oliver, or you'll encourage others to do the same."

"Yes, my lord."

Langley stood to indicate the interview was over, and Oliver expected him to ring for the butler. Instead, the earl walked to the study door to show Oliver out himself.

As Oliver walked down the hallway beside the earl, someone collided with his right arm. He turned and beheld a young lady with honey blonde hair and blue eyes, wearing a gown of cream sprigged muslin. She was standing in front of a doorway, and Oliver realized she must have walked out of a room and straight into him. The girl appeared to be lost in her own thoughts, and there was a depth to her eyes that suggested her thoughts were worth knowing. Oliver thought she was the most enchanting woman he had ever seen.

"I beg your pardon," Oliver said politely. He was keen to hear her voice and learn if it was as charming as the rest of her.

But the beauty barely nodded to him before turning and continuing down the hallway. Oliver felt as though he were invisible, and he reflected that to such a young lady, he probably was.

Langley cleared his throat, and Oliver realized his eyes had followed the girl down the hall.

"My wife's sister, Miss Isabelle Fleming," Langley told him. "She lives with us."

Oliver forced himself to look away from Miss Fleming's retreating figure, and for a moment, he regretted giving up his former life. As Stonecroft's temporary land agent, he could never aspire to court a young lady like Miss Isabelle Fleming.

Two

The Countess of Langley, formerly Miss Amelia Fleming, sat in the drawing room with a pile of letters in her hand. Amelia's appearance was little changed from that of the determined young lady who had captured the earl's heart a year ago. Although she now had a lady's maid, her red hair was styled in a simple knot, since she hated to spend time having it elaborately dressed. Her apple-green gown was simple too, although it had been made by one of London's most exclusive modistes, and its graceful lines concealed the fact that she was expecting her first child. The most significant change was in Amelia's expression, where her former look of anxiety had been replaced by one of contentment. She smiled when Isabelle entered the drawing room.

"It's about time you showed up," Amelia said to her younger sister. "I was getting impatient. Reading your letters is a highlight of my day, but I didn't want to start without you."

Nineteen-year-old Isabelle Fleming was enjoying a

very successful London Season. She was widely considered to be one of the most beautiful young ladies of the year, and had earned the nickname of the Irresistible Isabelle. The Langleys' townhouse was flooded with gifts from her many admirers, including flowers, fruit baskets, and poetry praising various parts of her anatomy. Since it was not entirely proper for Isabelle to receive letters from gentlemen, she and Amelia compromised by reading the letters together.

Amelia squinted at a letter and laughed. "Listen to this, Isabelle: Lord Islington writes that your eyes remind him of the sea in a storm." She glanced at her sister, who was staring out the window, apparently deep in thought. "Isabelle?"

"I'm sorry, Amelia, I wasn't listening," Isabelle said apologetically.

"Dreaming about one of your other suitors, no doubt," Amelia teased.

"Something like that," Isabelle said vaguely. She was actually thinking of the stranger from the hallway, and of the way his hazel eyes had gleamed with humour as he apologized for a collision that hadn't been his fault. Isabelle was trying to write a novel, and had been so distracted by a difficult plot point that she had walked out of the library without paying attention to where she was going. To make matters worse, she had been too flustered to acknowledge the stranger's apology, and had carried on as though nothing had happened. Isabelle hadn't recognized the man, but she had sensed his eyes on her as she continued down the hallway. She supposed he must think her impolite, or at best, very nearsighted.

The Earl of Langley strolled into the room and took a seat on the sofa next to his wife.

"Are you reading the letters?" he asked innocently.

"You can see that we are," Amelia said. She smiled at her husband before turning to Isabelle. "Robert would never admit it, but he enjoys the letters even more than I do."

Langley put an arm around Amelia's shoulders. "I enjoy anything that allows me to spend time with my wife."

"Well, you'll appreciate this," Amelia said with a chuckle. "Lord Islington compares Isabelle's eyes to the sea in a storm."

"I don't see why that's funny," Isabelle said mildly. Amelia had a practical disposition, and until she had fallen in love with the earl, she had had very little patience for poetry or sentiment. Although the love letters rarely touched Isabelle's emotions, she appreciated the courage it took to put thoughts down on a page, and she took a more tolerant view of her admirers' literary efforts.

"Well, during a storm the sea is grey, because the water reflects light from the clouds, or brown, because the waves stir up the sand," Amelia explained. "But your eyes are blue."

"I don't think it's meant to be taken quite so literally," Isabelle said, thinking that only her sister could take such a prosaic view. "I think he was trying to convey a sense of beauty and passion."

Amelia smiled. "If you say so. Let's see if the next one is any better."

"I'm not sure this kind of excitement is good for a lady

EMMA MELBOURNE

in your condition," Langley remarked. "Perhaps you should let me screen Isabelle's letters."

"Nonsense, Robert," Amelia said. "Although I'm increasing, I'm not an invalid. Besides, I think I'm a better judge of what's appropriate for an innocent young lady to read, since I have been a young lady and you have not."

Langley's lips twitched. "Do you no longer consider yourself a young lady?"

Amelia considered the question. "I suppose I'm still young, but no longer innocent."

Isabelle rolled her eyes. "I think your conversation is more scandalous than anything in the letters." She had lived with the Langleys since Amelia's marriage the year before, and while she couldn't ask for a better sister and brother-in-law, she often felt like she was intruding on a love story. Langley had always been an attentive husband, and he was spending even more time with Amelia as her pregnancy progressed.

Amelia unfolded another letter. "Oh, Isabelle, here's another poem from your Anonymous Admirer." Over the past several weeks, Isabelle had received several poems signed only 'An Admirer,' which had given Amelia and Langley a great deal of amusement. Amelia skimmed the poem and dissolved into giggles.

"If you're going to read the letters, it's only fair that you read them aloud," Langley complained. He looked over Amelia's shoulder to read the note.

Dear Miss Fleming, your cheekbones,
Are the loveliest I've ever known.
I love both the right and left,
And when you leave, I am bereft.

You are my destiny.
An Anonymous Admirer.

At that moment, Langley's brother, The Honourable Adrian Stone, walked in and found the countess convulsed with laughter and the earl speechless. At twenty-one, Adrian was as tall as the earl, but the resemblance ended there. While Langley was dark, Adrian was fair, with angelic features that belied his mischievous nature. He had recently come down from Oxford and decided it was time for him to move out of his brother's house, so he now lived in rented rooms on the edge of Mayfair. Since he wasn't ready to give up his brother's chef, Adrian still dined with the Langleys several times a week.

Adrian bowed to Isabelle. "What's all this?" he asked, looking at the letters curiously.

"I have received another poem from my Anonymous Admirer," Isabelle explained.

Adrian raised his eyebrows. "Is it a comic poem?"

"I don't think it's meant to be comic, but Amelia is easily amused," Isabelle said dryly.

Amelia finally found her voice. "Isabelle, you haven't even read it yet."

Adrian plucked the poem from Amelia's hand and read it aloud. "Lord, Isabelle, you should have told me you wanted poetry," he told her. "I could do much better than this, and I wouldn't even mention your cheekbones."

"You don't like my cheekbones?" Isabelle asked, in mock dismay.

"As cheekbones go, yours are exquisite," Adrian reassured her. "But I don't think I would put them in a poem."

"What would you put in a poem?" Amelia asked.

Adrian thought for a moment, then tried:

> Dear Isabelle, it is my duty,
> To tell you that you are a beauty.

Amelia frowned. "I'm not sure it's wise to tell a lady that you're complimenting her out of duty."

Adrian thought for a minute before trying again:

> Dear Isabelle, you're beautiful,
> I say this of my own free will.

This time, all three of his listeners laughed.

"I'm sure that even Lord Byron didn't get it right on his first attempt," Adrian said good-naturedly. "How about this?"

> Whenever I gaze upon Isabelle's face,
> My heart is set a-flutter.

He paused and wrinkled his forehead in concentration.

"I'd like to see what you find to rhyme with flutter," Amelia remarked.

Adrian thought for another minute, then smiled and completed his poem:

> Her eyes are as blue as the summer skies,
> Her hair is blonde, like butter.

"I'm pleased to learn you weren't wasting your time at Oxford," Langley said.

"Perhaps I'll become a poet," Adrian mused. "It can't be very difficult."

"Excellent idea," Langley agreed. "Let me know when you're earning enough money to support yourself."

Adrian looked at his brother with surprise. "Oh, I don't expect to earn any money from it."

"You just said you didn't think it would be difficult," Langley pointed out.

"I mean I wouldn't try to sell my work. That would cheapen it, don't you think?"

"On the contrary, I think it would make it more valuable," Langley replied.

"The value of art can't be measured in pounds and pence," Adrian said loftily. "I am above such worldly concerns."

"I'm pleased to hear you say so," Langley said with a wry smile. "Because I was thinking of decreasing your allowance."

"What?" Adrian exclaimed, looking affronted. "When I can hardly scrape by as it is! With prices what they are, it's a miracle I can keep a roof over my head. Just last week I had to pay Hoby twenty pounds for these boots!" He stretched out his legs to admire his Hessians. "But they are splendid, don't you think?"

"Works of art," Langley agreed. "I'm surprised Hoby could put a price on them."

Adrian looked at his brother suspiciously. "Are you roasting me, Robert?"

"Never," Langley lied. "Am I to understand that you would like me to continue your allowance?"

"Well, yes, unless you want me to give up my rooms and move back here," Adrian said.

"You make a good argument," Langley said.

Adrian looked gratified by the compliment. "Thank you, Robert."

"There are still several more letters to review," Amelia pointed out, as she unfolded another sheet.

Adrian smiled mischievously. "You know, Isabelle, you could just marry me and be done with all this nonsense from your suitors."

Isabelle had lost count of the number of times Adrian had asked her to marry him, and it had become something of a family joke. Everyone knew he didn't expect her to say yes, and he wouldn't know quite what to do if she did.

"Perhaps she is looking for a husband with the means to support her," Langley remarked. "Are you proposing to move her into your rooms?"

"Now, Robert, surely you would increase my allowance if I got married?" Adrian said.

Isabelle laughed. "Now I understand why you want to marry me."

"What? Oh, I've been asking Robert to increase my allowance for years, but I never thought of marriage until I saw you," Adrian said.

"You're a born romantic, Adrian," Langley said.

"Well, you promised to give Isabelle a dowry," Adrian pointed out.

"But there's really no need," Isabelle protested, looking at Lord Langley shyly. The earl had already been tremendously generous to her family. Two years ago, Isabelle's father had drowned in the Thames after losing a fortune to Langley at cards, and her family had been left in debt to the earl. Langley had not only forgiven the debt, he had also forgiven Isabelle's brother William for shooting him in a duel. It spoke to the depth of his love for Amelia, and Isabelle knew her sister was incredibly fortunate. She was beginning to despair of ever finding a man who would love her the way the Earl of Langley loved Amelia.

"Rest assured, Isabelle, that my motives are entirely selfish," Langley told her. "I am hoping to rid my house of your many admirers."

"But if Isabelle married me, it would solve the problem of her admirers," Adrian said. "And with the dowry, we could afford to set ourselves up in a house."

"I'm sorry, Adrian, but I couldn't give Isabelle a dowry if she married you," Langley said apologetically. "Her brother might think I approved of the match, and I would hate to be challenged to another duel."

"You shouldn't joke about duelling, Robert," Amelia said reproachfully. "When I think of how worried I was when you were shot–"

"I'm sorry, sweetheart," Langley said repentantly. "You have nothing to fear on that score. I have no wish to be shot again." He paused. "Although if I had the right woman to nurse me, the convalescence might not be so bad."

Amelia attempted to swat her husband on the arm, but he caught her hand easily and drew it onto his lap. She rested her head on his shoulder.

Adrian was still contemplating the problem of his allowance. After a moment's reflection, he turned back to his brother. "Robert," he asked hopefully. "Would you consider increasing my allowance if I promised not to marry Isabelle?"

Langley smiled. "I think that if you continue to pursue the matter, you risk having your allowance cut off completely."

Adrian's face fell. "But that's hardly reasonable," he argued.

"If you find your income inadequate for your needs, Adrian, I could offer you a job," Langley suggested.

"What sort of job?" Adrian asked suspiciously.

"Mr. Pettigrew's father is sick, so he will be away for several months," Langley explained. "I need someone to manage Stonecroft."

Adrian's brow furrowed. "I suppose I could try, Robert, but I have no experience in estate management."

"Would you like to learn?" Langley asked.

Adrian considered the question. "Probably not," he said honestly. "Pettigrew always seems to be working, and I think I would find that tedious. You might do better to hire a replacement for him."

Langley smiled. "All right."

"But I wouldn't mind going to Stonecroft," Adrian said thoughtfully. "And perhaps I could help with some of the work until Pettigrew's replacement starts."

"You're always welcome at Stonecroft, but I've already hired Pettigrew's replacement," Langley told him. "Mr. Oliver will start this week."

"Then why did you ask if I wanted to do it?" Adrian asked. "You hardly need two men for the job."

Langley sighed. "Would you believe I forgot about Mr. Oliver? I have a horrible memory, you know."

"I suppose it's to be expected as you get older," Adrian said kindly.

"I suppose it is," Langley agreed. "We're leaving for Stonecroft on Friday if you'd like to come with us."

"I believe I will," Adrian said. He noticed that Amelia was smothering a yawn. "Are you still keeping your lovely wife up at night?" he teased his brother good-naturedly.

"Don't forget that I can still rescind your invitation to Stonecroft," Langley replied. He turned to Amelia and searched her face for signs of fatigue. "Do you still plan to go to the Somertons' ball? If you're tired, perhaps you should stay home."

"I wouldn't mind staying home tonight," Isabelle said quickly. She had been to so many balls that she was beginning to find them wearisome.

"Nonsense, I am never tired, and it will do me good to get out of the house," Amelia said briskly.

"Then I will join you," Langley suggested.

Amelia laughed. "Don't be silly, Robert, I know how much you dislike going to balls. I thought you had plans to dine with Mr. Kincaid this evening?"

"Lucas would understand."

Amelia shrugged. "He might, but I would feel guilty for spoiling your evening." She smiled at her husband. "If it will make you feel better, I'll go up to rest for an hour."

"I'll go up with you," Isabelle said. She was eager to get back to her novel, as she thought she had found a solution to the problem with her plot.

"Come to my room for a minute," Amelia said, as they reached the top of the stairs. "I want to talk to you about something."

Amelia stretched out on her bed and gestured for Isabelle to take the chaise longue by the window.

"I'm sorry that you have to come to Stonecroft with us," Amelia said. "I talked to Robert about staying longer in London, but Pettigrew has already left, and Robert wants to go this week to ensure the new man can manage."

"Of course Lord Langley should go, and you should go with him," Isabelle replied. "I would hate for you to rearrange your plans because of me."

"But it's the middle of the Season, and you've become such a success," Amelia said. "With so many gentlemen competing for your interest, it seems a shame for you to leave."

"I don't mind," Isabelle said honestly. "I've been to enough balls to last me until next year."

The only person who didn't consider her Season a success was Isabelle herself. She was tired of balls, routs, and Venetian breakfasts, and bored with the gentlemen who gave her empty compliments. She knew that the men who called her the Irresistible Isabelle weren't referring to her character or her mind, since none of them could see past her looks. Although she had many loyal admirers, she also had critics; her beauty, coupled with her shyness and tendency to daydream, had led several gentlemen to conclude that she was proud. This opinion was shared by many young ladies and their ambitious mamas, and although Isabelle suspected they were jealous, their remarks still stung.

Amelia looked at her sister intently. "There aren't any gentlemen who have caught your eye?"

"No," Isabelle admitted.

"Well, there's certainly no rush for you to be married," Amelia said slowly. "Robert and I enjoy your company, and you're welcome to live with us for as long as you like." She paused, and a faint blush stained her cheeks. "But the thing is, Isabelle, I've found that marriage is quite enjoyable."

"I would never have guessed," Isabelle said dryly.

The blush on Amelia's cheeks deepened. "I'm sure that if you found the right person, you would enjoy it too."

Isabelle nodded. "I'm sure I would, but I can't will the right person into existence."

"Of course not," Amelia agreed. "But it's a matter of statistics, and the more gentlemen you meet, the greater the probability that you will find a connection with someone."

Isabelle rolled her eyes. "You make it sound like a mathematical exercise."

Amelia smiled. "Not exactly, but you're certainly more likely to meet someone in London than at Stonecroft. I'm sure Robert would let you stay in our townhouse if we could find you a chaperone. It's a shame that Aunt Lizzie got married." Aunt Lizzie, who had chaperoned Amelia and Isabelle the previous year, had married a vicar and moved to Somerset.

"Aunt Lizzie's very happy, Amelia, so it's hardly a shame," Isabelle replied.

"I told you marriage could be very enjoyable. I thought of asking Mama to chaperone you–"

"No," Isabelle interrupted vehemently. "Can you imagine Mama as a chaperone?" Their mother was the daughter of a French duke, and believed that the usual rules of polite behaviour did not apply to her. "She might try to steal my suitors."

Amelia laughed. The year before, their mother had married Mr. George Garland, a wealthy social climber who had previously been engaged to Amelia. "Since Mr. Garland is very much alive, I don't think there's much risk that Mama will steal your suitors."

"At least she's unlikely to marry them," Isabelle said thoughtfully.

"It might be a useful test," Amelia suggested. "Gentlemen who show too much interest in Mama aren't worth your time. But you should consider it, Isabelle. She could take you to parties, and she might not pay too much attention to you once you're there."

Isabelle shook her head. "Mama and Mr. Garland are still in France, and I think they intend to go to Yorkshire when they return to England."

Amelia chuckled. "Ah, yes. I suppose Mr. Garland must oversee the construction of his palace." Their stepfather had inherited several highly profitable textile mills, and he wished to spend his money creating an estate that would outshine those of the aristocracy. To that end, he had bought a large property in Yorkshire and was in the process of building a mansion.

"I think he calls it Garland Castle, Amelia," Isabelle corrected her sister with a smile. "But even if Mama was in London, I would much rather go to Stonecroft than stay with her."

"If you think so," Amelia said reluctantly.

"I do," Isabelle said firmly. She couldn't imagine anything more disastrous than trying to navigate society under her mother's chaperonage.

Three

"Lord Malthaner is looking at you again," Letitia Hunt whispered to Isabelle. After dancing the first four sets at the Somertons' ball, Isabelle and Letitia had rejoined their chaperones and were drinking lemonade.

Miss Letitia Hunt was the eldest daughter of a landed gentleman whose estate bordered Lord Langley's in Kent. Unfortunately, she suffered from both extreme shyness and an overbearing mother, and the combination could make her seem simple-minded. Amelia was inclined to dismiss her young neighbour as duller than ditchwater, but she was biased by the fact that she had once thought Langley was in love with Letitia. Since Isabelle was shy herself she sympathized with Letitia, and thought that when Letitia was removed from her mother's influence she was excellent company.

"I don't think Lord Malthaner has any particular interest in me," Isabelle said. "He hasn't asked me to dance more than once since I came to London." She smiled at her friend. "Perhaps he's looking at you, Letitia."

"Don't speak too loudly, or Mama will hear you," Letitia whispered. She glanced nervously over her shoulder at her mother, who was talking to Amelia. "I would hate to raise her expectations, when we both know that Malthaner hasn't had eyes for anyone but you all night."

While Isabelle was one of the most successful young ladies of the Season, Viscount Malthaner was unquestionably the most sought-after gentleman. Both his figure and fortune were handsome, and his dark hair and brooding expression led many to compare him to Lord Byron. He had inherited his title at the age of four, after his father died of an apoplectic fit, and his mother's considerable energies had been entirely devoted to his upbringing. Malthaner was now twenty-six, and he had made it known that he was looking for a bride. The ladies of the *ton* were aflutter at the prospect of a man who possessed a title, a fortune, and all of his teeth.

"Mama told me that last week, Lord Malthaner saved a young girl from being trampled by a mail coach," Letitia told Isabelle. "The child ran out in front of the horses and would have been killed if he hadn't pushed her out of the way." She smiled mischievously. "Of course, Mama heard it from her friend Mrs. Masterson, so the story was probably embellished. But he certainly looks like a hero, don't you think?"

Isabelle sneaked a look at the man in question, who was dancing a quadrille. He met her eye and winked, and she quickly looked away, embarrassed to have been caught staring. But Malthaner didn't seem to mind, and the dance had barely ended before he was in front of Isabelle. He bowed to her and Letitia, then addressed himself to Isabelle with a confident smile. Isabelle had never met a man who so closely resembled the romantic hero of her imagination.

"Miss Fleming, you are looking especially lovely tonight," Malthaner said. "I'm surprised to see you sitting with the wallflowers."

"It's very hot in here, and Letitia and I needed a rest."

"I'm sure you are wise. Now that you have rested, please tell me you have a dance free for me."

"I'm sorry, my lord," Isabelle said. "I am engaged for the rest of the evening."

"I don't believe it," Malthaner said. "I insist upon seeing your dance card."

Isabelle smiled nervously and handed him the little booklet. He frowned as he cast his eye down the column of names.

"Why Miss Fleming," Malthaner said. "I see you have Lord Calvert listed here for the next waltz."

Isabelle nodded. Lord Calvert was a stodgy but good-natured baron who had requested a dance early in the evening.

"Miss Fleming, you don't want to waltz with Lord Calvert," Malthaner said. "He's famous for stepping on his partners' toes." He used the little pencil attached to her dance card to cross out Calvert's name and write in his own. "You can dance with me instead."

"Lord Malthaner, I would be delighted to dance with you, but I don't think–"

"You don't have to think, Miss Fleming," Malthaner said in a teasing tone. "I will take care of it for you.

Calvert owes me a favour, and I'll let him know that I'll be taking his place."

"All right." Isabelle didn't have the courage to disagree.

~

Lord Malthaner was a skilled dancer, and Isabelle spent the first moments of the waltz enjoying the sensations of the movement and the music. After a while, the lack of conversation began to seem awkward, and Isabelle remembered the gossip she had heard from Letitia.

"I heard that you saved a young girl from being run over by the mail coach," Isabelle blurted. "Is it true?"

Malthaner smiled modestly. "You must know, Miss Fleming, that by the time such stories have spread through the *ton*, they bear little resemblance to the truth."

"I think it was awfully courageous," Isabelle remarked.

"Any gentleman would have done the same. But I would rather talk about you, Miss Fleming. That's an exquisite dress."

"Thank you," said Isabelle politely. She tried to think of a compliment to give Lord Malthaner, and cast her eye down his cream silk waistcoat and black pantaloons. The most remarkable item of his attire seemed to be his cravat, which was tied in a very complicated arrangement.

"That's a lovely cravat," Isabelle said shyly. She actually thought it looked rather silly, but Malthaner's gratified expression told her she had said the right thing.

"The style is my own creation," he told her. "I've named it the Avalanche, and my mother thinks it looks quite distinguished. But I don't suppose you're terribly interested in cravats, Miss Fleming?"

"Not terribly," she admitted.

"What are you interested in?"

Isabelle thought carefully about how to answer. She loved to read and write, but they weren't interests she wanted to discuss with Lord Malthaner. She wasn't afraid of being branded a bluestocking, but her writing felt too personal to share with someone with whom she was barely acquainted.

"I've always liked dogs," she finally said.

Malthaner smiled. "So have I. Do you have a dog, Miss Fleming?"

"No." While Isabelle was growing up, the Flemings had had a spaniel named Lucy, but Lucy had died two years ago. Isabelle still missed her.

"Do you know, Miss Fleming, I have a friend whose dog just had a litter of puppies. I'm sure he'd give me one for you."

"Thank you, Lord Malthaner, but I'm afraid it's not a good time for me to have a dog."

"What do you mean?"

Isabelle sighed. "I mean that in my current circumstances–"

"Ah, you live with your sister and brother-in-law, and you're worried they would object," Malthaner guessed.

"Not exactly," Isabelle hedged. She knew Amelia and Langley wouldn't object to her owning a dog; in fact, they had repeatedly urged her to treat their house as her own. But Isabelle still felt like a houseguest, and she didn't feel comfortable bringing a dog into a house that wasn't hers.

"I understand," said Malthaner. "I'm sure you'll have your own household soon, and perhaps it would be best to wait until then."

"Perhaps," Isabelle agreed. The waltz ended and she took his arm, expecting him to lead her back to the edge of the ballroom where Amelia was sitting.

"Do you like books, Miss Fleming?" Malthaner asked, as he led her across the room.

"Very much," she admitted, wondering how he had guessed.

"Then let me show you the library," Malthaner suggested. "I'm a close friend of the Somertons, and they won't mind if I give you a tour of the house."

"You are very kind, but I should return to my sister," Isabelle demurred.

But the path back to Amelia was blocked by a crowd of people who appeared to be watching an argument. Isabelle's view was limited by the other spectators, but as she got closer, she could see that Letitia was arguing with Mrs. Hunt. Beside them, a middle-aged man looked on with a predatory expression. Isabelle recognized him as Lord Braden, a widower who was rumoured to be in the market for a young wife.

"No, Mama, I won't do it," Letitia said firmly. The crowd had fallen silent, and her words carried through the ballroom.

"Be quiet, Letitia, you're causing a scene," her mother hissed.

"You have caused the scene, Mama, by trying to force me to dance when I've explained that I'm tired," Letitia replied. "I've danced with Lord Braden once already, and I'm sure he will understand that I need to rest."

Isabelle glanced at Lord Braden and thought that she wouldn't want to dance with him either. Braden was tall and rawboned, with harsh features and grey hair that he wore tied back in a neat queue. His face had turned red with annoyance, but the crowd made it impossible for him to leave.

"It's only a dance, Letitia," her mother said forcefully.

"I don't care if I die a spinster, Mama. I won't do it." Like Lord Braden, Letitia was trapped by the spectators. Since she couldn't escape the ballroom, she sat down and turned her face towards the wall.

"Fate has intervened to prevent me from returning you to your sister," Malthaner said to Isabelle. "Let me take you out of this crush, Miss Fleming."

"Miss Hunt is my friend," Isabelle began. She wanted to help Letitia, but she couldn't see a way to do so.

Malthaner chuckled. "You'll hardly help by standing here gawping. Come, I'll show you the library."

Before Isabelle could protest further, Malthaner had manoeuvred her past an elaborate display of hothouse flowers and out of the ballroom. She found herself in a shadowy hallway, and it took her eyes a minute to adjust to the darkness. Malthaner seemed to know where he was going, however, and he led her confidently down the hall until they reached a closed door.

"Lord Malthaner, I don't think–" Isabelle began nervously.

"I told you, Miss Fleming, you don't have to think," he said smoothly. He picked up a candle from a sconce on the wall and pushed open the door. "Just trust me."

Malthaner guided her through the door, and in the dim candlelight Isabelle could see that they were in a beautifully decorated sitting room.

"This isn't the library," she said in confusion.

"It's Lady Somerton's sitting room," Malthaner explained. "But look, she left a book on the table."

"It's a beautiful room," Isabelle began, "but–"

"You are the most beautiful thing in it," Malthaner said flirtatiously.

"Lord Malthaner, I think I should return to my sister." She realized he had closed the door, and although that lessened the risk that they would be discovered, it would make for a far greater scandal if they were. Isabelle was uncomfortable, but she couldn't deny that there was something exciting about a man who had the courage to break society's rules.

"Relax, Miss Fleming," Malthaner said with a teasing gleam in his eyes. "The scandal in the ballroom is absorbing everyone's attention. No one will miss us."

"But the impropriety of our situation–"

"I have a very important question to ask you," he interrupted. "And I would prefer to do it without an audience." He leaned close to her and lowered his voice, and she could smell the sandalwood of his cologne. "Miss Fleming," he said seriously, "will you dance with me at Almack's next week?"

"A-Almack's?" she stammered.

Her confusion seemed to amuse him. "Surely you're familiar with it. Thinly sliced bread, warm lemonade?"

Isabelle collected herself. "I won't be in London next week. I'm going to Stonecroft with Lord and Lady Langley on Friday."

"That is a disappointment indeed," Malthaner said. "When do you return?"

"I don't know," Isabelle said. "Likely not until the autumn."

"And you are determined to go with your sister?" he asked. "It wouldn't be possible for you to stay with your mother?"

"Mama is in Paris."

"A friend, then?"

Isabelle hesitated. Lord Malthaner was the most interesting man she had met in a long time. For the first time, she wished she didn't have to leave London, but she couldn't see an alternative. Her closest friend in London was Letitia Hunt, but she knew that Mrs. Hunt would never allow Isabelle to stay with them. For that matter, Amelia would not want Isabelle to stay in town under the chaperonage of Mrs. Hunt.

"I'm looking forward to going to Stonecroft," she said. "I like the country, and I'm ready for a change."

"Then it seems I will have to be patient," Malthaner said with a sigh. "Do you know what my mother says about patience, Miss Fleming?"

"No."

"She says it's a virtue that I don't possess." He brought Isabelle's hand to his lips and kissed it. "But I think, my dear Miss Fleming, that you are worth waiting for."

Isabelle blushed. Despite her many admirers, she had very little practice in the art of flirtation, and she couldn't think of how to reply.

"Come," Malthaner said. "I expect the excitement will be over. Let me return you to your sister."

The dancing had resumed when they returned to the

ballroom, and Isabelle saw no sign of Letitia or Lord Braden. She found Amelia standing along the wall, talking to an acquaintance.

"There you are," Amelia said. "Where have you been?"

Malthaner bowed. "I apologize, Lady Langley. There was such a crowd of people in this part of the room that I couldn't bring Miss Fleming back to you when the dance ended. I thought I should take her out of the crush."

It was a weak explanation, but Amelia seemed to accept it. Malthaner winked at Isabelle and walked away.

"What happened to Letitia?" Isabelle asked her sister as soon as Malthaner had left.

"Oh Isabelle, I don't think I've ever been so angry in my life!" Amelia exclaimed. "I didn't have a chance to speak to Letitia before her mother took her home, but I think Lord Braden tried to take liberties when he danced with her the first time. And Mrs. Hunt still insisted that she dance with him again. That woman is shameless! I wanted to intervene, but I feared it would only make things worse." She sighed. "I wish Robert had come."

Amelia spoke with the confidence of a woman who believed her husband could do anything, but since Mrs. Hunt was encouraging Lord Braden's advances, Isabelle wasn't sure what Langley could have done to help Letitia. What Letitia really needed was a chivalrous gentleman to offer to marry her and protect her from Lord Braden. Failing that, the next best thing would be for someone else to cause an even bigger scandal to distract the *ton* from Letitia's troubles.

And if there was little that Langley could do for Leti-

THE MYSTERIOUS MR. OLIVER

tia, Isabelle could do even less. It was a lowering reflection.

"I'm sorry, Amelia, I'm not feeling well," she said. "Would you mind if we went home?"

"Not at all," Amelia said kindly. She looked at Isabelle with concern. "You're looking very pale."

They were standing in the entrance hall, waiting for the coach to be brought round, when Isabelle felt a hand on her arm. She turned to see Lord Malthaner smiling down at her.

"Leaving so soon, Miss Fleming?" he inquired politely. "That's disappointing. I hoped to have the pleasure of dancing with you again."

"I'm sorry to disappoint you," Isabelle said.

"I can't persuade you to stay?"

Isabelle was tempted. She was upset about Letitia, but Malthaner's attention was flattering.

The silence grew awkward, and Amelia stepped into the breach. "Miss Fleming is feeling unwell, and we are going home."

Malthaner's face took on an expression of sympathy. "I'm sorry to hear that, Miss Fleming. Do you think it was something at supper? I was a little suspicious of the crab puffs."

"I'm sure it wasn't the crab," Isabelle said quickly. "I am just tired."

"In that case, I won't keep you." He bowed. "Good night, Lady Langley, Miss Fleming. I hope to see you again soon."

His flirtatious tone seemed to rob Isabelle of rational thought. "I'm not sure when we'll have the opportunity," she said. "Since we are leaving town on Friday."

Malthaner smiled. "You'll find, Miss Fleming, that I make my own opportunities."

∼

Isabelle and Amelia tried to call upon Letitia Hunt the following afternoon, but the Hunts' butler informed them that the family had gone out of town.

"They must have gone to their house in Kent," Amelia remarked to Isabelle, as they walked back to their carriage. "I'm sure we'll see Letitia when we go to Stonecroft."

"I hope so," Isabelle said. "I just wish I had been able to speak to Letitia after the shocking scene with Lord Braden last night. She needs friends, since she certainly won't get any support from her mother." She turned to her sister. "Will you come with me to see her in Kent?"

"Of course. But if I know Mrs. Hunt, we won't have to go to them," Amelia said with a smile. "She will bring Letitia to us."

Four

Stonecroft, Kent
One week later

"If you'll excuse my saying so, sir, I wasn't expecting to see you this morning," a tenant farmer told Oliver. "Mr. Pettigrew always came around in the afternoon." The words were polite enough, but the man's tone made it clear that he considered Pettigrew's approach far superior to Oliver's.

Oliver had only been at Stonecroft for a week, but he was already sick of hearing about how Mr. Pettigrew did things. He didn't wish Pettigrew ill exactly, but he wouldn't have been sorry to learn that his predecessor had made an error. Ideally, it would be an error that Oliver could put right, thereby earning Lord Langley's gratitude and respect. So far, however, he had found no fault with Mr. Pettigrew's management.

He turned back to the farmer. "I am not Mr. Pettigrew," he said simply, fixing the man with a stare. The

35

farmer nodded and turned away, grumbling to himself. Oliver decided he had earned a break and walked towards the cottage that served as his office.

The Old Cottage had been the land agent's residence until several years earlier, when Langley had decided to replace it with a more comfortable dwelling. The only problem with the New Cottage was that it was considerably farther away from the tenant farms, so the Old Cottage had been repurposed as the land agent's office. Most days, Oliver took some bread and cheese up to the Old Cottage to eat during his midday break.

Oliver was surprised to find Isabelle sitting behind his desk with a stack of paper in front of her and a pen in her hand. He had thought of Isabelle several times since she had run into him in the hallway of the Langleys' townhouse, and he recognized her immediately. A lock of blonde hair had escaped from her chignon, and there was a smudge of ink on her nose. The overall effect was perfectly lovely, and Oliver was infuriated.

"What are you doing here?" he asked irritably.

Isabelle rose to her feet. She recognized Oliver from their encounter in the hallway, but she couldn't understand what he was doing in the land agent's cottage. "I'm not bothering anyone," she said defensively. "This cottage is for the use of the land agent, but he doesn't use it, so there's no reason–"

"I'm the land agent, and I use it," Oliver ground out.

Isabelle blushed. "Oh. I apologize, Mr. Oliver," she said, looking adorably flustered.

Oliver was irrationally pleased that Isabelle knew his name, but he tried to keep his emotions from showing.

"Have we met?" he asked.

"We haven't been introduced, but Lord Langley mentioned he had hired you to replace Mr. Pettigrew," Isabelle stammered. "And I remember seeing you at the Langleys' townhouse last week, although I didn't know your name at the time."

"I'm surprised you remember me."

"I don't see why you would be," she replied. "I'm not in the habit of running into people, and I don't think I'm losing my memory, so it's unlikely that I would forget." She could have added that she hadn't forgotten his hazel eyes, square jaw, and the high-bridged nose that was slightly too long but still suited his face.

"I apologize," Oliver said. "I didn't mean to imply that you were losing your memory."

Isabelle smiled. "I suppose I should apologize to you. I realized that I didn't stop to speak to you after I ran into you, even though I'm afraid it was my fault."

"Yes," he agreed. "I'm afraid it was."

"Well, I apologize," she said. "I hope I didn't cause you any lasting injury."

"I have recovered."

There was a beat of silence, and Isabelle realized she hadn't introduced herself. "My name is Isabelle Fleming. I'm Lady Langley's sister."

"I know. Lord Langley explained who you were." Oliver realized he was blushing too, and he forced himself to focus on the problem of her presence in his cottage. It was quickly becoming obvious that Miss Isabelle Fleming had the power to cause his heart a very serious injury indeed.

"I see," Isabelle said.

"What are you doing in my cottage?" he asked bluntly.

It came out more harshly than he intended, and his conscience pricked him when he saw her flinch.

"I didn't realize you were using this cottage," she explained. "Mr. Pettigrew never did."

"While Pettigrew may have had time to waste walking back to his house whenever he needed a desk or a meal–"

"I don't think Mr. Pettigrew wanted to put the maids to the trouble of coming to clean it," Isabelle retorted. She drew a finger along the surface of the desk and held it up for his inspection. "It's filthy. I was planning to clean it the next time I came."

"It's been cleaned."

Isabelle looked dubiously around the cottage, which didn't look particularly clean.

"I cleaned it myself," Oliver ground out. He had taken a feather duster to the more visible dust and cobwebs on the furniture, and swept the worst of the dirt out the front door.

"Oh," she said, and the furrow on her brow cleared. "Well, I suppose that explains it."

"You don't think I can clean a cottage?"

"I'm sure it's cleaner than it was before you started," Isabelle said kindly. "Since you plan to make use of it, I'll ask Mrs. Prescott to send someone out to clean it."

"That won't be necessary," Oliver ground out. "I would hate to put them to the trouble."

"As you wish," she said, but her expression made it clear she didn't agree with him. "Although I'm not sure that working in such an environment is good for your health."

"You shouldn't come here if it offends you," Oliver retorted. "In fact, you shouldn't come here even if it doesn't." His gaze fell to the papers spread out on the desk in front of her. "What are you doing with those papers?"

"Nothing." Isabelle quickly gathered her papers and clutched them against her chest.

"It's clearly not nothing," Oliver said in frustration. "Let me see them." He was worried that she had found the rent records, and he was embarrassed that he had left the cottage unlocked. He suspected that few of the tenant farmers could read well enough to make sense of his records, but nonetheless, it was unprofessional.

"It's not nothing, but it's personal," Isabelle explained.

"I need to see them. If you've found the rent records–"

Isabelle laughed. "The rent records? Do you really think I came here to read Lord Langley's rent records?"

As soon as she said it, Oliver realized the absurdity of his accusation, but Isabelle continued before he could apologize.

"Perhaps you think I intend to alter some numbers and skim off some of the money?"

Against his will, Oliver smiled. "I admit that seems unlikely."

"More than unlikely, it's almost impossible. Even if I could alter the records, I don't know how I would steal the money, unless you also leave the rent money in an unlocked cottage?"

"I don't."

"I'm pleased to hear it. There's also the fact that I would never steal from Lord Langley. He and my sister have been incredibly generous to me."

"I didn't mean to imply that you would," Oliver said. "But you still haven't explained why you're here."

Isabelle sighed. "Sometimes I need to get away from my sister and Lord Langley. They still behave like newlyweds, and it can be very awkward."

Oliver smiled with amusement. "Are they not still newlyweds?"

"They've been married for a year!" Isabelle exclaimed. "I expected them to have moved past this stage by now, but they're still besotted. There's so much innuendo, and the way they look at each other! They think I don't notice it, but I'm not a complete innocent."

"So you come here to escape?" Oliver asked.

Isabelle nodded. "Yes. I know it's irrational, but sometimes the main house feels confining."

Oliver looked at her skeptically. "And you prefer this cottage?"

"Yes."

"You're right, it is irrational," he said, but there was no criticism in his tone.

She nodded again. "Perhaps I could continue to work in the cottage when you're not using it?"

"No," he said simply.

Isabelle looked surprised, and Oliver suspected she wasn't used to having men say no to her.

"Why not?" she asked. "I won't disturb any of your papers, and whenever you want to use the cottage, I'll go. You'll hardly ever know I'm here."

"I'm sorry, Miss Fleming, but that's impossible." For a young lady who claimed she wasn't a complete innocent, she was remarkably ignorant of the rules of propriety.

"I'll clean it for you," she offered.

"No, you will not," he bit out. "I'm sorry, Miss Fleming, but I use this cottage as my office, and I must ask you to stay out of it."

He hadn't intended to speak so sharply, and he saw her face fall before she gathered her pride and stood.

"I understand, Mr. Oliver," she said stiffly. "I apologize for inconveniencing you, and I assure you it won't happen again." She swept out of the cottage with her head high.

Oliver sat behind his desk and stared at the wall. He hadn't handled the confrontation well, but he knew that allowing Isabelle to use his cottage would set him on the road to madness. Isabelle represented everything he disliked about the nobility; she did what she liked, without thinking of how her actions might affect other people. She certainly hadn't been concerned about the consequences Oliver would face if they were seen in the cottage together.

Oliver was familiar with the attitudes of the nobility because he had been born into it. His real name was Oliver James Montgomery St. Clair, and he was the second son of the Duke of Edgeworth, one of the richest and most influential men in the country. Edgeworth was known for both his intelligence and his austerity; he held himself to a high standard of behaviour, and he expected the same of his sons. Oliver's elder brother, Rupert, was the duke's heir first and his son second, and Oliver felt like an afterthought. Since Oliver's mother had taken her husband's opinions along with his name upon her marriage, she hadn't tried to influence the duke's treatment of their sons.

Despite this, Oliver had enjoyed a happy childhood in the care of a nurse and then a tutor. This had changed when he went to Eton at age ten, where it had quickly become clear that Oliver was not only a better athlete and scholar than Rupert, he was also more popular. Oliver had felt as though his father blamed him for exposing Rupert's inadequacies, and he had learned to strive for mediocrity.

When he had returned home for the summers, Oliver had made it his mission to avoid his father, and had consequently spent many hours outdoors with the estate's land agent. He was happiest when he was outdoors, and he had dreamed of eventually managing the ducal estates for his brother. Unfortunately, his father hadn't sympathized with this dream, and had insisted that Oliver would join the army when he graduated from Cambridge. Oliver had hated the idea of becoming a soldier, and he had told his father he wouldn't do it.

Oliver had worked hard at Cambridge in the hope that he could enter the church, but after he graduated with honours he had realized he didn't want to be a clergyman. The duke had still wanted him to join the army, but Oliver had defied him and gone to live in London. In town, he had gone to the theatre, dabbled in gambling, and enjoyed a liaison with an adventurous widow. Although his exploits had been tame compared to those of many young noblemen, his father had thought he was living a life of debauchery, and Oliver hadn't tried to correct him.

The conflict had reached a peak when the duke heard rumours about Oliver's affair with the widow, who was hoping Oliver would marry her. Oliver had been summoned home, where his father had announced his intention to buy him a commission in the army. When

Oliver had refused to comply, the duke had declared him an embarrassment to the family and cut off his allowance. Oliver had returned to London, where he learned that the adventurous widow had moved on, and was enjoying a dalliance with a wealthy viscount. He had been near the end of his resources when he won a small fortune at cards, and in an act of supreme irony, he had bought a commission in a cavalry regiment.

Oliver had been determined that any honour or shame that resulted from his career in the army would be his alone. To that end, he had reinvented himself as Mr. James Oliver, the son of an entirely fictitious landed gentleman from Derbyshire. He hadn't told his family or friends that he was enlisting, and to his knowledge, they had never looked for him. Oliver imagined his father could have found him if he had bothered to look; he had taken his first name as his surname, after all.

Perhaps his choice of name had been foolish, but Oliver had been afraid that if he chose something different, he would forget to answer to it. He had chosen to buy a commission rather than enlisting in the general infantry for much the same reason; his accent was clearly upper class, and life in the army was hard enough without trying to disguise his speech. In his experience, lies were most successful when they were close to the truth.

And Oliver knew he was lying to himself about Miss Isabelle Fleming. The real reason he had been infuriated to find her in his cottage was that despite her flaws, she was the most attractive woman he had ever seen, and he wanted her in a way he hadn't wanted a woman in years.

Five

Letter from Miss Isabelle Fleming to her brother William, Lord Cliveden

Dear William,

We have arrived safely at Stonecroft, and it is a relief to be out of London! The only news here is that the land agent, Mr. Pettigrew, has left because his father is unwell. Lord Langley has hired a new man, Mr. Oliver, on a temporary basis. Mr. Oliver seems to take his work seriously, but I'm sorry to say that he has little else in common with Mr. Pettigrew. While Mr. Pettigrew was all amiability, Mr. Oliver looks as though he never learned how to smile.

Yesterday Mr. Oliver found me doing some writing in an empty cottage, and he acted as though I had broken into his home! To be fair, the cottage is theoretically for the land agent to use as an office, but Mr. Pettigrew never did so. There was really no need for Mr. Oliver to be so unpleasant about it.

Amelia remains sickeningly in love with Lord Langley,

and while I am pleased that they are so happy, their displays of affection grow tiresome.

Yours,
Isabelle

∼

Dear Isabelle,
I think you may be judging Mr. Oliver too harshly. Perhaps he was simply focused on his work, and found you a distraction. Especially since the cottage is (theoretically) his office. But if you chase him away from Stonecroft, feel free to send him to Cliveden Manor. I have a hard time convincing my land agent to get off his backside and do any work.

William

∼

The news that the Earl and Countess of Langley had returned to Stonecroft spread quickly through the village, and was quickly followed by the intelligence that the countess was expecting a child. The local physician, Dr. Carter, took a great interest in this report; he was young, ambitious, and frustrated by the fact that he had yet to meet the earl. A year before, Dr. Carter had been summoned to Stonecroft after Lord Langley was shot in a duel, but a houseguest named Miss Amelia Fleming had disagreed with his proposed treatment and thrown him out of the house.

But Dr. Carter saw the countess's pregnancy for the

opportunity that it was, and he was determined he would not let it pass him by. After spending a morning mustering his courage, he knocked on the door of Stonecroft and told the butler, Matthews, that he wished to see the earl.

"Is he expecting you?" Matthews asked.

"Not exactly, but I think he will want to see me," Dr. Carter said optimistically.

Matthews didn't share Dr. Carter's optimism, and he left him standing in the hall while he went to inform Langley that he had a visitor. After pacing for a few moments, Dr. Carter concluded that Matthews was incompetent, and decided to search for the earl himself. He passed through an open door and found himself in the morning room, where Amelia sat behind a rosewood desk, reviewing the household accounts.

"Dr. Carter, what an unexpected surprise," Amelia said smoothly. She didn't rise to greet him.

Dr. Carter would never forget the houseguest who had foolishly prevented him from treating the earl the year before, and he could hardly believe he had found Amelia there again. "Miss Fleming," he said, bowing stiffly.

Amelia didn't correct him. "I didn't know you were coming," she said casually.

"Lady Langley may not feel the need to inform you of all the household decisions," he said superciliously.

Amelia raised her eyebrows. "Perhaps not. Did Lady Langley summon you?"

Dr. Carter was tempted to lie, but since Amelia seemed to be inexplicably good friends with the earl and his family, he thought a lie was likely to be caught. "Not exactly," he admitted.

"Ah," Amelia said with an enigmatic smile. "Lord Langley then?"

"No," admitted Dr. Carter.

"I see. A social call?"

"It is a private matter," Dr. Carter said stiffly.

At that moment, Langley strolled in, looking every inch the aristocrat in a navy waistcoat, buckskin breeches, and Hessian boots. Dr. Carter correctly assumed he was the earl, and bowed deeply.

"I am honoured to make your acquaintance, my lord," Dr. Carter said. "I am Dr. Carter, the county physician."

Langley nodded, but his attention was focused on his wife. "Are you unwell, Amelia?" he asked with concern. She appeared to be in her usual good health, but he knew she would have to be at death's door to send for Dr. Carter.

"I'm perfectly well, Robert, and I don't know why Dr. Carter is here."

"I see. Perhaps he will enlighten us." Langley looked at Dr. Carter expectantly.

Dr. Carter cleared his throat. "My lord, I have come to offer you my professional services," he began pompously.

"I wasn't aware I was in need of them," Langley replied.

Dr. Carter glanced at Amelia before looking back at the earl. "I was hoping to speak to you privately, sir. I heard about . . ." he trailed off and stared towards the doorway. Amelia and Lord Langley followed his gaze and saw Isabelle standing there.

"I'm sorry, I didn't mean to interrupt," Isabelle said. "I

came to ask if you wanted to go for a walk in the garden, Amelia, but I'll come back later."

Isabelle was a vision of loveliness in a blue muslin gown, and Dr. Carter took her for the countess. He felt a rush of jealousy; not only was Langley blessed with looks, wealth, and a title, he had also won the hand of one of the most beautiful ladies Dr. Carter had ever seen. Although it was hardly a surprise that a rich man of noble birth had found himself a lovely wife, it still didn't seem fair.

Dr. Carter collected his wits and bowed deeply to Isabelle. "My lady," he said obsequiously. "It's an honour to make your acquaintance. I am Dr. Carter."

Isabelle's first concern was for her sister's health. "Amelia, are you unwell?" she asked anxiously. "I didn't know you had sent for the doctor."

"I didn't send for him, and I am perfectly fine," Amelia reassured her sister. "I was just telling Robert that I don't know why Dr. Carter is here."

Dr. Carter looked at Amelia with irritation. "My business is with the Earl and Countess of Langley," he said in a condescending tone. "If you'll excuse us–"

Amelia smiled. "I can assure you, Dr. Carter, the Countess of Langley has no secrets from me."

Dr. Carter looked at Langley, who nodded. "She's right," Langley said, with a gleam of amusement in his eyes. "What did you wish to discuss, Dr. Carter?"

Dr. Carter was still reluctant to proceed with Amelia present. "My lord, before I begin, I should explain that I met Miss Fleming last year, and we had different opinions on the best course of treatment for your injured shoulder."

"I heard about that," Langley acknowledged. "Fortunately, the outcome was good."

"Yes, although I still think you would have recovered more quickly with bloodletting."

"I suppose we will never know."

"Likely not, although if you ever suffer a similar injury–"

Langley smiled. "I have promised my wife I won't fight another duel, so I am hoping to avoid being shot again."

Dr. Carter looked disappointed, then he brightened. "Perhaps I will have an opportunity to treat another patient with a similar injury."

"I suppose you can hope," Langley said ironically. "But I don't imagine you came to discuss my shoulder?"

"I didn't, my lord, but if you are feeling any lingering effects from the injury, I would be happy to advise you."

Langley smiled. "My shoulder is fine. Why are you here, Dr. Carter?"

"My lord, I understand your wife is in a delicate condition–"

"She is not in the least delicate, but she is expecting a child," Amelia interrupted.

Dr. Carter refused to acknowledge Amelia, but continued to speak to Langley. "I wished to offer my congratulations."

"Thank you."

"If you haven't already engaged a physician to attend to Lady Langley, I would be honoured to do so. This is a perilous time, and one can never be too careful." He glanced at Isabelle. Her slender figure showed no signs that she was expecting, and he supposed she wasn't as far along as gossip had claimed. "For example, I'm surprised that you permit Lady Langley to walk in the garden when the sun is near its peak."

Amelia snorted. "I'd like to see him forbid it." She had given up riding early in her pregnancy after Langley expressed concern about the risk, but the earl had been wise enough to phrase it as a request rather than an order.

Dr. Carter frowned at Amelia and turned back to Langley. "You will certainly want a physician to be present for the confinement," he said hopefully. "I trained at St. Bartholomew's in London, and I have a great deal of experience."

Amelia's eyes widened. "Definitely not. We have already made arrangements with a midwife."

Dr. Carter's eyes widened in shock, and he turned to the earl. "A midwife? But surely, my lord, you would want a physician for the Countess of Langley?" He looked reverently at Isabelle.

Langley nodded. "My wife prefers the assistance of a midwife, but I have also arranged for a physician to come from London."

Dr. Carter appeared deflated by this news. "I see."

Amelia wrinkled her brow. "Robert, I really don't think that's necessary. The village midwife has delivered hundreds of babies, and I'm sure she's as capable as any London doctor."

Langley moved to stand beside Amelia and put an arm around her shoulders. "The physician is for me, my darling. I think I will find your confinement stressful, and I would like to have a physician available in case I suffer a nervous attack."

Langley's expression left no doubt of the fact that he was deeply in love with Amelia, and Dr. Carter gaped at them. "You are the Countess of Langley?" he said to Amelia incredulously. "But how?"

"The usual way," Amelia told him matter-of-factly. "I married the earl."

Dr. Carter turned to Isabelle in astonishment. "But I thought you were the countess?"

Isabelle pressed her lips together to suppress a laugh. "No," she said simply.

"Dr. Carter, allow me to introduce my wife's sister, Miss Isabelle Fleming," Langley said.

Dr. Carter collected the shreds of his dignity and bowed to Isabelle again. "I am pleased to meet you, Miss Fleming."

Isabelle curtsied politely.

"You are staying with your sister?" Dr. Carter asked inanely.

"I am," Isabelle said.

"I am the only physician in the neighbourhood, Miss Fleming," he said pompously. "And I assure you that if you need a physician while you are in Kent, it would be my pleasure to serve you."

"Thank you."

"That's not to say I would be pleased to hear you were ill," Dr. Carter clarified. He was feeling disoriented by Isabelle's beauty. "Merely that if you do happen to fall ill, I would be honoured to help you in any way I could."

Amelia was quivering with silent laughter, and even Langley's lips were twitching. Isabelle took pity on the doctor. "You are very kind, Dr. Carter," she said seriously.

"And as the only physician in the neighbourhood, I know how valuable your time must be."

Dr. Carter preened. "I pride myself on efficiency, Miss Fleming."

Isabelle nodded. "Then since we are all in good health, we won't delay you any longer. I'm sure you have many patients awaiting your expertise."

Dr. Carter's disappointment was obvious, but he was unable to think of a reason to stay, so he bowed and took his leave.

Six

"I was hoping to visit the Hunts today," Isabelle said to Amelia at the breakfast table the next morning. "I'd like to see Letitia."

"According to Mrs. Prescott, the Hunts are not in the neighbourhood," Amelia said. Although no one would call the housekeeper, Mrs. Prescott, a gossip, she seemed to know everything that went on in the county.

Isabelle frowned. "Where do you think they've gone?" As far as she knew, the Hunts' only country home was the estate that bordered Stonecroft.

Amelia shrugged. "Perhaps they're staying with family until the scandal dies down."

Isabelle frowned. "How bad do you think it is? The scandal, I mean?"

"I expect it will pass quickly," Amelia said optimistically. "Letitia showed a lot of courage, and anyone with sense will see that the scene with Lord Braden wasn't her fault. Some people may even think better of her for it."

"Perhaps." Try as she might, Isabelle couldn't share

her sister's confidence. Her time in London had taught her that the people with the loudest voices usually had the least sense. But she knew there was nothing she could do to help Letitia, and dwelling on the subject wouldn't benefit anyone. "Do you have plans for the day?" she asked Amelia.

"I was planning to visit some of the tenant farmers," Amelia replied. "Mrs. Prescott told me that one of the farmers' wives has just had a baby, and is having a difficult time. I expect what she really needs is someone to help with the housework, but she's unlikely to let me do that, so I'll take her some scones and fruit." She rolled her eyes. "One of the tenant families had influenza last autumn, and I tried to help with some of the washing up. I think the farmer's wife was more distressed by my efforts to help than by the influenza!"

"Maybe she was afraid you didn't know what you were doing," Isabelle teased her sister.

Amelia smiled. "She would have been surprised to learn that before I married Robert, I did a fair amount of washing up." Before Amelia's marriage the Flemings hadn't had many servants, so Amelia and Isabelle had done some of the housework themselves.

"I expect she would have been," Isabelle agreed. "I'd like to come with you to visit the tenants."

Amelia sighed. "I'm feeling a little tired today, so I think I'll go tomorrow instead."

Isabelle raised her eyebrows in mock surprise. "Tired?"

"Don't tell Robert, or he may call Dr. Carter back," Amelia grumbled. "If you must know, the baby has started to kick, and she wakes me up at night."

"Where is Lord Langley?" Isabelle asked. Langley and Amelia were in the habit of coming down to breakfast together, and it was unusual for him to be absent.

"One of the tenant cottages has a leaking roof, so Robert has gone to look at it with Mr. Oliver," Amelia replied. "I didn't think it was possible, but it seems that Mr. Oliver is even more industrious than Mr. Pettigrew. He says he starts early so he can get his outdoor work done before the heat of the day."

"I see," Isabelle said. "But surely Mr. Oliver didn't need to drag Lord Langley out before breakfast. It seems rather inconsiderate."

Amelia laughed. "Robert said the same thing as he was leaving this morning, but he didn't mean it. He only pretends to be lazy, you know."

"I know." Isabelle studied her sister carefully and thought that Amelia did look tired. "I could visit the tenants by myself today," she suggested.

Amelia agreed without protest, and half an hour later Isabelle was walking across the fields towards the tenant cottages, carrying a basket of scones and fruit. Amelia had suggested she have the coachman drive her in the gig, but Isabelle had insisted she preferred to walk. By the time she reached the cottages, her arms ached from the effort of carrying the basket, and she wished she had gone in the gig.

Amelia had given her directions to the home of the family with the new baby, and the sound of a crying infant told Isabelle she had come to the right place. There was no answer to her knock, but the door was unlocked, so Isabelle cautiously let herself in. She almost cried herself when she saw the state of the cottage. The single table was piled with dirty dishes, and a puppy appeared to be asleep on a heap of laundry in the corner of the room. A red-faced woman paced the floor, trying to soothe an equally red-faced baby.

Mrs. Daniels was too exhausted to be ashamed of the state of her cottage, or to protest when Isabelle announced that she would help to clean it up. By the time Isabelle had washed the dishes, dusted the furniture, and swept the floor, the baby had stopped crying. She asked if she could hold him, and Mrs. Daniels handed him over without hesitation. Baby Edward seemed to like Isabelle, and promptly fell asleep in her arms. Isabelle, who had very little experience with babies, thought he was incredibly sweet and impossibly small.

The sun was high in the sky when Isabelle set off to return to the house, and the path beside the fields offered little shade. It wasn't long before she was sweaty and miserable, and she berated herself for refusing Amelia's offer of the carriage. She was halfway home when she caught her foot on a tree root and tripped.

Isabelle sat up and took an inventory of her injuries. Her palms were scraped and her dress was torn, but the most significant problem seemed to be with her right ankle. She had twisted her foot when she fell, and her ankle was now throbbing in pain. She removed her boot and stocking to inspect the joint, and was relieved to see nothing visibly wrong with it.

Isabelle carefully replaced her boot and got to her feet, then gritted her teeth and tried to walk. Her right ankle protested every step, and after she had gone about ten feet it was clear that she wouldn't make it home without help. She knew Amelia would eventually send someone out to look for her, but she worried it could be hours before her sister grew concerned. She hobbled back to the shade of the tree and prepared to wait.

She had barely sat down when she saw a horse and rider coming towards her, and she sighed with relief. Her relief was short-lived, however, when she identified the rider as Mr. Oliver. She remembered their last conversation in the Old Cottage, and for a moment she wished he would ride past.

Oliver reined in his horse and dismounted. "Miss Fleming," he said with concern. "Have you injured your leg?"

"No," she said emphatically. "I am perfectly fine."

"I saw you limping, Miss Fleming."

"I wasn't limping," she protested.

"So you were jumping on one foot for your own amusement?"

"Perhaps it was for your amusement, Mr. Oliver. You looked so dour when we last met that I thought I would entertain you with the spectacle."

The corner of Oliver's mouth lifted. "I wasn't entertained by the spectacle, but I can't say the same for your conversation."

"I am pleased to provide you with amusement," Isabelle said sarcastically.

Oliver held out a hand to help her to her feet, and she winced as she put weight on her ankle. "If you try to walk on an injured joint, you'll only make it worse," he told her. "Is it your knee?"

"My ankle," Isabelle admitted. "I tripped on a tree root and twisted it."

Oliver nodded. "You can ride my horse back to the house."

Isabelle was terrified by the thought of riding his horse, and she hoped her expression didn't betray her fear. She had taken a bad fall off a horse at the age of twelve, and she hadn't been comfortable on a horse since. She rode only when she couldn't avoid it, and she hadn't been on a horse in months.

"I can walk back, I just need a moment to rest first," she told him.

"You're as bad as a soldier," Oliver said, in mock disgust.

"What do you mean?"

"Soldiers always downplay their injuries on the battlefield. They don't want others to put themselves at risk trying to help them." As soon as he said it, Oliver wished he hadn't. He had no desire to talk about the war.

"I don't see the parallel, Mr. Oliver. This is hardly a situation where you will put yourself at risk trying to help me."

"Perhaps you don't want to inconvenience me."

"I am not at all concerned with your convenience, Mr. Oliver. I simply don't want your help."

"But you were concerned about my dour expression," he mused. "It's a paradox, really."

"I suppose it is," Isabelle agreed. "But while I appreciate your concern, I don't need your help. I am perfectly able to walk."

Oliver raised his eyebrows but said nothing.

"I am!" Isabelle insisted. "I just need a short rest first."

"I can't leave you sitting under a tree," Oliver said.

"If the tree troubles you, I will move out to the open field," Isabelle retorted.

Oliver rolled his eyes. "What I mean is that I can't leave you here."

"I'm sure you can, Mr. Oliver," Isabelle said. "What you mean is that you won't."

"You're right, Miss Fleming," he said. "I won't leave you here. If you don't wish to ride the horse, I will carry you back to the house."

Her blue eyes widened. "You can't carry me!" she exclaimed.

He interrupted with a smile. "I think you mean to say that I shouldn't carry you. I'm confident that I could carry you if I wished."

"I see. Do you have much experience in carrying ladies?"

"None at all," he admitted. He did, however, have some experience in carrying wounded men off the battlefield, but that was not a subject he wished to discuss with Isabelle.

"Well, Mr. Oliver, if you have no experience with ladies, I suppose I will opt for the horse."

Oliver smiled at her choice of words, but he was secretly glad she chose to ride. He wasn't as well conditioned as he had been in the army, and he didn't think he would be able to carry her back to the house without stopping to rest.

Isabelle stared up at the horse, which appeared to be a particularly large beast. "I've never ridden astride, and I'm not sure I'll be able to with my skirts," she explained hesitantly.

Oliver seemed to sense her anxiety, for the teasing

note left his voice. "You won't have to," he said reassuringly. "You can keep both your legs on one side. I'll lead the horse, and we'll go slowly."

"All right," Isabelle agreed. Without giving her any more time to worry, Oliver put his hands on her waist and swung her easily onto the horse. He kept hold of the reins with one hand and took her hand with his other.

"All right?" he asked.

"I think so," Isabelle said nervously.

"Turn yourself a little towards his head, and bend your front knee a little," he advised.

Isabelle carefully followed his instructions, and found the small change in position made it easier to balance.

"Better?" Oliver asked.

"A little, but it still feels awkward," she admitted.

"Try not to look down," he advised. "Focus on something in the distance, like the house. If it's easier, you can close your eyes."

To her dismay, Isabelle realized her anxiety was causing sweat to bead on her forehead and palms. Oliver's hand was strong and dry.

"Is your ankle bothering you?" he asked gently.

"No, I'm just nervous," she confessed.

"Don't worry, Miss Fleming," he said reassuringly. "Rufus is one of my favourite horses. In all the time I've known him, I've never seen him throw a lady."

"How long have you known him?"

"Since I came to Stonecroft last week."

"I see," said Isabelle. "And have you ever seen a lady ride him?"

"You're the first," Oliver confessed, with a sparkle of humour in his hazel eyes.

"Thank you, Mr. Oliver, that's very reassuring," Isabelle murmured.

"The worst thing that can happen is you'll fall, and I'll catch you."

"Would that be worse than if I fell and you didn't catch me?"

"That's impossible," he said confidently. "You know I'll catch you if you fall."

Isabelle laughed. "You are very sure of yourself, Mr. Oliver."

"Not at all," he said. "It's merely that I can't imagine having to tell Lord Langley that I allowed his sister-in-law to fall off a horse. I imagine you are his favourite sister-in-law?"

Isabelle laughed. "I am his only sister-in-law."

Oliver nodded. "So you must see why I don't want to tell him I allowed you to fall off a horse. He might raise an eyebrow and stare at me through his quizzing glass, and I might further embarrass myself by swooning under the scrutiny. There is no alternative, Miss Fleming. If you fall, I will catch you."

Isabelle laughed. "You're being ridiculous."

He smiled. "You can't deny that your brother-in-law is formidable."

"He is, but I can't imagine you swooning in front of him." Isabelle didn't think there were many men who could stand up to Lord Langley, but she imagined Mr. Oliver could.

They walked in silence for a few minutes. The horse seemed to understand that Oliver was not a man to be trifled with, and he was on his best behaviour.

"Miss Fleming, what were you working on when I

found you in my cottage the other day?" Oliver asked suddenly. Isabelle realized he had waited until she was comfortable on the horse to begin his inquisition.

"I don't see why that interests you," she said lightly.

"Since you chose to do it in my cottage, I think it's only fair for you to give me an explanation."

"I wasn't hurting anything," she said defensively. "Were you worried I would steal your things?"

"Not my possessions, only my reputation and my position here. Can you imagine if someone had seen you leaving my cottage? I doubt Lord Langley would approve of his land agent having a tryst with his sister-in-law."

"But it was nothing like that," Isabelle protested. "I would have explained that you didn't know I was using the cottage until you found me there."

"And Langley might have believed it," Oliver said. "Or he might not."

"But it was the middle of the day!" Isabelle protested. "Surely no one would suspect impropriety in broad daylight." She flushed. "I mean, I'm not sure–"

Oliver bit back a laugh. When faced with a beauty like Isabelle, a man would be tempted to do improper things at any time of day.

Isabelle noticed the gleam in his eyes. "I suppose you think I'm naïve."

"I didn't say that."

"You didn't have to, I could see it in your eyes."

Oliver's only reply was an amused smile.

"Oh, and now you're not even going to answer me?" Isabelle asked, nettled.

"Since you can read my thoughts, it seems I don't

have to." Oliver couldn't recall when he had last had a more childish conversation, or a more enjoyable one.

"You're right," Isabelle admitted. "I shouldn't have been in your cottage. If you must know, I am writing a novel, and I find it easier to write in a quiet place." She blushed. "You probably think it's silly."

"Why would I think that?" he asked, looking genuinely curious.

"Well, it's unlikely that anything I write will ever be published," she said hesitantly. Her family saw her scribbling as an eccentric habit. Amelia and William were kind about it, but she knew they didn't understand it.

"Writing is an outlet for creative expression," Oliver said. "The world would be a much better place if more people made time for such things."

Isabelle smiled. "My mother says no one will want to marry me if word gets out that I write."

"Perhaps you should use it as a test," Oliver suggested lightly. In his opinion, Isabelle could take up any hobby she wanted and still have men fighting for her hand. "Advertise your hobby and see how people respond. Men who are scared off by such a thing aren't worthy of your consideration."

"That's an interesting idea," Isabelle said thoughtfully.

"Although I doubt many men would be put off, Miss Fleming. If you expressed an interest in collecting insects, you would likely have men knocking on your door and asking to see your collection."

"Because of my looks," Isabelle said with resignation.

Oliver had absolutely been thinking of her looks, and

he had thought of little else since he had found her in his cottage. But he sensed that answer wouldn't please her.

"Because you would be the only young lady in London with an insect collection," he said lightly. "And because you're an interesting conversationalist."

She smiled. "No one's ever told me that before."

"The men in London must be particularly dull-witted."

"Some of them are," Isabelle admitted. "But most of them can't get past the subject of my appearance."

Oliver feigned confusion. "What's wrong with your appearance?"

Isabelle flushed. "Nothing's wrong with it exactly, it's just that–" she broke off, ashamed to put it in words.

"Yes?"

"Many men find me beautiful," Isabelle blurted.

Oliver nodded. "I'm not a good judge of the matter, as I prefer women who are tall and dark," he told her. "But you are certainly very pretty, Miss Fleming."

"Don't feel obliged to praise me, just because I'm your employer's sister-in-law," she said tartly. After complaining that most men couldn't see past her appearance, she knew it was irrational to be piqued by Oliver's faint praise, but she couldn't help herself.

Oliver smiled at her. "I've never praised a lady out of obligation, Miss Fleming."

They were nearing the house, and Isabelle realized that if they went any farther, they would be within view of the windows.

"I will get down here," she said stiffly.

Oliver pulled on the reins to signal the horse to stop,

then stood staring at her expectantly, with the ghost of a smile on his lips.

"Would you be so kind as to help me down?" she finally asked.

He reached up and lifted her down easily. Isabelle thought his hands lingered on her waist for an instant longer than necessary.

"Thank you," she said.

Oliver nodded and held out his arm to help her up to the house, but she declined it with a little shake of her head.

"My ankle feels much better already, and I can make it inside without help." She set off for the house before Oliver could argue the point, and since she seemed to be walking without a limp, he didn't chase after her.

Seven

Three days later, Oliver left Langley's study feeling happier than he had in weeks. He was beginning to feel at home at Stonecroft, and he thought the staff and tenant farmers were starting to trust him. The earl had just reviewed his accounts and told him they appeared to be in order, which Oliver took as high praise. Best of all, unlike everyone else on the estate, Langley hadn't once compared him to Mr. Pettigrew.

Oliver had planned to return to his cottage, but the sound of feminine voices in the drawing room made him pause. He had thought of Isabelle often since he had helped her ride back to the house, and he had even asked her maid about her in the servants' hall. Daisy had told him that Isabelle was enjoying playing the invalid, and hadn't left her bedchamber since the injury. Oliver was surprised by this, as Isabelle had seemed to be walking easily after he lifted her down from the horse, and he wondered if she had downplayed her injury to prevent him from carrying her into the house.

He was almost certain that one of the voices in the drawing room belonged to Isabelle, so he knocked on the door and entered. He found Isabelle and Amelia sitting opposite each other, with books open on their laps. Isabelle's right foot was propped on a table, and six inches of stocking were visible above her slipper.

"I'm sorry," Oliver said, embarrassed to have caught Isabelle in such a position.

"Come in, Mr. Oliver," Amelia said politely. "You've come at a good time. I am getting very frustrated with the characters in this novel, and I need an excuse to put it down."

"What are you reading?" he asked.

"It's called *Emma*," Amelia explained. "Isabelle recommended it."

"But you wouldn't? Recommend it, I mean?"

"I find it rather silly. The heroine, Emma, is unjustly criticized for trying to help her friends."

"Amelia can sympathize with her," Isabelle said, with a teasing smile.

"Yes, I can," Amelia agreed. "It's hard to watch people make poor decisions when some well-timed advice might save them from grief."

"There's a little more to it than that," Isabelle protested. "And Emma's advice isn't always good."

"Oh, there's a lot more to it than that," Amelia agreed. "It's taking me ages to get through it."

"You don't have to read it if you're not enjoying it," Isabelle told her.

Amelia sighed. "The problem with novels is that I get frustrated when the characters behave irrationally."

Isabelle turned to Oliver. "Do you read novels, Mr. Oliver?"

"No," he replied, startled by the question. "I don't have time." He had enjoyed reading as a boy, and later at Cambridge, but he hadn't read anything for pleasure since he had joined the army.

"What do you do in the evenings?" Isabelle asked him.

"I work, and then I sleep." Oliver didn't tell her that he spent his time between work and sleep drinking alone in his cottage and then tossing and turning in bed, haunted by memories of the war.

Isabelle's forehead wrinkled in concern. "You work in the evenings?"

"Sometimes," he admitted. "There are always accounts to review and reports to read."

"So all you do is work and sleep? What do you do for amusement?"

He was tempted to say that talking to Isabelle was the most entertaining thing he had done in months, but he realized how pathetic it would sound. "I enjoy being outdoors, and I take pride in my work."

Isabelle looked troubled. "I'm sure Lord Langley wouldn't mind if you borrowed a book from his library," she said thoughtfully.

"You should take this one," Amelia said decisively, holding out the first volume of *Emma*. "I don't think I'm going to get through it."

"Thank you, Lady Langley, but I won't have time to read it," Oliver said politely.

"I wouldn't have thought Lord Langley was such a demanding employer," Isabelle remarked.

"He's not," Oliver admitted. "But I'm still learning how the estate runs, so I'm not as efficient as I could be. I expect things will get easier with time."

"But if I understand correctly, you're only here on a temporary basis?" Isabelle asked. "It seems likely that by the time you've learned how things run, Mr. Pettigrew will be back."

Oliver smiled. "Stonecroft is one of the finest estates in the country, and I'm sure the knowledge will benefit me regardless of what I do next."

"Do you know what that might be?" Isabelle asked.

"No," Oliver said honestly. "But I'm confident I'll find a new position."

"If there's so much work to be done, perhaps Lord Langley will wish to keep you on when Mr. Pettigrew returns," Isabelle suggested. "You could assist him."

"I'm afraid that's impossible," Oliver said.

"Why?" Isabelle asked. "I think Lord Langley would consider it. I know he looks intimidating, but–"

"He doesn't look intimidating," Amelia protested.

"To those of us who are not married to him, he often looks intimidating," Isabelle continued. "But I've found that he's actually very kind."

"Langley might consider it, but I wouldn't," Oliver said firmly.

"It wouldn't be charity," Isabelle insisted. "You said yourself that there are always accounts to review and reports to read. It seems like too much work for one person."

"The truth, Miss Fleming, is that I don't think I could work with Mr. Pettigrew," Oliver said lightly. "People would be forever comparing the two of us, and I understand he's a man of extraordinary talents. Can you imagine what such a situation would do to my confidence?"

"I'm not sure the comparison would be unfavourable," Isabelle said, before she noticed the gleam of humour in Oliver's eyes.

"You are very kind, Miss Fleming," he said. "I came to ask about your ankle. I hope it's feeling better?"

"Yes, much better," Isabelle said. "Amelia convinced me to rest it again today, but it's really almost healed."

"I'm pleased to hear it."

"How did you know about her injury?" Amelia asked curiously.

"Daisy was concerned about her, and mentioned it in the servants' hall," Oliver lied.

Amelia looked skeptical of this explanation, so Isabelle decided to tell her the truth. "Actually, Amelia, Mr. Oliver found me on the path after I hurt my ankle, and he was kind enough to let me ride his horse back to the house."

"I see," Amelia said, with a penetrating look at Oliver.

"I don't remember if I thanked you for your help," Isabelle told Oliver shyly. "I'm not sure what I would have done if you hadn't found me there."

Oliver gave her a look of surprise. "If I recall correctly, you said you were perfectly able to walk, and had merely stopped for a rest under a tree."

Isabelle blushed. "I may have underestimated the injury," she said carefully. "I appreciated your kindness."

"It was a pleasure, Miss Fleming," Oliver said with a smile.

Matthews appeared to announce Dr. Carter, and the

doctor bustled into the room before Amelia could protest. He bowed to Amelia and Isabelle before looking inquiringly at Mr. Oliver, and Amelia reluctantly performed the introductions. If Dr. Carter thought it was unusual to find the land agent in the drawing room with the countess and her sister, he kept his opinion to himself.

"Miss Fleming, I came as soon as I heard of your injury," he told Isabelle pompously.

"How did you hear of it?" Amelia asked bluntly. "I don't think anyone sent for you."

He gave her a reproving look. "No one sent for me, which is most unfortunate, as I understand Miss Fleming has been suffering for the past three days. I had to hear the news in the village."

"People are talking about my ankle in the village?" Isabelle asked in disbelief. "Have they nothing better to discuss?"

"Likely they don't," Amelia remarked.

Dr. Carter nodded. "I believe word spread through the servants. *Some* people in this household are concerned about you, Miss Fleming."

"I suppose that's kind of them, but I think they're making a fuss over nothing. The injury is trivial, and although it was quite painful when it happened, it's really almost better. I think I'll be able to resume my usual activities tomorrow."

"Now, Miss Fleming," Dr. Carter said, with a condescending smile. "I insist that you give the injury time to heal, and it may take several days still. If you'll allow me to examine your ankle, I will tell you when you may resume your usual activities."

"How fortunate that you are here to tell us what to do," Amelia said dryly.

Dr. Carter chose not to reply to this, but turned to Oliver instead. "I'm certain you don't want to watch me examine Isabelle's ankle?"

Oliver thought he might enjoy watching the examination of Isabelle's ankle very much. Propriety won out, however, and he bowed to the ladies and took his leave.

"Take the book," Isabelle encouraged him, and Oliver reluctantly accepted the first volume of *Emma* from Amelia.

After a thorough examination of Isabelle's ankle, Dr. Carter concluded she had suffered a sprain.

"You are fortunate it wasn't more serious," he told her. "I recommend another week of rest. The joint is weak, and if you return to your usual activities too quickly you will risk another injury."

"Thank you," Isabelle said politely. She had no intention of taking his advice, but she recognized that argument would be futile.

Dr. Carter turned to Amelia. "How are you feeling, Lady Langley?"

"Perfectly splendid, thank you."

Dr. Carter seemed disappointed by her answer. "I hope you aren't overexerting yourself?"

"If I am, it's no one's business but my own."

"Lord Langley might consider it his business," Dr. Carter said.

"Quite likely he does, but he's intelligent enough to keep his thoughts to himself." She smiled demurely. "He knows that an argument wouldn't be good for the baby."

Dr. Carter frowned. "But you must see that–"

"I wonder, Dr. Carter," Isabelle interrupted. She had recognized the dangerous gleam in Amelia's eyes, and unlike her sister, she disliked conflict. "Would you recommend that ladies who are with child avoid both physical and mental exertion?"

Dr. Carter was chagrined to realize that he was once again discussing a delicate subject with an unmarried young lady. "I would indeed, Miss Fleming," he said carefully.

Isabelle nodded. "I thought so. I've found that conflict can excite my sister, so I try not to disagree with her."

Dr. Carter gave Isabelle an approving look. "I think that's wise."

Amelia rolled her eyes at her sister and rose to pull the bell. "Matthews will show you out, Dr. Carter."

Dr. Carter bowed and followed the butler out of the drawing room.

As soon as the door had closed, Amelia turned to Isabelle. "I never knew you thought of me as a half-wit."

"He means well, and I didn't want to sit through a quarrel."

Amelia smiled. "Dr. Carter may disagree with me, but he will never really quarrel. It's one of the benefits of having a title; Dr. Carter is so desperate to attend the birth of Lord Langley's heir that he will stay polite, regardless of what I say to him." She chuckled. "I'm sure that if I wasn't a countess, Dr. Carter wouldn't want anything to do with me."

"Now I understand why you married Lord Langley," Isabelle teased. "The title allows you to say impertinent things to country doctors."

"You know I didn't marry Robert for his title," Amelia said mischievously. "It was for his fortune."

"I think society places too much importance on rank and fortune," Isabelle said thoughtfully. "A man can't control the circumstances of his birth, and it doesn't seem right to judge him on them. It's more impressive when a man starts without advantages and makes something of himself."

Isabelle's words were overheard by Dr. Carter, who was pacing in the hallway while he waited for Matthews to fetch his coat. The doctor left Stonecroft in excellent spirits, confident that at least one of the estate's noble residents recognized his worth.

"Dr. Carter was here again, but there's no need for concern," Amelia told Langley, when he and Adrian entered the drawing room a short time later. "We didn't send for him, but he heard about Isabelle's ankle. I'm afraid you've just missed him."

"I think I'll survive the disappointment," Langley said. He handed Isabelle a letter. "This came for you in today's post."

Isabelle's thoughts went immediately to Lord Malthaner, and she blushed. She hadn't expected to receive many letters at Stonecroft, and so far, she had been proven right; the men who had pledged their eternal admiration had forgotten her as soon as she left town. She had hoped, however, that Lord Malthaner would be the exception.

"If you're blushing, perhaps I should read it first," Amelia suggested.

Isabelle ignored her sister and opened the letter to find a poem.

The sun's gone to sleep
And it rains all day
Nothing but storm clouds
Since Isabelle went away

The curtain is down
At the end of the play
The lights have gone out
Since Isabelle went away

And yet I keep dreaming
I live for the day
That I see her again
Since Isabelle went away

You are my destiny.
I hope to see you soon.
An Anonymous Admirer.

"Is it from a gentleman?" Amelia asked slyly.

"I think so. It's from the Anonymous Admirer." Isabelle tried to smile, but found she couldn't do it. There was something unsettling about the whole business, and her admirer's decision to keep his identity secret seemed more bizarre than romantic.

"I'm feeling a little tired, so I think I'll go upstairs," she said, dropping the letter on the table.

"Do you mind if we read it?" Amelia asked.

"You may keep it," Isabelle replied from the doorway.

Amelia skimmed the letter, then handed it to Langley before following her sister out of the room. Adrian stood close to Langley so he could read over his shoulder.

"I think that's one of the worst yet," Adrian remarked. He took the letter from his brother and turned it over, hoping to find a clue to the identity of the sender. "It's not even franked," Adrian said in disgust. "If I wanted to send a girl love-poetry, I'd take the trouble to get a frank."

"Whom would you ask to frank it?"

Adrian looked surprised. "You, of course."

Langley smiled. "But if you sent it anonymously, people might think I had written it."

Adrian laughed. "Now, Robert, surely no one would suspect you of writing love-poetry." He paused. "And you're not the sort of scoundrel who would try to take credit for another man's work."

Langley assured his brother that he was not that sort of scoundrel.

"Still, someone should tell this fellow to show his admiration in a way that doesn't cost us anything to receive," Adrian remarked.

"I wasn't aware that you paid to receive the post at Stonecroft, Adrian," Langley said gently. "But if you would like to take over the responsibility, I wouldn't object."

"What?" Adrian grinned. "No, Robert, but it's the principle of the thing. It doesn't seem right for you to pay for such drivel."

"I appreciate your concern for my finances, Adrian, but I believe I can stand the expense."

"You don't mean to encourage this Anonymous Admirer?"

"Of course not. I can understand why you're jealous of a rival for Isabelle's affection, but I hardly think the poetry is helping his cause."

"About that, Robert," Adrian said sheepishly. "I know I've made a fool of myself over Isabelle, but now I think of her as a sister."

Langley smiled. "I know."

"You know?"

Langley sighed. "You don't think I'd let you stay at Stonecroft if I thought you had a serious interest in Isabelle?"

Adrian bristled. "She could do a lot worse, you know."

"'I don't doubt it, but I prefer not to dwell on the thought. We must trust in Isabelle's good judgment."

"Do you think she has good judgment?" Adrian asked doubtfully. "She never gave me any encouragement."

Langley smiled at his brother. "There's no accounting for a lady's preferences."

Eight

Oliver started reading *Emma* that evening and was surprised to find himself enjoying it. He finished the first volume the following day and wanted to ask Isabelle about the second, but to his frustration, two days passed with no sight of her. On the afternoon of the third day he decided to look for her in the library, but to his disappointment, the only person there was Lord Langley.

"Looking for a book, Oliver?" Langley asked.

"Yes," Oliver said quickly. The earl's eyes were shrewd, and Oliver felt as though Langley knew he was really hoping to find a young lady. "That is, I would like to borrow something to read in the evenings, provided you have no objection."

"You're welcome to borrow anything you like," Langley said. "But come to my study for a moment first. I have a dilemma, and I want to ask your opinion."

"Of course, sir," Oliver agreed, turning to follow the earl down the hall.

THE MYSTERIOUS MR. OLIVER

"Have a seat, Oliver," Langley said, gesturing to the chair opposite his desk. "Cognac?"

Oliver nodded. Langley poured drinks for them both, then leaned back in his chair. "Isabelle has an admirer," the earl began.

Oliver choked on a sip of cognac. He assumed that Langley had discovered how he felt about Isabelle and was trying to warn him off, and he supposed he shouldn't be surprised. He wondered if the earl knew about their encounter in the Old Cottage, or that Oliver had helped her home after she injured her ankle.

"What makes you think so?" Oliver asked carefully.

"He sends her bad poetry and signs it 'An Anonymous Admirer,'" Langley said dryly.

"*Poetry*, sir?" Although Oliver was relieved to learn that Langley hadn't been referring to him, he hated the thought of another man sending poetry to Isabelle.

"It wouldn't be my style either," Langley agreed. He handed Oliver a letter. "This arrived two days ago, and I'm afraid Isabelle was upset by it."

Oliver read the poem, and like Isabelle, he found it upsetting. "You don't know who sent it?"

Langley shook his head. "She's received similar notes in London, but I never took them seriously. I thought that a man who wrote poetry like that was probably harmless, but now I don't know." He sipped his cognac and sighed. "If he sends more letters, I don't know whether to give them to Isabelle or destroy them."

Oliver thought for a minute. "I think you should give them to Miss Fleming," he said finally. "If you don't, and she learns about them later, she'll think you didn't trust her to deal with them herself."

"That was my inclination too," Langley said. "I suppose she shouldn't be receiving letters from gentlemen, but I don't see how she can decide if she likes a man if she can't communicate with him."

"Do you think there is a gentleman in particular that she likes?" Oliver asked casually. Langley gave him a strange look, and Oliver hastened to explain himself. "Because I'm sure the letters will stop once she's married. Even a fool can see that Isabelle's not the type to carry on an affair."

"I'm afraid our poet is likely a fool," Langley said. "But at least if the letters continue after her marriage, it will be a problem for her husband." He stood and smiled at Oliver. "I'll let you get back to the library."

When Oliver returned to the library, he still didn't find Isabelle, but he did find the second volume of *Emma*. He started back to his cottage, but paused when he saw an unusual vehicle sweep up the drive and stop in front of the house. The large carriage was painted a deep shade of purple and had a stylized 'G' painted on the panel in gold. A footman rushed out to let down the steps, and Oliver stared at the man who descended them. The visitor had fair hair and a florid complexion, and appeared to be in his late thirties. As Oliver watched, he removed his many-caped driving coat to reveal a green and white pinstriped waistcoat that nipped in at the waist. Oliver suspected that the man's wasp-waist was the result of a tightly laced corset, and he didn't envy his valet.

Next to descend was a delicate blonde lady, wearing a purple silk gown that almost exactly matched the colour of the coach. Diamonds dripped from her ears and glittered on the buckles of her shoes, and Oliver was amazed that she had worn such ostentatious clothing to travel. Her liberal use of cosmetics made it difficult to guess her age, but Oliver thought she was several years older than her companion.

"I can't believe it's so hot in May," the man complained, wiping sweat from his brow.

His companion wasn't listening to him, for she had spotted Oliver and was staring at him intently.

"But I know you!" she said, walking towards him with narrowed eyes.

Oliver held his breath. He was certain he had never met the lady, but it was quite possible that she was acquainted with one of his relatives.

"I beg your pardon, ma'am, but I don't think–" he began carefully.

"Lady Marguerite," she interrupted. "I am Lady Marguerite Garland. This is my husband, Mr. George Garland." She surveyed Oliver intently. "But I should know who you are!"

"People often mistake me for someone of their acquaintance," Oliver said smoothly. "I have that sort of face."

"But no, I think your features are very distinctive. In fact, you are very attractive," Lady Marguerite said candidly.

Oliver's cheeks heated. "Thank you, ma'am," he said. "But I don't believe we've met. My name is Mr. Oliver."

"My first husband's valet!" Lady Marguerite exclaimed triumphantly. "You look just like him. He was very attractive too, and he never laughed when my husband did foolish things. I told him he should be on the stage, because he was so good at hiding his thoughts. But it seems he enjoyed being a valet." Lady Marguerite shrugged her shoulders to show that such a preference was incomprehensible to her.

"I must get out of this heat," Garland said peevishly.

"Yes, yes, we will go inside," Lady Marguerite agreed. "You will come too, Mr. Oliver." Before Oliver knew what was happening, she had taken his arm and led him up the steps to the door. Matthews uttered an inarticulate protest as Lady Marguerite and Oliver swept past him towards the drawing room, with Mr. Garland close behind them.

The residents of Stonecroft had assembled in the drawing room for tea, and the sight of the visitors had an interesting effect on the party. Isabelle blanched, Amelia almost dropped the teapot, and Adrian looked pleased by the diversion. Only Langley's expression remained inscrutable.

Adrian spoke first. "Lovely dress, Lady Marguerite," he remarked. "Did you dress to match your carriage? Do you still have the purple one?"

Lady Marguerite didn't deign to reply to that, but Garland beamed. "The proper name for the colour is aubergine, but it is lovely, isn't it?" he asked proudly. "We now have both a phaeton and a travelling coach in aubergine. We came in the travelling coach, of course, because of the luggage."

"Luggage?" Amelia asked weakly.

"We have come to visit you," Lady Marguerite announced, as though she was conferring a great favour.

"Wonderful," Langley remarked blandly. "I suppose the letter advising us of your visit was lost in the post?"

Lady Marguerite frowned in confusion. "There was no letter," she said matter-of-factly. "We have just returned from France, and we planned to stay at your townhouse, but you were not there. Mr. Garland didn't want to stay at your house while you were away, so we have come to Stonecroft."

"We are honoured," Langley said ironically. "May I ask why you didn't want to stay at your own house?"

Garland grimaced. "Our townhouse is closed," he explained simply.

"Ah," Langley said. "And you didn't consider reopening it?"

"We have given the staff a holiday," Garland replied.

"We have spent so much money on the construction of Garland Castle that we couldn't afford to open the house," Lady Marguerite said in frustration.

Amelia looked panicked. "Surely you don't mean to sell the townhouse?"

"Of course we do not mean to sell it," Garland blustered. "This is a temporary retrenchment. My textile mills are still turning a handsome profit, and everything is proceeding as it should."

"Nothing is proceeding as it should," Lady Marguerite retorted. "We are building a home in Yorkshire," she explained to Oliver. "It was going to be magnificent, but we have had to alter the plans, and now it will hardly be bigger than Stonecroft!"

"I can see how that would be a disappointment," Langley said wryly.

Garland surveyed the drawing room with a critical

eye. "But Garland Castle will have far more Italian marble than Stonecroft does."

"George insisted on Italian marble, but there has been such difficulty in getting it shipped to Yorkshire," Lady Marguerite said. "It has been a tremendous piece of mismanagement, and you wouldn't believe the money we have spent."

"We might have borne the cost of the marble quite easily if you hadn't spent so much money on new dresses," Garland said irritably.

"But that is nonsensical!" Lady Marguerite said. "Your business is in textiles, George, so when I buy dresses, I am supporting it."

"But you ordered your clothes in France!" Garland protested.

"Ah," said Lady Marguerite, in a conciliatory tone. "You own English mills, so you are upset that I didn't buy my clothes here. I haven't found anyone in England who understands silk as well as Madame Mireille, but for you, George, I will visit the English modistes."

"But my angel, you bought so many gowns in France, you can hardly need more," Garland said.

"Perhaps not," Lady Marguerite said nobly. "But I will buy them, George, since I wish to please you. Not in Kent, however. I will wait until we return to London."

"How long do you intend to honour us with your presence?" Langley asked politely.

"We're not entirely certain," Garland began. "We planned to go to Yorkshire to oversee the construction of Garland Castle, but Lady Marguerite wanted to see Amelia. Isabelle too, of course," he added as an afterthought. "And you know, a mother's visit to her daughters can never last long enough."

Oliver had wondered about the Garlands' relationship to the family at Stonecroft, but he would never have guessed that Lady Marguerite was Isabelle's mother. Now that he looked for it he could see the resemblance, although Lady Marguerite had unsuccessfully tried to augment her charms with powder and paint.

"I only hope you won't neglect Garland Castle," Langley said smoothly. "I've never built a house, but I've heard it's important to be on site to supervise the construction."

"I can vouch for the truth of that," Garland said, pleased to have found a subject on which he had greater expertise than the Earl of Langley. "It's very hard to find reliable workers. Some are cheating scoundrels, but I think most are just lazy."

"It certainly sounds as though you're needed in Yorkshire," Adrian remarked.

"I am, but my first duty is to Lady Marguerite," Garland said. "And she's accustomed to noble society." He turned to Oliver. "Her brother's a duke, you know," he said proudly. "Her father was too."

Oliver realized that Garland was waiting for him to reply, so he murmured: "Congratulations."

"Thank you," Garland said. "When Garland Castle is done, we will hold house parties, but that is impossible while it's under construction. So Lady Marguerite gets bored in Yorkshire, don't you, my angel?"

"Of course I get bored, there is nothing to do!" Lady Marguerite exclaimed. "We must stay in a cottage while the castle is built, and there is no society there."

"I fear you may find the entertainment somewhat lacking here," Langley said apologetically.

"Then it is fortunate that we have come!" Lady Marguerite said, turning to Amelia. "There is nothing worse than a quiet existence for a lady who is with child. She will fret over every imagined ailment, and the child will be born timid!" She looked at Langley through narrowed eyes. "I hope you are not cosseting Amelia."

Langley fixed Lady Marguerite with an icy stare. "Do I look like the sort of man who would cosset his wife?"

Adrian snickered, and Lady Marguerite looked at Langley suspiciously.

"Do you know, I think you do," she said thoughtfully. "It's always the men one least expects. Yes, it is fortunate that we have come."

"I'm feeling rather ill," Garland announced. "I think I must lie down."

"I'll ask Mrs. Prescott to have a guest room prepared," Amelia said. "Would you care for some tea?"

"Nothing hot," Garland said with a shudder. He lowered himself into a wing chair with a creaking of corsets.

Langley took pity on him. "Brandy, Garland?" he asked.

"Please," Garland said gratefully. "I need something to settle my stomach." He lowered his voice as though to impart a confidence. "I suffer from dyspepsia, you know, and I am a patient of Dr. Henry Reynolds. In fact, we stopped to see him in London before we came here."

"Brandy certainly won't help you!" Lady Marguerite said scornfully. "But I will take some, for I have never understood your English fascination with tea."

Langley poured two glasses of brandy, and Lady Marguerite frowned when Garland accepted one. "If you would only give up spirits, and stop lacing your corsets so tightly, you would feel much better, and you wouldn't need Dr. Reynolds," she told her husband. "A little exercise would help too."

"I don't expect someone who has never suffered from dyspepsia to understand," Garland said nobly.

"Do you think Dr. Reynolds has experienced dyspepsia?" Lady Marguerite asked. "No doubt he pretends to be sympathetic, so he can collect his fee. I don't think English doctors know what they're about. The doctor you consulted in France said there was nothing wrong with you."

Garland frowned. "That's not true," he said defensively. "Dr. Lefebvre said I had *absolument rien.*"

"That sounds unpleasant," Adrian remarked. "Is it dangerous?"

"I don't know," Garland said in frustration. "Dr. Lefebvre would only speak French, and when I asked Dr. Reynolds about it, he said he couldn't say." He turned to Lord Langley. "Have you heard of this condition?"

A smile tugged at Langley's lips as he considered his reply, but Lady Marguerite spoke before he could answer.

"*Absolument rien!* The doctor said absolutely nothing is wrong!" Lady Marguerite huffed. "I have explained this to George, but he does not believe me."

"I think you have mistaken the translation," Garland said, wincing as he shifted in his chair.

"Would you like me to summon the doctor, Garland?" Langley asked politely.

Garland sighed. "I suppose it's some country man?"

"We are in the country," Amelia pointed out.

"But I understand Dr. Carter trained at St. Bartholomew's in London," Langley said with a small smile.

Garland brightened. "Then I suppose I had better see him."

A footman was dispatched to fetch the doctor, and Oliver tried to slip out of the room in his wake. He knew he should have left the drawing room long ago, but he hadn't been able to draw himself away from the bizarre family reunion.

"But where are you going?" Lady Marguerite asked Oliver.

"I must get back to work," he replied.

Lady Marguerite looked perplexed. "My daughter has some strange ideas, it is true, but surely she doesn't expect her guests to work?"

Oliver smiled. "But I am not a guest, Lady Marguerite. I am the land agent."

Lady Marguerite frowned. "But you look nothing at all like a land agent," she protested.

"I am sorry to disappoint you," Oliver said politely. "If it makes you feel better, I only have the position on a temporary basis." He could see that she was eager to explore the subject, so he quickly bowed and made his exit.

Dr. Carter was overjoyed to be summoned to Stonecroft, and presented himself as quickly as he could. The footman hadn't told him who needed his services, and his elation dimmed slightly when he realized the patient was only the countess's stepfather. But he put a brave face on it, and spent over an hour closeted with Garland in one of the guest bedchambers.

Back in the drawing room, Amelia sighed. "I suppose I should invite Dr. Carter to stay for dinner," she said, looking displeased at the idea.

"But then we will be seven at the table," Lady Marguerite remarked. "An uneven number is bad luck."

"Perhaps Mr. Garland will be too unwell to come to dinner," Adrian said innocently.

"Mr. Garland is never too unwell to eat," Lady Marguerite scoffed. "We must have the land agent!"

Isabelle looked at her mother in confusion. "Do you mean Mr. Oliver?"

"Yes, the one who looks like a valet. The attractive one."

"Mr. Oliver doesn't want to dine with us," Amelia explained. "I've invited him before, but he always declines. I think he fears it would be awkward. And if he comes, we will have five gentlemen and only three ladies."

"Nonsense," Lady Marguerite scoffed. "An attractive man is always a welcome addition to the table." She turned to Isabelle. "Isabelle. Go tell Mr. Oliver that we want him at dinner."

Isabelle flushed. "I will invite Mr. Oliver, Mama, but I can't force him to come."

"Nonsense. If he's concerned that he doesn't have the right clothes, tell him he can have his pick of Mr. Garland's wardrobe. He can borrow his valet, too."

"I'm not sure it's just about clothes, Mama," Isabelle said carefully.

"You must be decisive, Isabelle. Tell Mr. Oliver that if he doesn't appear, I will fetch him myself."

~

Isabelle walked down to Oliver's cottage and knocked on the door. He didn't answer immediately, and she had raised her hand to knock again when the door swung open.

"Miss Fleming," he said, looking surprised. Isabelle's pale green gown made her blue eyes look turquoise, and she looked young and very lovely. Oliver understood why she inspired men to write poetry.

"Good evening, Mr. Oliver," she said. She opened her mouth to invite him to dinner, then closed it again. For some reason, a dinner invitation seemed fraught with meaning, so instead she blurted: "Did you read the book?"

"I beg your pardon?"

"*Emma,*" Isabelle explained. "I thought I saw you carrying it this afternoon, so I wondered if you had read it."

"You are remarkably observant, Miss Fleming. I have finished the first volume."

"What did you think?"

"I liked it well enough to look for the second volume."

"Is that all?" she asked, her disappointment plain. *Emma* was one of her favourite novels.

"I'll withhold judgment until I've finished the whole," he said with a smile. "Did you walk down here just to ask me that?"

"My mother sent me to invite you to dinner."

"Do you wish to invite me to dinner?"

Isabelle blushed. "Of course."

"You don't look certain, Miss Fleming," he said in a teasing tone.

"The thing is, Amelia feels obligated to invite Dr. Carter, and that will give us an uneven number, so my mother insisted we ask you."

"I see. I'm being invited to make up the numbers."

"You're being invited because we would like your company," Isabelle rallied.

"I'm flattered, Miss Fleming, but I don't think it's a good idea."

"If you're worried you don't have the right clothes, my mother has offered to lend you something from Mr. Garland's wardrobe, along with the use of his valet."

Oliver smiled. "I hope Lady Marguerite doesn't expect me to wear a corset."

Isabelle laughed. "You would hardly need one," she remarked without thinking.

Oliver's eyes twinkled. "You don't think so?"

"I just meant we won't be dressed formally," she said quickly. Oliver hadn't thought she could look lovelier, but the blush stealing across her cheeks was charming.

"That's a relief, because I don't think a corset would be comfortable," he said.

"I'm sure it wouldn't," Isabelle said. "And I think men in corsets look foolish."

"The Prince Regent would be devastated to hear you say that," Oliver teased.

"Do you think he really wears corsets?" Isabelle asked. "I thought that was just a rumour."

"Oh, he certainly does. You can often hear the creaking before you see the man."

"Have you met the Prince Regent?" Isabelle asked curiously.

"No," Oliver lied. He had actually met the Regent on several occasions before he entered the army. "But I've heard him described."

"I see," Isabelle said. "I understand why you might not want to borrow from Mr. Garland, but I'm sure Lord Langley would lend you a set of evening clothes. I can ask him if you like."

"You are very concerned about my clothing, Miss Fleming," Oliver said lightly.

Isabelle's cheeks coloured again. "I don't care what you wear, but I thought it might matter to you."

Oliver thought of the set of formal clothes packed in the bottom of his trunk, a relic from a time in his life when he had thought his clothes mattered very much. They were at least five years out of date and he wasn't sure if they still fit, but the thought of showing up to dinner dressed as a London dandy brought a smile to his lips.

"If I come to dinner, Miss Fleming, I will wear my own clothes." He wouldn't wear the old formal clothes either; if he went, he would go as Mr. Oliver, not Lord Oliver St. Clair.

"I hope you come," Isabelle said. "Mama said that if you refused, she would come to fetch you herself."

"In that case, I suppose I have no choice." Oliver was tempted to ask if Isabelle would sit next to him, but he thought better of it.

Isabelle looked pleased. "You will join us?"

"Yes."

"Will you walk back with me now?"

Oliver checked his fob watch. "Surely it's too early? Everyone will still be dressing."

"Yes," Isabelle admitted slowly. "I just thought–"

"Don't worry, you can trust me to appear," he said dryly.

Isabelle smiled. "I will see you soon, then, Mr. Oliver."

Nine

Isabelle returned to the house and went upstairs to her bedchamber, where her maid was waiting to help her change for dinner.

"You're late, Miss," Daisy said reproachfully. "I was thinking the white satin–"

"I'm not changing tonight, Daisy," Isabelle interrupted. "So we just need to do something with my hair."

"Not changing?" Daisy asked in surprise.

"It's not a formal dinner, so this dress will be fine."

Daisy's expression made it clear that she didn't agree. "But Miss, I heard your mother plans to wear a new dress from France."

"All of her dresses are from France," Isabelle said.

"With a diamond necklace," Daisy continued.

"How do you know? She only arrived this afternoon."

"I heard it from her maid, Marie. Marie said the necklace was once owned by a Princess of the Far East."

"I see." Isabelle wondered if that story had sprung

from her mother's fertile imagination or that of her maid. "Do you talk about my jewellery downstairs, Daisy?"

"No, Miss Fleming," Daisy said sadly. "There is very little to discuss. But I thought you might wear your strand of pearls tonight, with your white satin gown."

"I am not changing my dress, Daisy, and I'm not wearing jewellery either," Isabelle said firmly.

"Very well, Miss," Daisy said, in a tone of resignation. "I heard your mama invited Mr. Oliver to dinner."

"You are very well-informed."

"He's a very handsome man," Daisy said, with an uncharacteristic giggle. "Even though he looks unhappy all the time. Do you think he has a tragic past?"

"I don't know," Isabelle said dismissively, although she had wondered the same thing.

"He has sad eyes, and there's something mysterious about him," Daisy continued.

"Now you're being fanciful, Daisy."

"Perhaps he's been disappointed in love," Daisy speculated. "But I can't understand why a girl would throw him over, because he's ever so polite, and he has the most charming table manners. He never chews with his mouth open, like some of the footmen."

Isabelle smiled but said nothing.

"I expect he's lonely, but he's not likely to find a young lady while he's at Stonecroft," Daisy continued "I'm sure he considers himself far too good for the likes of me, but he could never look as high as someone like you."

"That's nonsense, Daisy," Isabelle said. "If you've finished with my hair, I will go down."

"So, Dr. Carter, have you found the reason for my husband's symptoms?" Lady Marguerite asked across the dinner table. Unlike her daughters, who still wore morning dresses, Lady Marguerite had changed into an ivory silk evening gown accessorized with a choker of diamonds. Although the gown was simply cut, it was remarkable for its plunging neckline and clinging skirts.

Dr. Carter turned to Lady Marguerite, and found his eyes drawn first to her diamond necklace and then to her décolletage. He made an effort to lift his gaze to her face. "I don't think it's appropriate to discuss your husband's health at the dinner table, ma'am."

"If you don't know, Dr. Carter, you would do better to say so," Lady Marguerite admonished.

"We have had a successful initial consultation, and there are several possible reasons for his symptoms," Dr. Carter said stiffly.

Lady Marguerite snorted. "Yes, I have been telling him so for months. The reasons are tight lacing, an excess of rich food, and a lack of exercise."

Garland frowned. "Now Marguerite, Dr. Carter does not think it is that simple."

"Of course he doesn't," Lady Marguerite said scornfully. "He is hoping you will continue to request his services, so it's in his interest to tell you what you want to hear." She sighed. "I have no patience with people who fancy themselves sick. They run from one doctor to another, quack themselves with useless treatments, and bore their acquaintances by telling them about it." She glared at Dr. Carter. "And you English doctors indulge these people, because you lack the courage to tell them their problems are all in their heads."

"If doctors have nothing useful to offer, why do people continue to consult them?" Dr. Carter asked acidly.

"Because their friends no longer wish to visit them, for fear of hearing about their ailments!" Lady Marguerite said triumphantly. "So they are forced to summon the doctor for company."

Isabelle took pity on Dr. Carter. "I think medicine is a noble profession," she said kindly.

Dr. Carter preened. "Indeed it is, Miss Fleming," he said, beaming at her. "But it is more than a profession, it is a calling."

"I cannot conceive of anything so tedious," Lady Marguerite said.

"Then it's fortunate you're not a physician, Lady Marguerite," Dr. Carter replied.

"Certainly, it's fortunate for me, but perhaps not so fortunate for the patients," Lady Marguerite said. "I would give excellent advice."

"You must see many interesting things, Dr. Carter," Isabelle said diplomatically.

Dr. Carter smiled warmly at Isabelle. He thought it was remarkable that she had grown up to be such an intelligent young lady, in spite of the corrupting influences of her mother and elder sister. "I do, Miss Fleming," he said.

"Do you truly find it interesting to listen to your patients complain?" Lady Marguerite asked skeptically. "I don't imagine you would be so keen to listen to them if you weren't being paid to do so."

"I have many less fortunate patients who are unable to pay my full fee," Dr. Carter said nobly. "Some can't pay anything at all, and I treat them out of charity. Many of my patients suffer from serious illnesses and wouldn't survive without medical care."

"If you were truly charitable, you wouldn't tell us about it," Lady Marguerite said dismissively. "You probably boast of your charity work to all of your paying patients. And I expect the patients who are able to pay are the ones who are least likely to be ill." She turned to Mr. Oliver. "It is usually women who fancy themselves sick, and you must see a difference between ladies of the nobility and those of your own class. Working-class women don't have the luxury of imaginary complaints."

"Mama!" Isabelle exclaimed. "Mr. Oliver's father is a landowner. He is hardly of the working class."

"But Isabelle, he's working, and he's not of the nobility, so he's of the working class." Lady Marguerite turned back to Oliver and smiled. "I hope I don't offend you?"

"Not at all, Lady Marguerite," Oliver assured her, looking amused. "I'm not ashamed of working."

Lady Marguerite gave him an approving nod. "And would you agree that working-class women don't have the luxury of imagining themselves sick? If they were too soft, they wouldn't survive."

"In general, I think you're right, Lady Marguerite," Oliver agreed. "But I think many aristocratic women are much stronger than they look."

Oliver's eyes found Isabelle's as he spoke, and she blushed and turned to Garland. "When do you think Garland Castle will be completed?" she asked, in an effort to change the subject.

"There have been a few setbacks," Garland admitted. "We had to take down several trees to make room for the house, and then our architect quit. His vision did not agree with mine."

"I told Mr. Garland to hire a French architect, but he did not listen to me," Lady Marguerite said.

"Despite the problems, I still expect it to be magnificent," Garland said. "I am thinking of opening it to the public, with a small fee for admission. We don't need the money, of course," he said quickly. "But you can never have too much money. Don't you agree, Lord Langley?"

"I think you're more ambitious than I am," Langley replied.

"It's a shame the estate is so far from London," Garland said thoughtfully. "If we were closer to town, as you are here at Stonecroft, it would be far more convenient for people to visit."

"I'm not sure about that," Langley said. "I think your location is ideal."

Lady Marguerite looked at him through narrowed eyes.

"In Yorkshire, you will only get visitors with the commitment and means to make the journey," Langley explained. "If you were too close to London, you would have to contend with the scaff and raff of town."

"The challenge will be in drawing the guests north," Garland mused.

"Have you considered a circus?" Adrian suggested. "Something like Astley's Amphitheatre. You could get performing animals, monkeys, that sort of thing."

Garland appeared to consider it. "You don't think it would be vulgar?"

"Oh, you'd hire well-born animals," Adrian said easily.

"And you think people would want to see it?" Garland asked curiously.

"Lord, yes. I can't count the number of times I've been to Astley's."

"Perhaps Garland could hire you as the circus manager," Langley suggested.

Adrian smiled. "I think it would be too far from town for me."

A footman interrupted with a message for Dr. Carter, which he read with a frown. "I'm afraid I must go," he said, with a bow to Amelia. "I have been summoned to see a patient, and it's a matter of some urgency."

"Of course you must go," Amelia agreed. "Thank you for coming, Dr. Carter."

"Convenient thing about being a physician," Adrian commented, as soon as Dr. Carter had left. "If I were a doctor, I'd have my man send me messages whenever I went to a dinner party. That way, if I got bored, I could leave with the excuse that I had been called to see a patient."

"Why would you need an excuse?" Lady Marguerite asked, looking at Adrian in confusion. "It isn't difficult to leave a dull party. The challenge is for those who wish to be rid of the doctor."

Adrian was silent for a moment while he considered this. "Perhaps you could send the doctor a false message, saying one of his patients needed him urgently," he suggested.

Lady Marguerite nodded. "It is an idea, that. Although I think the mistake was inviting Dr. Carter to dinner in the first place."

Isabelle thought that Dr. Carter had served a useful

purpose, as he had kept Lady Marguerite's mind off her daughters' shortcomings. That changed during the pudding course.

"And you are not betrothed yet, Isabelle," her mother said with disappointment. "You inherited my beauty, so it's *incroyable* that you do not have gentlemen falling at your feet."

"I wouldn't know what to do with gentlemen who fell at my feet," Isabelle said mildly.

Adrian nodded his agreement. "She might trip over them. It would be a dashed nuisance."

Lady Marguerite ignored Adrian and pursed her lips. "Perhaps it is because they think you're a bluestocking. You haven't let it be known that you read books? Or that you write stories?"

"No, Mama," Isabelle said calmly.

"And no one has caught your interest? You may not have thought of it, Isabelle, but if you don't marry, you will be a charge on your brother and sister for the rest of your life!"

"Not a charge on you, Mama?" Isabelle asked innocently.

Her mother looked surprised. "It would not make sense for you to live with Mr. Garland and me. We do not intend to have children."

Mr. Garland looked uncomfortable. "Well, as to that, Lady Marguerite, we haven't entirely decided–"

Lady Marguerite silenced her husband with a look. "We have decided, George. And since we will not have children, it is only sensible for Isabelle to live with Amelia, so she can help take care of her nieces and nephews."

Isabelle smiled. "I will enjoy being an aunt."

Lady Marguerite looked at her doubtfully. "Yes, but it is one thing to be an aunt when you are only visiting from time to time, and quite another when you are living there. You will become an unpaid drudge."

"Mama, Isabelle will always be welcome to live with us," Amelia said firmly. "And I hope we will never take advantage of her."

Lady Marguerite eyed Isabelle speculatively. "If you are fond of a particular gentleman, you could always try to manoeuvre yourself into a compromising situation with him. It would only work if he were honourable, and honourable men are often dull, but it might be better than life as a drudge."

Isabelle turned red with embarrassment. "Mama!" she exclaimed.

"Well, it's not as though you would try to entrap anyone here," Lady Marguerite said practically.

Langley looked at Adrian. "I don't know if that means she doesn't think you're eligible, or she doesn't think you're honourable," he remarked.

Adrian took the teasing in good humour. "There's no need for Isabelle to entrap me. I'd marry her tomorrow if she'd have me."

Lady Marguerite raised an eyebrow. "If Isabelle were foolish enough to marry a man without a title or a fortune, she might as well marry Mr. Oliver."

Isabelle's cheeks burned, and Oliver coughed.

"You know, Isabelle, he's quite attractive," her mother continued, surveying Oliver critically. "It's a pity he's only a land agent."

"Mama!" Isabelle protested. "How can you say–"

"It's nothing to be ashamed of, Isabelle," Lady Marguerite interrupted. "I said I find him attractive, which is a compliment, and as to being a land agent, I'm sure he knew that already."

"But Mama–" Isabelle tried again.

"*Bien*, don't say you haven't thought of him," Lady Marguerite said unabashedly. "He's tall, and handsome, and from what I have seen, he doesn't talk too much. Why, if I wasn't married to Mr. Garland, I would consider it myself."

The table fell silent for a moment, and Amelia gestured to a footman for another serving of blancmange. Her mother looked at her critically.

"Be careful, Amelia," her mother said. "I know you're increasing, but if you increase too much, you'll never regain your figure."

"I was thinking Amelia was looking particularly beautiful this evening," Langley said, in a tone of voice that would have silenced most guests.

But Lady Marguerite was not like most guests. "I don't believe in polite lies, Lord Langley," she said, in the manner of a parent teaching a principle to a young child. "It's false kindness, especially when there is a remedy for the situation." She gazed at her eldest daughter with disapproval. "Amelia could eat less pudding, and she would be better for it. Isabelle could stop talking of books, and she would be far more likely to find a husband. In the long run, it's far more compassionate to tell someone the truth."

"In that case, Mama, I should tell you that your dress is indecent," Isabelle said bravely. "The neckline is far too low."

Lady Marguerite stared at her daughter incredulously. "If you think, Isabelle–"

"I must say, Lady Marguerite, that I agree with Miss Fleming," Oliver interrupted. "And white dresses are really better suited to young ladies."

"I say," Garland sputtered. "There's no need to be offensive." His usually florid complexion had turned puce.

Oliver smiled. "You might find the statement offensive, but I think your wife would consider it a kindness."

Garland was breathing heavily. "I have half a mind to call you out, Mr. Oliver."

Oliver sighed. "I hate to disappoint you, Mr. Garland, but I don't fight with men who are missing half their minds. It isn't sporting."

Garland stood so abruptly that he knocked his chair backwards, then hesitated. He wasn't confident he could beat Oliver in a fight, so he tried to think of a way to extricate himself from the situation without losing face. Everyone was staring at him except for Oliver himself, who was sipping his wine with apparent indifference.

It was Lady Marguerite who finally saved her husband. "But this is ridiculous!" she exclaimed. "Sit down, George. We will leave the melodrama to the bourgeoisie." She lifted her wineglass to Oliver. "Mr. Oliver has made a witticism, and I congratulate him."

It was hard to justify fighting to avenge a wife who found the situation humorous. Garland tried to sit, but forgot that he had knocked over his chair, and he stumbled. A footman rushed over to assist him, and Amelia rose to signal that it was time for the ladies to withdraw.

Lady Marguerite turned to her husband. "George, you will come with us," she said autocratically. "If you drink any more port, you will snore like a pig all night, and I won't get any sleep. My first husband was the same. I don't know what it is with men and port." Garland followed her meekly from the room, leaving Langley, Adrian, and Oliver at the table.

Oliver turned to Langley. "My lord, I wish to apologize," he said stiffly. "I shouldn't have insulted your guests."

Langley smiled. "On the contrary, Oliver, I think you showed great restraint in your comments to Lady Marguerite. I was tempted to tell her she looked like a courtesan, and that might have given Garland an apoplexy."

Adrian smirked at his brother. "How would you know what a courtesan looks like, Robert?"

"I have a vivid imagination, Adrian," Langley replied blandly. "But I admit that I lack personal experience, so your knowledge of the subject may be more accurate than mine."

Adrian flushed. "Robert, you of all people should know that I don't have the funds to go into the petticoat line."

Langley sighed. "And yet I'm still not motivated to increase your allowance."

Adrian turned to Oliver. "My brother has interesting in-laws, wouldn't you say?"

Oliver smiled. "Lady Marguerite is certainly an original."

"As Mr. Garland delights in reminding us, Lady Marguerite is the daughter of a duke," Langley remarked.

"I don't think she was raised to consider anyone's feelings but her own."

Oliver nodded. "I see."

"It's only the children of dukes that you need to beware of, Oliver," Adrian said. "In my experience, the children of earls are invariably polite."

"Invariably," Langley agreed, smiling at his brother in a way that made it clear that there was true affection between them. Oliver envied them, and wished he had a similar relationship with his brother. Rupert had never wanted to have much to do with Oliver when they were growing up, and the brothers had never been close. In retrospect, Oliver thought his father might have been to blame for that, too. Rupert had known he fell short of father's expectations, and he hadn't wanted to compete with Oliver for his father's attention.

Oliver rose and bowed. "I should take my leave."

Langley gestured to the decanter. "Have another glass of port."

Adrian smiled. "Yes, do. Unlike poor Mr. Garland, you don't need to worry about keeping anyone up with your snoring." He turned to his brother. "Whereas you, Robert, should be careful."

"I don't snore, Adrian," Langley said with dignity.

"You don't know if you snore," Adrian corrected him. "Amelia is so infatuated with you that she wouldn't tell you if you did."

Langley frowned at his brother, but there was a hint of a smile in his dark eyes. "If you mean to remain at Stonecroft, Adrian, I insist that you speak of my wife with respect."

"I have a great respect for Amelia, but you must admit

she's not entirely rational where you're concerned. She seems to think you are without fault."

Langley was smiling in earnest now. "Amelia has excellent judgment."

"The two of you are certainly well-matched," Adrian remarked. "Really, Robert, you owe me a debt for having brought the match about."

Langley raised an eyebrow. "I wasn't aware that you had–er–brought the match about."

"You didn't realize you were in love with her until you thought I had eloped with her," Adrian argued. "Although since you give me such a paltry allowance, you should have known I didn't have the means to elope."

Oliver's expression betrayed his curiosity, and Langley sighed. "Before I married Amelia, she came to visit us at Stonecroft, and Adrian was foolish enough to offer her a ride back to London in his curricle," he explained.

"I didn't exactly offer, Robert, she insisted that I take her with me," Adrian protested.

"Fortunately, Adrian was obliging enough to drive his curricle into a ditch, thus allowing me to catch up with them," Langley explained.

Adrian smiled mischievously at Oliver. "You should have seen the look on Robert's face when he found us. I've never seen him so furious."

"I'm not sure if you've seen my brother drive," Langley said to Oliver. "But if you have, you'll understand why no responsible host would allow a guest to ride in Adrian's curricle."

"That accident wasn't my fault," Adrian protested. "I had to swerve to avoid another vehicle. And really, Robert, you know that's not why you were furious."

"I don't know what you mean," Langley said.

Adrian smiled slyly at his brother. "You were madly in love with her, and I can't believe I didn't see it at the time. Do you remember when I suggested that you set her up as your mistress? I thought you were going to knock me down."

"I probably should have," Langley replied.

"Do you have any siblings, Oliver?" Adrian asked.

"An elder brother."

"And is he as difficult as Robert?"

"We're not close," Oliver said stiffly.

Adrian gave him a look of pity. "That's a shame."

Ten

Letter from Isabelle to her brother William

Dear William,

Mama and Mr. Garland arrived yesterday for a surprise visit. Apparently they are overextended, and they have closed their London house to economize. They insist the situation is temporary, but they haven't told us how long they plan to stay. They may visit you at Cliveden Manor next.

Mama seems to be infatuated with Mr. Oliver, and her behaviour has been rather embarrassing. She insisted he join us for dinner yesterday and made several comments about how handsome he was. To be fair to Mama, Mr. Oliver is not bad looking. He's tall, with enough muscle to lift heavy objects, but not so much that he appears grotesque. He has the most interesting hair; it looks as though it can't decide whether to be blond or brown, and whether to wave or curl.

Yours, Isabelle

∼

Dear Isabelle,

It's probably for the best that Mama and Mr. Garland went to Stonecroft. I'm sure they will have far more entertainment with you than they would at Cliveden Manor. If they ask about Cliveden, tell them there is a great deal of work to be done at the home farm, and I would be very grateful for Garland's help.

Wouldn't it be funny if Mama left Garland and ran off with Mr. Oliver? But I suppose they would need a place to go, and since I can't imagine Mama living in a cottage, there's a chance the pair of them would end up at Cliveden Manor. All in all, you probably shouldn't encourage the idea.

William

∼

Isabelle had been embarrassed by her mother's behaviour towards Mr. Oliver, so the following morning she went for a walk around the grounds in the hope she would run into him. After she had walked for half an hour, she found him painting a fence that enclosed a sheep pasture.

"Good morning, Mr. Oliver," she said. "Aren't there labourers to do that sort of work?"

"Good morning, Miss Fleming," he replied politely. "Yes, there are labourers, but this section hasn't been done, so I decided to do it. If it's left much longer, the wood will rot. " He grinned. "If I sit in an office all day, I'll get soft."

He was wearing a loose cotton shirt, but Isabelle could still see the outline of his muscles as he painted, and she thought he looked anything but soft. "I don't think there's much risk of that," she said thoughtfully. "Perhaps you should have left it to the labourers."

Oliver laughed. "Do you think I'm above painting a fence?"

"Not at all. I fear you're not qualified to do it." She peered at the fence critically. "You missed a spot up there."

"If I missed a spot, it's because you were distracting me. And this is only the first coat."

"Well, if you do it right the first time, you might not need a second coat. Think of all the paint you would save."

"Stonecroft is hardly short of paint."

Isabelle smiled. "Let me help you."

"I thought your sister was the one with an interest in this sort of work?"

"Amelia's not the only one who can do practical things," Isabelle said defensively. "I'm perfectly capable of painting a fence."

"You might be, but I don't have a second paintbrush."

"I'm sure you need a rest. We could take turns."

Oliver gazed at her blue muslin dress. "You're hardly dressed for painting."

"This is an old gown," Isabelle lied, "and I think I can manage to get the paint on the fence rather than on myself."

Oliver smiled. "I'm sorry, Miss Fleming, but my pride won't let me stand here and watch you paint the fence."

"Oh." Isabelle realized she wasn't going to win the

argument, so she decided to change the subject. "Mr. Oliver, I hope you weren't uncomfortable at dinner last night."

"Why, Miss Fleming, since you were kind enough to explain that I could come without a corset, I was perfectly comfortable. I can't recall when I last spent a more interesting evening."

Isabelle laughed, then her expression turned serious. "My mother often speaks without thinking. I know some of her remarks were insensitive, and I hope you weren't offended."

Oliver set down his paintbrush. "Do you mean her references to people of my social class, or her suggestion that you might marry me if I had a title and fortune?"

Isabelle's cheeks burned. "Both. I hope you weren't insulted."

Oliver smiled. "Since your mother managed to find fault with everyone present, I was flattered that she thought me worthy of her notice."

Isabelle laughed. "She was particularly hard on poor Dr. Carter."

"You should be careful with Dr. Carter," Oliver said, in a tone of voice that was no longer teasing. "He's more than halfway in love with you already, and it's cruel to raise a man's expectations if you have no intention of fulfilling them."

"His expectations of what?" Isabelle asked in confusion.

Oliver almost laughed. He had seen the way Dr. Carter looked at Isabelle the evening before, and it had left him in no doubt of the other man's feelings. "Dr. Carter wants to marry you, Isabelle."

Her expression made it clear that he had shocked her. "That's ridiculous," she protested. "I haven't done anything to raise his expectations."

Oliver raised an eyebrow. "You were kind to him, which was a great contrast to the behaviour of your mother and sister. And you smiled at him."

"You're accusing me of raising his expectations because I smiled at him?" she asked incredulously.

It was clear to Oliver that Isabelle didn't understand the power of her smile. "I didn't say it was rational, Isabelle, but be careful. Men are more fragile than they look."

"Perhaps instead of all the fighting, Wellington should have sent a young lady to smile at Napoleon. She could have bewitched him into surrendering," Isabelle said with a laugh. "Perhaps that's what actually happened, and that's why you don't want to talk about the war. It wouldn't be nearly as impressive as a victory in battle."

Oliver's expression changed. "That isn't funny, Isabelle," he said stiffly.

"I'm sorry, Mr. Oliver. I was only trying to make a joke."

"The war wasn't a joke."

"Of course not," Isabelle agreed.

Oliver turned back to the fence and resumed painting, much faster than he had before. He barely seemed to notice that he was dripping paint on the ground and leaving large spots of the fence unpainted.

"What was life like in the army?" Isabelle asked.

"I don't like to talk about it." Oliver spent far too much time trying not to think about his time in the army.

"You don't have to talk about the battles, or share military secrets," Isabelle said, trying to tease him out of his bad humour. "What did you do when you weren't fighting?"

"Tried to forget about fighting," he said grimly. "Then prepared to fight again." He continued to work, throwing paint on the fence with harsh, angry strokes.

"I'm sorry I asked," Isabelle said. When Oliver didn't reply, she turned and walked back to the house.

The following day was rainy, and after several hours in the drawing room with her mother and stepfather, Isabelle sought refuge in the library. She was scanning the shelves for a book to read when she was interrupted by Dr. Carter.

"Luck is on my side today," Dr. Carter said, in a tone of satisfaction. "I came to inquire after Mr. Garland but had the good fortune to find you instead."

Isabelle thought the library was an unusual place to look for Mr. Garland, but she forced herself to smile politely. "I think Mr. Garland and Mama are in the drawing room," she said. "I'm surprised Matthews didn't show you the way. I'll take you to them."

"Stay a minute, Miss Fleming," Dr. Carter said. "I have a confession to make."

"Oh?"

"I lied to your butler," he said, looking very pleased with himself. "I told him Mr. Garland had summoned me secretly, because he didn't want your mother to know of it. I was to go up to his bedchamber quietly."

"I see," said Isabelle cautiously. "But Mr. Garland didn't summon you?"

Dr. Carter frowned. "I expect he will want to consult me again, but he didn't send for me," he confessed. "That was a ruse to gain entry to Stonecroft."

Isabelle hid a smile. "For what purpose, Dr. Carter? Are you hoping to steal a book?"

"I am hoping for a much more valuable prize." Dr. Carter dropped to one knee in front of her. "Miss Fleming, I am hoping to steal your heart."

Isabelle stared at him, speechless.

"I see I have surprised you, but I'm not ignorant of your feelings," Dr. Carter continued. "I know you feigned the injury to your ankle in order to see me again."

"I didn't feign an injury!" Isabelle protested. "I turned my ankle. And I never sent for you. You simply appeared with a story that there was gossip about my ankle in the village. Which seemed entirely ridiculous, if you must know."

"But Miss Fleming, when I arrived you insisted that there was nothing wrong with your ankle."

"Because it had improved by the time you examined it."

"If that's how you want to play it," Dr. Carter agreed, with a knowing smile. "I suppose you want to punish me for not coming to examine it sooner, but the news of your injury didn't reach me for several days."

"I certainly didn't want to punish you!" Isabelle exclaimed. "Really, Dr. Carter–"

"And then you told your sister that you thought society placed too much importance on rank," he interrupted. "I could guess what brought that to your mind."

Isabelle was certain that he couldn't.

"While I can't offer you a title or a fortune, I flatter myself that I have built a good reputation in the neighbourhood," Dr. Carter continued. "I am confident that I will be able to support you in comfort. You will not have as many servants as your sister, but with your nobility of mind, I'm sure that such a consideration will not weigh with you."

Isabelle took a deep breath. "Dr. Carter, I am honoured by your proposal, but I'm afraid I must decline it."

"Ah," he said. "You are afraid of what your family will think."

"No, I'm not," Isabelle said honestly. Her mother would make a fuss if she accepted Dr. Carter, but she thought her brother William would give his consent if he believed it was what she wanted. The problem was that she didn't want to marry Dr. Carter. Her heart didn't speed up when he entered the room, and there was no *frisson* of excitement when he touched her hand.

"I am aware that some members of your family hold views that are not as enlightened as your own, but I don't think they would stand in the way of true love," Dr. Carter said.

Isabelle smothered a giggle. It seemed the sour-faced Dr. Carter was a romantic.

"I am sorry, Dr. Carter, but I do not return your affection," she said gently.

"I see," he said abruptly. "Is this your sister's doing?"

"Of course not."

"Then Miss Fleming, I don't understand. After giving me every encouragement, you now say that you don't return my affection. I can only conclude that either sinister influences have poisoned your mind, or that you delight in trifling with the feelings of an honest man."

It was clear that Dr. Carter was genuinely upset, and Isabelle considered what to do. She knew that if Amelia were in this situation, she would treat Dr. Carter to a scathing speech that would effectively depress his pretensions. Isabelle, however, was too tender-hearted. She could hear Oliver's voice, saying it was cruel to raise a man's expectations if you had no intention of fulfilling them. Intentionally or not, it seemed she had raised Dr. Carter's expectations, and she needed to convince him that his suit was unwelcome.

"To tell you the truth, Dr. Carter, I want to marry into the nobility," she said, in what she hoped was a haughty tone. "I am determined not to settle for anything less than an earl."

"But you told your sister–"

"Amelia is inclined to make too much of her rank," Isabelle lied. "I thought she needed to be put in her place."

Dr. Carter could certainly sympathize with that wish.

"And you are resolved?" he asked stiffly.

Isabelle nodded.

"Then I suppose there is nothing more to be said."

"I suppose not," Isabelle agreed, relieved to see the end of a painful conversation.

"Although," Dr. Carter began, and Isabelle groaned inwardly. "I must say, Miss Fleming, I am disappointed. I thought your views were more advanced than those of your mother and sister, but it seems I was mistaken."

Isabelle heard the library door open, and she turned.

"There you are, Isabelle," Adrian said, as he swept into the room with Lady Marguerite on his heels. He frowned when he saw Dr. Carter. "Are you unwell, Isabelle, or have you simply gained another admirer?"

"I believe Dr. Carter came to inquire after Mr. Garland's dyspepsia," Isabelle replied.

"The library seems like a dashed silly place to look for Mr. Garland," said Adrian, with a gleam of devilment in his eyes. "Take care, Isabelle. If you continue to tryst with Dr. Carter, your mama might insist that you marry him."

"Ha!" exclaimed Lady Marguerite. "My daughter, marry a doctor? I've never heard such a ridiculous notion."

Dr. Carter bowed stiffly. "Let me assure you, ma'am, that your daughter shares your views on the subject."

Lady Marguerite stared at him in disbelief. "You don't mean to say that you asked Isabelle to marry you?"

"It was an error in judgment, ma'am, and one that will not be repeated," Dr. Carter said, before bowing again and leaving the room.

Eleven

"I wonder if you could do me a favour, Mr. Oliver," Langley asked the following day.

"Of course," Oliver answered quickly. When Langley had summoned him for a meeting in his study, he had worried the earl had found a problem with his work, so the request for a favour came as a relief.

"You should wait to hear what it is first," Langley said enigmatically. "Lady Marguerite and Mr. Garland have asked about a tour of the estate, and I thought you would be the best person to show them the grounds."

"If you wish, sir, but I don't know nearly as much about the history of the estate as you do," Oliver said cautiously.

"The Garlands don't know the history either, which should give you some scope for creativity."

"I see. Do they wish to walk or ride?"

"One or the other," Langley said vaguely. "I'll leave it to your judgment. Since it may take you several hours to cover the grounds, you could ask the cook to put together a hamper of food to take along."

"A hamper of food," Oliver repeated.

"Lovely day for it, don't you think? Although if you would rather not tour the estate, you could take the Garlands for a drive. Morgan could take you," he suggested, referring to his coachman, "so you can devote yourself to the Garlands' entertainment. If you go to Maidstone, you could stop at the Maidstone Arms for refreshments."

"And the tour of the estate?" Oliver asked.

"Save it for another time," Langley said. "Unless you're keen to do it today, in which case you should. As I said, I trust your judgment. What do you think?"

"I think I will enjoy spending the day with Lady Marguerite and Mr. Garland, sir."

"I knew I could rely on you, Oliver," Langley replied, pleased that Oliver understood that his real objective was to get the Garlands out of the house.

Oliver left the study and made his way to the drawing room, where he found Lady Marguerite arguing with Isabelle.

"This is folly, Isabelle," Lady Marguerite said. She turned and saw Oliver in the doorway. "Ah, Mr. Oliver. Tell my daughter she is being foolish."

"I'm afraid I don't know what you're discussing, Lady Marguerite," Oliver said. "But I came to ask if you and Mr. Garland would like to accompany me on a tour of the estate."

"That is exactly what we are discussing," Lady Marguerite told him. "I want Isabelle to come too."

"You are welcome to join us, Miss Fleming," Oliver said politely.

"Thank you, but I would prefer to stay here."

"The truth, Mr. Oliver, is that Isabelle is afraid of horses," Lady Marguerite explained. "She had a bad fall several years ago, and she hasn't wanted to ride ever since."

Oliver turned to Isabelle. "Were you badly hurt?" he asked gently.

She nodded. "I hit my head. The doctor was concerned, and I spent four days in bed."

"Yes, but that was years ago, and you recovered," Lady Marguerite pointed out. "The only way to get over your fear is to face it."

"If Miss Fleming was hurt riding, I don't think she is foolish to be cautious," Oliver said. "That seems to demonstrate good sense."

"I doubt you would say that if she were a man," Lady Marguerite said.

Oliver smiled. "I suppose we'll never know."

"I understand you were in the military, Mr. Oliver," Lady Marguerite continued. "Can you imagine what would happen if a soldier refused to get back on a horse after taking a fall? Or refused to go back into battle after seeing some sort of disaster?"

Oliver's expression shuttered. "But Miss Fleming is not in the military, and we are no longer at war," he said curtly. "So, Lady Marguerite, I think this subject is foolish."

"I have ridden since the accident, Mama," Isabelle said. "But I prefer to ride at a slower pace than you do."

Lady Marguerite smiled. "That is because I am not ruled by fear, Isabelle."

"I am afraid this discussion is pointless," Oliver said. "I remembered that I must go to Maidstone today, so I won't be able to take you on a tour of the estate."

Lady Marguerite's brow furrowed. "But why didn't you mention this earlier? Couldn't you go to Maidstone another day?"

"I'm afraid not," Oliver lied. "I must attend to an urgent matter of business. But you, Mr. Garland, and Miss Fleming are welcome to come with me."

Lady Marguerite frowned. "I suppose we might as well, since there is nothing else to do here."

The weather was fine and the scenery beautiful, so the drive to Maidstone would have been pleasant if it weren't for Lady Marguerite's fixation on Isabelle's marriage prospects. Oliver had taken Langley's suggestion and asked Morgan to drive them, but rather than entertaining the Garlands, he found himself listening to Lady Marguerite.

"I don't understand, Isabelle," she lectured. "A young lady with your looks will receive offers of marriage unless she is doing something to chase the men away. Don't you agree, Mr. Oliver?"

"I'm afraid I have very little knowledge of the subject, ma'am."

"I think, Isabelle, that I should chaperone you myself next Season," Lady Marguerite continued.

"But will you have a house in town?" Isabelle asked innocently.

"I will have to," she said simply. "George knows I never agreed with his decision to close the house, but he relies on the advice of his man of business, and his man of business is an imbecile."

"It's not that simple, Marguerite," Garland said.

"But it should be," she retorted. "If you can't convince your man of business to change his advice, you should change your man of business. Then we will reopen the house."

"I would prefer to live with Amelia," Isabelle said firmly.

"But she will have a young child, and she may not want to spend her time taking you to balls," Lady Marguerite said. "Some ladies are funny that way."

Isabelle would never admit it to her mother, but that fear had crossed her mind.

"What's more," Lady Marguerite continued, "Amelia has no sense of her duty as a chaperone. Why, if I hadn't intervened, you might have found yourself betrothed to Dr. Carter!"

Mr. Garland perked up. "If you're interested in marrying a doctor, Isabelle, you might consider Sir Henry Reynolds," he suggested. "He's a widower, you know, and it would be convenient to have him in the family. Dr. Carter might do for country folk, but I have a lot more faith in Reynolds."

"Isabelle does not want to marry a doctor!" Lady Marguerite exclaimed. "Dr. Carter wished to marry her! I don't know what she said to encourage him, but I find the whole affair *incroyable!*"

Isabelle was thankful that she was sitting beside Mr. Oliver instead of opposite him, so she wasn't forced to meet his eye. "I didn't encourage him, Mama," she said. "But perhaps I wasn't doing anything to chase him away."

Isabelle's meaning was lost on Lady Marguerite, but Oliver pressed his lips together to hide a smile.

When they finally reached Maidstone, Oliver left the rest of the party at the Maidstone Arms and spent forty-five minutes walking up and down the main street. When he thought that enough time had passed to support his lie of having come to town on a matter of business, he returned to the inn. The proprietor explained that since there was no private parlour available, the Garlands were in the main dining room, and Oliver prepared himself for complaints about the inadequacy of the inn. He had made it to the doorway of the dining room when the sight of a young lady stopped him short.

The lady was on her way out of the dining room, but she froze when she saw Oliver. She was of medium height, with pleasant but nondescript features, and she appeared to be about Oliver's age. Isabelle, who had an excellent view of the doorway, thought the most remarkable thing about the lady was her effect on Mr. Oliver. His eyes widened and his face blanched, but he recovered himself quickly and bowed.

"Good afternoon, Mrs. Coates," he said politely. "You're looking well." She was the widow of Francis Coates, who had been Oliver's closest friend in the army until Coates' death at Waterloo. Oliver had known her well; she was one of the brave women who had travelled with the army because she couldn't bear to be separated from her husband. After Coates' death, she had gone home to live with her parents.

"I am Mrs. Henderson now," the lady said awkwardly.

"I was married last month, and we have just returned from our wedding trip. Mr. Henderson has gone out to check on the horses."

"I see," Oliver said, trying to keep a neutral expression. "Congratulations, ma'am."

"It's been two years," she said, a little defensively.

"I know." As though Oliver could ever forget.

An uncomfortable silence fell, and Oliver racked his brain for something to say.

"Where did you go for your wedding trip?" he finally managed.

"Ramsgate," she answered quickly. "We stayed in a hotel by the sea."

"It sounds very nice," Oliver said inanely.

"It was."

There was another awkward pause before Mrs. Henderson spoke again. "I didn't think I would marry again, but I was very lonely," she confided. "And I thought that if I had been the one to die, I wouldn't have wanted Francis to spend the rest of his life in mourning."

"Of course not," Oliver agreed, his expression wooden.

"I would have wanted him to move on, and to be happy," she continued. "And I think he would have wanted the same for me." She clasped her hands in front of her, almost protectively, and Oliver realized she was playing with her wedding ring through her glove.

"I'm sure he would. I wish you well, ma'am," Oliver said, before bowing and taking his leave of her.

"At last!" Lady Marguerite said dramatically, when Oliver reached their table. "You can tell the coachman we're ready to leave. If you can believe it, this establishment has only one private parlour, and it's occupied."

"Of course," Oliver agreed stiffly. "I'll find Morgan and ask him to get the carriage ready."

"Mama, we should let Mr. Oliver have something to eat first," Isabelle said, gesturing to the platter of meat and cheese on the table.

"Thank you, Miss Fleming, but I'm not hungry."

Morgan had the coach ready quickly, and the drive back to Stonecroft passed uneventfully. After Oliver helped the others descend, he walked off towards the stables. Isabelle told her mother she was going to walk in the garden, and she spent five minutes wandering through the rosebushes before slipping down to the stables. She found Mr. Oliver brushing a horse with sure, rhythmic strokes.

Oliver nodded to Isabelle before turning back to the horse, and they stood in silence for several minutes. Isabelle reflected that although she would never be truly at ease around horses, there was something comforting about the smell of the stables. She wanted to ask Oliver about the lady he had encountered at the Maidstone Arms, but she sensed it wasn't the time.

"You were right about Dr. Carter," she finally said.

Oliver finally looked at her properly, and she looked so miserable that he felt no satisfaction in having been right.

"Was it a difficult decision?" he asked lightly.

Isabelle sighed. "The decision wasn't difficult, but the process was. I couldn't make him believe that I didn't want to marry him."

"He has a high opinion of himself," Oliver remarked.

"I doubt many country doctors would have the presumption to court a viscount's sister."

Isabelle sighed again. "And that was the argument I finally had to make. I told him I was determined to marry a man with a title."

"It shouldn't have come as a surprise to him."

"I think it did," Isabelle said sadly. "But it isn't true."

Oliver gave her a cynical look. "You don't want a man with a title?"

"That's not what I said. But if I loved a man, it wouldn't matter if he had a title or a fortune."

"I see," Oliver said skeptically. "So you don't care about a man's rank or wealth? You would marry a farmer, or a shopkeeper, if you fell in love with him?"

"I don't know," Isabelle said honestly. "I've never been acquainted with a farmer or a shopkeeper, so this is all theoretical."

It was on the tip of Oliver's tongue to ask her opinion on land agents, but he knew that would be dangerous.

"I think you mean hypothetical," he said instead.

Isabelle's brow furrowed. "Isn't it the same thing?"

"A theory is based on a principle that has already been proven through experimentation, while a hypothesis is untested. So, since you have never been acquainted with a farmer or a shopkeeper, you can't theorize about how you would behave towards one. You can only hypothesize."

"I have learned something new today," she said with a smile. "I didn't realize you were a scholar."

"I did graduate from Cambridge," he said dryly, irritated that she was surprised.

Isabelle laughed, and Oliver couldn't help but appreciate the flush it brought to her cheeks.

"I'm sorry," she said, once she collected herself. "It's just that your comment reminded me of Mr. Garland. He never tires of reminding us that he went to Cambridge."

"I suppose we have that in common," Oliver said stiffly.

Isabelle grinned. "I think it's the only thing you have in common with Mr. Garland. I don't think he graduated, and I doubt he would know the difference between a hypothesis and a theory. But I imagine you were academically inclined?"

"I got by." Oliver had, in fact, graduated with a first. "You should get back, Miss Fleming," he said gently. "People will wonder where you are."

Isabelle wanted to protest, but she knew he was right, so she nodded and walked back to the house to dress for dinner.

The following day, Isabelle packed some fruit into a basket and set off for the tenant cottages to pay another call on Mrs. Daniels and her baby. Mrs. Daniels looked surprised to see Isabelle again, but she thanked her profusely for the fruit and insisted that she come in for tea. In contrast to Isabelle's first visit, the cottage was now as neat as a pin, and the baby was sleeping peacefully in his crib. It was clear that Mrs. Daniels no longer needed help, and Isabelle was wise enough not to offer any. She drank her tea as quickly as she could and took her leave.

On her way out the door, Isabelle tripped and almost

lost her footing. When she looked down, she realized she had collided with a puppy. He was a tiny creature, only a ball of brown fur with legs, and he stared up at Isabelle with a reproachful expression.

"I beg your pardon, Miss Fleming," Mrs. Daniels said apologetically.

"It's all right," Isabelle said with a laugh. "I think I should be begging this fellow's pardon. I didn't see him there." She bent down and picked up the dog, who squirmed in her hands but settled when she held him against her chest. "I think he was asleep the first time I came, so I haven't had a chance to meet him yet. He is a boy, isn't he?"

"Yes, he is," Mrs. Daniels said uncomfortably.

"What's his name?"

"He doesn't have a name yet."

"I see," said Isabelle, although she didn't really understand how one could neglect to name a dog. Her feelings must have shown on her face, because Mrs. Daniels launched into an explanation.

"I haven't named him because I don't think I'll be able to keep him," she said quietly, as though sharing a secret. "Our dog had a litter almost two months ago, and my husband got rid of the pups, but somehow this one escaped. When Joe came back from taking care of the others, he didn't have the heart to get rid of him too."

Isabelle drew the puppy closer to her chest and tried not to think about the fate of its siblings.

"I promised Joe I'd give him away as soon as he was old enough to leave his mother." Mrs. Daniels explained with a sigh. "We can't keep a second dog."

"Who will you give him to?"

Mrs. Daniels frowned. "I don't know yet."

"I'll take him," Isabelle said impulsively.

Mrs. Daniels looked skeptical. "Are you sure?"

"Yes," Isabelle said decisively. "That is, if you're really not hoping to keep him yourself."

"Oh no," Mrs. Daniels said. "Joe was quite clear about it."

As Isabelle walked home with the puppy in her arms, she encountered Mr. Oliver crossing the fields.

"Good morning, Mr. Oliver," she said.

"Miss Fleming," he said, nodding politely. Isabelle thought of him spending his evenings alone in his cottage, and she made another impulsive decision.

"I wonder if you could do me a favour," she asked. "I've acquired a puppy rather unexpectedly, and he's in need of a home. Would you consider taking him?"

As Isabelle still held the dog against her chest, it was impossible to look at him without looking at her chest. Oliver glanced at the puppy for just long enough to confirm that he was, indeed, a puppy, before drawing his eyes back up to meet Isabelle's.

"Are you sure that's a puppy?" he asked. "He's very small."

"All puppies are small," Isabelle said defensively.

Oliver looked at her skeptically. "But this one looks more like a rodent. What breed did you say he was?"

"I didn't say," Isabelle replied. "But I think he's a mixed breed."

"Ah," Oliver said knowingly. "Part dog and part rat."

"It's unkind to judge him by his looks," Isabelle retorted. "I expected better of you, Mr. Oliver."

"You're right," Oliver acknowledged, with a teasing

gleam in his eyes. He sneaked another glance at the dog. "Fortunately, he's asleep, so he won't have heard my observations. Where did you find him?"

"One of the tenant farmers," Isabelle explained. "Their dog had a litter, and the rest of the siblings were–" she paused. "Got rid of. This one escaped, but the farmer told his wife she would have to find another home for him."

"You don't want him yourself?"

Isabelle did, but she thought Oliver needed the puppy more than she did. "I don't think I can keep him," she said regretfully. "He'll have to be let outside at night. It's not practical for me to take him out myself, and I can't ask the servants to do it."

"Except me," Oliver said.

"What do you mean?" Isabelle asked, confused.

"You said you can't ask the servants, but you can ask me."

"But you're not a servant."

"I am," he pointed out.

"But you're different," she argued. "And you have your own cottage, so it will be easier for you to take him out at night."

"I'm not sure Lord Langley would approve."

"Lord Langley won't even notice," Isabelle said airily.

"I don't think there's much that escapes his notice."

"Well, he might notice, but I don't imagine he'll care," Isabelle amended.

"A puppy will be a lot of work," Oliver remarked.

"I can help with him," Isabelle offered. "I'll play with him and take him for walks."

Oliver appeared to think about it. "Did Mr. Pettigrew have a dog?" he finally asked.

Isabelle looked at him in confusion. "I beg your pardon?"

"Mr. Pettigrew, the previous land agent. Did he have a dog?"

"I barely knew Mr. Pettigrew," Isabelle explained. "So I wouldn't know if he had a dog."

For this first time since his arrival at Stonecroft, Oliver pitied his predecessor. "You're right," he said, trying to hide a smile. "It doesn't matter."

"I understand if you don't want him," Isabelle said, turning to walk away. "Good day, Mr. Oliver."

"I didn't say I didn't want him." Oliver held out his hands, and Isabelle gave him the puppy. "What's his name?"

"Hermes," Isabelle said decisively.

"The god of travellers and thieves," Oliver commented.

"I just thought he looked mischievous," Isabelle explained. "You can change his name, of course."

"He does look like a Hermes," Oliver said. Hermes opened his eyes, squinted up at Oliver, and promptly fell back asleep. "I suppose I should take him back to my cottage and see if he needs a meal."

Isabelle held out her hands to take Hermes back. "I can carry him."

Oliver raised an eyebrow and kept hold of his puppy. "I thought you gave him to me?"

"You're right, I did." Isabelle smiled. "Thank you, Mr. Oliver."

Oliver stopped at the Stonecroft kitchen to get some

scraps from the cook, then took Hermes back to his cottage and fed him. He set out a water bowl and blanket in the corner of his small sitting room, and told the little dog he had a new home.

Oliver quickly learned that if he left his puppy alone in the cottage for more than two hours, Hermes would relieve himself on the floor. Whenever he could, he took Hermes with him as he went about his work, and within a week, the residents of Stonecroft were used to seeing Oliver with a puppy at his heels. Hermes, however, had very little interest in the other residents of Stonecroft, as his affection was all for Oliver. It didn't matter that Isabelle had been the one to save him from an uncertain fate at the Daniels' farm; Hermes saw Oliver as his rescuer, and Oliver enjoyed the novel experience of being a hero in the eyes of a dog.

Twelve

Letter from Isabelle to her brother William

Dear William,

Yesterday I acquired a dog from the wife of one of the tenant farmers. He's really only a puppy, with mischievous brown eyes and the sweetest little tail. I named him Hermes. Mr. Oliver said Hermes looks like he's part rat, but I don't think he meant to be unkind.

I gave Hermes to Mr. Oliver. I thought they would be good company for each other.

Yours,
Isabelle

After the Garlands had been at Stonecroft for a week, Langley instructed Matthews to start serving inferior wine with dinner. Lady Marguerite remarked upon it, and even told Langley where in France he might find superior vintages, but neither she nor her husband spoke of leaving. After two weeks, Isabelle overheard Langley ask Amelia if he should tell the Garlands to go, but Amelia just laughed and said that they weren't really bothering her. Isabelle wanted to say that the Garlands were certainly bothering her, but she held her tongue, remembering that she was a guest at Stonecroft herself.

But the burden of entertaining the Garlands fell largely upon Isabelle. Amelia had taken to resting in her bedchamber in the afternoons and Langley often joined her there, leaving Isabelle to amuse her mother and step-father. The Garlands disliked most outdoor activities, so Isabelle spent most of her time in the drawing room, listening to her mother talk. She had little time to read, or work on her novel, or wander the grounds in the hope of encountering a certain land agent and his new puppy.

One sunny afternoon Isabelle was listening to her mother complain about the Stonecroft servants, while Mr. Garland snored gently on the sofa. Matthews provided a welcome distraction when he announced that Mrs. Hunt and her daughter had called.

Mr. Garland startled awake, and Lady Marguerite wrinkled her nose. "I don't believe I know any Hunts."

Matthews resented Lady Marguerite's tendency to act as the mistress of Stonecroft, so he turned to Isabelle. "I believe Lady Langley is resting, Miss Fleming," he said. "Shall I tell the Hunts that no one is home?"

"Oh, please send them in," Isabelle said quickly, for she was eager to see Letitia. "And Matthews, could you please send in tea?"

"Certainly, Miss Fleming," Matthews replied. Unlike her mother's autocratic ways, Isabelle's gentle manners had quickly endeared her to the Stonecroft servants.

Mrs. Hunt swept into the room, followed closely by Letitia. Isabelle was relieved to see that Letitia looked reasonably well, despite being dressed in an unflattering shade of pink. Mrs. Hunt had decided that Letitia was more likely to be noticed if she wore bright colours, but the vibrant shades overwhelmed her fair complexion and delicate features.

Isabelle performed the introductions, and Mr. Garland tried to improve upon them.

"Lady Marguerite is the daughter of a French duke," he said proudly, since Isabelle had inexplicably forgotten to mention this.

"How delightful," Mrs. Hunt said coolly.

Amelia and Langley joined them then, and a maid followed soon after with tea.

"Please allow me to pour the tea, my dear Lady Langley," Mrs. Hunt said solicitously.

"Thank you, Mrs. Hunt, but I am perfectly able to pour out," Amelia replied.

"Yes, indeed," Lady Marguerite said. "My daughter is not an invalid, she is simply with child. But if she needed someone to perform the task for her, surely, as her mother, I would be the best person to do so."

Garland was quick to support his wife. "Lady Marguerite is very good at pouring tea," he said loyally. "It was one of the first things I noticed about her."

"Well, I'm not sure," Mrs. Hunt said. "I understand you are from France, Lady Marguerite, and I'm not sure the French appreciate tea the way the English do. There is an art to serving it properly, and my friends often comment on how well I pour a cup of tea. I have taught Letitia, and she can pour out just as well as I do."

Lady Marguerite gave Letitia a condescending look. "How nice for you to have an accomplishment."

Letitia blushed but said nothing.

"Letitia has many accomplishments, Mama," Isabelle said. "And she is one of the kindest people I know. I've never heard her speak an unkind word to anyone."

Lady Marguerite snorted. "I don't consider kindness an accomplishment. It indicates either timidity or a lack of imagination."

Mrs. Hunt's eyes flashed. "I'm afraid that people who think their rudeness will be excused simply because they have courtesy titles are sorely mistaken."

Lady Marguerite smiled. "No one would accuse you of timidity, Mrs. Hunt, but I'm afraid you are the one who is mistaken. I don't expect you to excuse my rudeness; I don't care what you think of me."

Amelia had been handing round the tea while her mother sparred with Mrs. Hunt. Adrian wandered in, bowed to the Hunts, and was turning to walk back out when a look from Langley caused him to sit down.

"If I might make a suggestion," Langley said casually, "we have recently bought a set of balls for lawn bowling, and once we have finished the tea, you might all enjoy a game."

Adrian brightened. "In the mood to be beaten again, Robert?"

"Adrian is remarkably skilled at lawn bowling," Langley explained. "I've never managed to beat him. In fact, I don't know anyone who has."

"I'd like to try," Lady Marguerite said, looking at Adrian through narrowed eyes. "It's a French game, you know. We call it *boules*."

"It sounds interesting," said Garland. "Can we play in pairs?"

"You can play however you like," Langley assured him.

"You won't be joining us?" Adrian asked.

"I think I'll stay and keep Amelia company," Langley said nobly.

Amelia's eyes sparkled with devilment. "What if I want to participate?"

Langley sighed. "Amelia, I don't think lawn bowling is advisable, but if you insist, we can send for Dr. Carter and ask for his opinion on the subject."

"There's no need for Dr. Carter, Robert," she said quickly. "But there's also no need for you to keep me company. I'll be perfectly happy reading a book and drinking this excellent tea."

Langley glanced out the window in search of another excuse, and was relieved to see Oliver crossing the lawn. He turned back to his wife and smiled. "That's fortunate, my darling, because I just remembered that I have to meet with Mr. Oliver."

Langley sent a footman to inform Mr. Oliver of his wish to meet with him, and the lawn bowlers set out for the south lawn. Isabelle and Letitia allowed themselves to fall behind the rest of the group.

"How have you been, Letitia?" Isabelle asked her friend quietly. "Amelia and I tried to visit you in London, after the Somertons' ball, but we were told you had gone to the country."

"We went to my grandmother's house in Tunbridge Wells," Letitia explained. "Mama wanted to go somewhere none of her friends would find us. She has the sort of friends who say they have come to sympathize when they have really come to gloat." She smiled philosophically. "I suppose it's no surprise, for it's how she behaves herself."

"She should never have encouraged Lord Braden," Isabelle said. "He must be three times your age."

"Almost three times, yes. But Mama still thinks that the scene at the ball was my fault, and I should have agreed to dance with him a second time." Letitia blushed and lowered her voice. "I wouldn't have minded dancing with him, but the way he put his hands on me made me uncomfortable."

Isabelle's eyes widened. "Did you explain that to your mother?"

"I did," Letitia confirmed. "But Mama's still hoping he'll make me an offer of marriage."

Isabelle's brow furrowed. "But why Lord Braden?"

Letitia shrugged. "He's rich, and he has a title. She's worried that no one else will offer for me."

"Oh, Letitia," Isabelle said sympathetically. "I'm sorry."

Letitia sighed. "In her defence, I think she truly believes I'll be happier with him than I would be as a spinster, or married to a man without a title."

Isabelle didn't think that was a particularly good defence. "What does your father say?"

"Father's never been able to stand up to Mama," Letitia explained. "I don't expect him to start now."

"What will you do?"

"I'm not going to marry Lord Braden," Letitia said firmly. "I'm fairly sure that even Mama hasn't found a way to marry me to a man without my participation in the ceremony. If she drags me to the church, I'll refuse to say the vows." She smiled. "Now that I've caused one scandal, I'm not as afraid of causing another."

Isabelle could see the sense in that. "Have you told your mother how you feel?"

"Oh, she won't listen to me," Letitia said matter-of-factly. "If I have an opportunity, I may try to tell Lord Braden. I'm afraid he may be coming to stay with us next week. Mama's very excited because a nobleman is coming to visit, but she refuses to tell me who it is."

"It might not be Lord Braden," Isabelle said optimistically.

Letitia laughed bitterly. "I can't think of another nobleman who would want to visit us."

Isabelle tried to think of a way to help her friend, and quickly reached the disheartening conclusion that there was very little that she could do. She imagined that if Letitia could avoid Lord Braden he would lose interest in her, but she couldn't see how that could be managed if he came to stay with the Hunts. If Isabelle were married and had her own establishment she could invite Letitia to stay, but she wasn't in a position to invite her to Stonecroft. It was almost enough to make Isabelle wish she had encouraged one of her admirers, but she reminded herself that if she were married, she wouldn't be able to invite a friend to stay without her husband's permission. Marriage would only improve her situation if she could find the right man.

They reached the south lawn and joined the others.

After a brief argument about whether to play by French or English rules, Adrian threw out the white ball to serve as the target.

"This field appears to have a slope," Lady Marguerite complained.

"Quite possibly," Adrian agreed cheerfully. "If you don't think you're up to the challenge, you can concede."

Mr. Garland quickly discovered that his coat was moulded so tightly to his shoulders that it was difficult to throw a ball. His second throw split a seam under his arm, and he bustled into the house to deliver the coat to his valet's tender care.

To Adrian's surprise, Letitia was his closest competitor, and although he took the first two rounds, she won the third. Isabelle played a respectable game, while Lady Marguerite and Mrs. Hunt were consistently the farthest from the target.

On the fifth round, Lady Marguerite was more successful, and it wasn't clear whether her ball or Letitia's was closest to the target. She and Letitia walked out to inspect the distances, and when Letitia appeared to be distracted, Lady Marguerite nudged her ball towards the target with her foot.

"You kicked your ball, Marguerite!" Mrs. Hunt exclaimed.

"I did no such thing!" Lady Marguerite protested indignantly. "I may have stumbled and touched the ball with my foot, but I certainly did not kick it!"

"You did!" insisted Mrs. Hunt. "You kicked the ball."

"Are you accusing me of cheating?" Lady Marguerite asked.

"Yes," said Mrs. Hunt bluntly. "I know what I saw."

"Now Mama," said Letitia, at the same time as Isabelle said: "Mama, I don't think–"

"This is a matter of honour, Letitia," said Mrs. Hunt grimly.

"Yes, a problem of honour," agreed Lady Marguerite. "You have none. You are willing to lie to help your daughter win a game of lawn bowling."

"And you are willing to cheat to win a game of lawn bowling. It's pathetic."

Lady Marguerite marched back to the house in high dudgeon, with the rest of the party trailing after her. Lord Langley heard the commotion in the entrance hall and emerged from his study, where he and Oliver had been enjoying a glass of brandy.

"Lord Langley," Lady Marguerite began. "Mrs. Hunt has accused me of cheating. I can't believe I have suffered such an insult in your house."

"It wasn't actually in the house, it was on the south lawn," Adrian put in helpfully.

Langley's lips twitched. "Now, Lady Marguerite, surely there has been a misunderstanding," he said calmly.

"There's no misunderstanding," Mrs. Hunt said firmly. "She deliberately kicked the ball. I saw her cheat, my lord."

Lady Marguerite glared at Mrs. Hunt. "Lord Langley, that woman is a liar," she said hotly. "She must be banished from the house."

"Lady Marguerite, you must see that I'm unable to–er–banish Mrs. Hunt from Stonecroft," Langley said diplomatically. "She is a close neighbour and friend."

"You would take her side over mine?" Lady

Marguerite asked in disbelief. "Let me remind you that you are married to my daughter!"

"Lady Marguerite, this quarrel has nothing to do with me. You and Mrs. Hunt will have to sort it out between yourselves."

Lady Marguerite's cheeks flamed, and her eyes flashed fire. "This is more than a quarrel, Lord Langley. That woman has impugned my character." She looked at Mrs. Hunt with loathing. "I cannot stay another night in a house where a woman like her is welcome!"

"I'm sorry to hear that, Lady Marguerite," Langley said smoothly.

"Now Marguerite, let's not be hasty," Garland said, looking nervously at Langley. "Lord Langley has been a considerate host, and I'm sure we both appreciate his hospitality."

"A considerate host would not allow such a woman into his home," Lady Marguerite said hotly. "What is more, she may corrupt my daughters, so I believe I have an obligation to remove them from this house–"

"I'm afraid I would object to that," Langley interrupted.

"I suppose I should be grateful you have the courage to object to something," Lady Marguerite said disdainfully. "I would hate to think that my daughter had married a man who was entirely spineless."

"Indeed," Langley remarked.

"I understand why you wish to keep Amelia here, since you are married to her," Lady Marguerite said grudgingly. "And if she is corrupted by the company you keep, you will be the one to suffer for it."

"I have no wish to corrupt your daughters," Mrs. Hunt

said indignantly. "But they may benefit from learning the value of fair play, as I doubt they learned the lesson growing up."

Lady Marguerite ignored this barb, and turned to her younger daughter. "Isabelle, I don't think you should stay here any longer."

Isabelle held her breath, worried that her mother was about to suggest she come to London with her and Mr. Garland.

"I think you should go to Cliveden Manor and stay with William," Lady Marguerite announced.

Oliver felt a tightness in his chest. He had been enjoying the spectacle until Lady Marguerite had broached the idea of removing her daughters. He hadn't known of Isabelle's existence when he applied for the post at Stonecroft, but now he couldn't imagine Stonecroft without her.

"But Mama, William is busy working on the estate, and there is no one to chaperone me," Isabelle pointed out.

"You hardly need a chaperone if you're living with your brother," her mother said dismissively.

"But I would need a chaperone if I wanted to visit anyone," Isabelle said. "And I might be lonely." Oliver thought he saw her eyes flicker in his direction when she spoke of loneliness.

"I suppose it is your decision," Lady Marguerite said reluctantly. She turned to Langley. "If it isn't too much trouble, perhaps you could ask your staff to assist with preparing our coach."

"No trouble," Langley said quickly, gesturing to a footman.

"My dear," Garland said, in a conciliatory tone. "It is approaching the dinner-hour, so I wonder if we would be better to stay until the morning. We haven't even decided where we will go."

"It doesn't matter where we go, but we must leave here," Lady Marguerite exclaimed. "We can't be far from an inn."

"If you are heading towards London, the Bull is less than an hour away," Langley supplied helpfully.

"Yes," said Garland slowly. "But we stopped there on the journey here, and their food was tolerable at best. Whereas your cook, Lord Langley, is truly excellent. All things considered, I think we would be better to leave tomorrow morning."

"You're being ridiculous, George," Lady Marguerite said. "It wouldn't hurt you to miss dinner."

But Garland appeared to think it might hurt him considerably. "My dear Marguerite, I fear–"

"Perhaps a hamper for the road," Oliver interrupted, before Garland could share his fears. "I'll ask the cook to prepare one."

Garland brightened, and Isabelle gave Oliver a look of gratitude.

The staff made haste to prepare the purple travelling coach and pack a hamper of delicacies, and the Garlands departed within the hour.

~

The Hunts were invited to stay for dinner.

"We will soon have a noble visitor staying with us,"

Mrs. Hunt said proudly, as the footmen served fruit and cheese. "It is quite an unexpected honour."

"How is it unexpected?" Adrian asked. "It sounds as though you're expecting him."

"Or her," Amelia pointed out. "It could be a lady."

"It's true that we are expecting him now," Mrs. Hunt said, ignoring Amelia's comment. "But I could hardly believe my eyes when I read his letter. You'll never guess who it is."

"The King?" Adrian asked innocently.

Mrs. Hunt appeared to deflate a little. "No."

"The Prince Regent?" Adrian tried.

"No."

"Can you give us a hint?" Adrian asked.

Mrs. Hunt smiled. "I'm afraid I cannot. The visitor emphasized the need for the utmost discretion."

"So naturally you're telling us about it," Amelia remarked.

"I haven't told you who it is," Mrs. Hunt pointed out.

"But we've already ruled out the King and the Prince Regent," Adrian said. "So we've started to narrow it down."

"I think instead of guessing specific people, you should start with broader questions," Amelia suggested.

"That's clever," Adrian agreed, before turning back to Mrs. Hunt. "Does your noble visitor hold a rank of earl or higher?"

"No," Mrs. Hunt said reluctantly.

"One of the lower nobles then. Viscount?"

"I'm not at liberty to say," Mrs. Hunt said coyly.

"It's a viscount," Adrian concluded, and Mrs. Hunt didn't dispute the point. Isabelle looked at Letitia sympathetically. Lord Braden was a viscount, so it seemed Letitia's fears were well-founded.

"Perhaps it's Lady Langley's brother," Adrian suggested.

"If William wanted to come to Kent, surely he would stay with us?" Amelia said.

"Maybe he wants to see you, but he doesn't want to impose," Adrian suggested. "It's quite a good idea, actually."

"So he would impose upon the Hunts?" Amelia asked skeptically.

Adrian shrugged. "Mrs. Hunt seems eager to have him."

Mrs. Hunt smiled. "I will bring our visitor to call upon you when he arrives, and I daresay you will be surprised."

Thirteen

Life at Stonecroft was far more comfortable after the Garlands' departure, and Isabelle filled her days with reading, writing, and walks around the estate. Adrian taught her to play cribbage, and Amelia frequently joined them. Langley's concern that his wife would overexert herself proved unfounded; Amelia had the sense to admit that pregnancy made her tired, and she was content to leave the estate business to Oliver.

Oliver enjoyed most of his work, but he hated collecting rent. The bailiff collected rent from most of the tenants, but Oliver was responsible for the difficult ones. Pettigrew's records suggested that some of the tenants never paid without a fight, and that Mr. Clark belonged to this group. Oliver found Clark on a chair outside his cottage, enjoying the spring sunshine and drinking a mug of ale.

"Good morning," Oliver said politely. "Mr. Clark?"

The man nodded insolently.

"My name is Mr. Oliver, and I've taken over from Mr.

Pettigrew as Lord Langley's land agent. I've come to collect your rent."

"I know who you are," Clark drawled. "But I don't 'ave the rent."

Oliver thought Clark would be more likely to have the money for his rent if he spent more time working and less drinking ale on his porch. "Is there a reason you're not able to pay?"

Clark laughed. "I don't 'ave the money. I can't give you somethin' I don't 'ave."

Langley was a generous landlord, and he had told Oliver not to push the tenants for payment if they were unwell or there were other extenuating circumstances. But so far, Mr. Clark hadn't provided an excuse. Oliver was familiar with his type, and knew that if he didn't stand up to him, Clark would never make any effort to pay his rent. Worse, other tenants would be encouraged to follow his example, and before he knew it, Oliver would have lost control.

"You're three months behind on your rent, Mr. Clark," Oliver said. "If you're unable to pay, I'll have to ask you to leave." He hoped it wouldn't come to that. He had no experience with evicting tenants, and he didn't know how he would force Clark to leave if he refused to go.

"You can't do that." Clark stood and walked towards Oliver with a mean look on his face. He spat on the ground, inches from Oliver's boots, and Oliver had to fight the urge to step away.

"You'll find that I can," Oliver said calmly. "I have the authority to act on Lord Langley's behalf. He can't afford to keep tenants who don't pay rent."

"Langley don't need the money," Clark scoffed.

"That may be so, but it's irrelevant. Your lease states that you will pay rent."

Clark took a step closer, and Oliver could smell the ale on his breath. "I don't like the lease."

Oliver stood his ground. "Then I expect you to leave by the end of the week."

Clark wound up and took a swing at Oliver's face, but Oliver saw him coming and sidestepped the punch. Oliver had done some boxing in his youth, and his time in the military had sharpened his reflexes. Although Clark was heavier than Oliver, he lacked his conditioning and his experience.

Clark grunted and came at him again. Oliver danced out of the way but he wasn't quite fast enough, and Clark managed to land a blow on his upper arm.

Oliver realized that a fight was inevitable. The next time Clark charged, Oliver hit him in the face, and he crumpled like a deadweight. Oliver stood over him, worried he was seriously hurt, but after a moment Clark rose to his knees and shook his head, looking stunned.

"I'll be back next week for the rent," Oliver said crisply. "If you don't have it, you'll need to make arrangements to move."

Clark glared at Oliver before staggering to his feet and stumbling back to his cottage. When Oliver turned to leave, he saw Isabelle Fleming leaning against a fence, fewer than twenty feet away, and his heart sank. He wasn't sure how long she had been there, but he hoped she had seen that Clark had been the one to start the fight.

"I suppose you think I'm heartless," Oliver said, a

little defensively. "I hate to threaten tenants with eviction, but–"

"It had to be done," Isabelle said matter-of-factly. "If you hadn't stood up to him, he would never have paid, and it would have encouraged the other tenants to do the same. Lord Langley wouldn't miss one farmer's rent, but it would set a bad precedent."

"Yes, exactly," Oliver said, surprised by her quick understanding of the situation. "I can assure you that I'm not in the habit of fighting with the tenants."

"Actually, I thought you were brilliant," Isabelle said, beaming up at him. "I was worried he would hurt you, but you seemed to dance out of the way of his fists. I've never seen anything like it."

"I would hope not," Oliver said ruefully. "I'm sorry you saw that. I didn't know you were there."

"Where did you learn to fight?" she asked curiously.

"Here and there," he said evasively. "Play-fighting with my friends as a boy, mostly." His father had actually hired experts to teach Oliver to box and fence.

"Are you hurt?" Isabelle asked, looking at Oliver's right hand. Oliver noticed he had scratched his knuckle, and it was bleeding a little. Isabelle took his hand to examine the scratch and the sensation of her hands on his almost undid him. He jerked his arm away.

"Did I hurt you?" Isabelle asked in concern. "I was trying to be gentle."

"It's nothing. It will mend," he said shortly. "I've suffered much worse, believe me."

"Of course," Isabelle said stiffly.

"But I appreciate your concern, Miss Fleming," he

said kindly. "I know it's a lot to ask, but I would rather you didn't tell Lord Langley that you saw me fighting with one of his tenants." He thought Langley would understand why he had hit Clark, but the earl likely wouldn't be pleased that Isabelle had witnessed it.

"I have no intention of telling Lord Langley about it," Isabelle said. "But perhaps you could do me a favour in return."

"What sort of favour?" Oliver asked warily.

"I want you to teach me how to box."

"I beg your pardon?" Oliver said incredulously. He looked at the sprite-like young lady in front of him and wondered if he had heard her correctly.

"I want to learn to fight," Isabelle repeated. "Mr. Clark is bigger than you, but you still managed to knock him down. There's clearly a science to it, and I want to learn."

"But Miss Fleming," he began, still shocked by what she was asking.

"Please, Mr. Oliver?" she asked hopefully.

"I can't teach you to box," he said firmly.

She looked at him thoughtfully. "Do you mean you can't teach, or you don't think I can learn? Or that you simply refuse to do it?"

"All of that," he said quickly. Isabelle's face fell, and he revised his answer. "That is, I expect you could learn, but I have no experience with teaching, and it would be most improper."

"So you refuse to do it," she clarified.

"Yes."

"Why would it be improper? It's common for young ladies to have dancing masters, and this would hardly be different."

"If you consider fist-fighting similar to dancing, I'd like to see you at a ball," Oliver said dryly. "If it's just like a dancing lesson, would we ask your sister to chaperone?"

Isabelle considered the question. She didn't think Amelia would be as shocked by the idea as Oliver thought, but she realized she would prefer to learn without her sister watching.

"Amelia might want to take part in the lessons, and I don't think it would be wise in her condition," Isabelle improvised. She didn't really think her sister would want to learn to box while she was expecting a child, but she couldn't think of a better excuse. "Lord Langley definitely wouldn't like it."

"I suppose not," Oliver agreed. "Why don't you ask Lord Langley to teach you to fight?" Oliver asked. "He's better qualified than I am."

"What makes you say that?"

"He has the look of an athlete," Oliver said. Langley frequented Jackson's Boxing Saloon and was known to be a formidable opponent, but that wasn't the sort of thing that a land agent was likely to know.

"I'd rather not ask Lord Langley, I find him a little intimidating," Isabelle explained.

"But you're not intimidated by me?"

"No," she said simply.

Oliver didn't know whether to be insulted or flattered. "There's still the problem of impropriety," he pointed out.

"I don't see why it would be improper," she protested. "Would you be tempted to take liberties?"

Yes, he thought. "Of course not," he ground out.

"I think you're actually the perfect person to teach me to box, since I'm not the sort of woman you find attractive," she reminded him. "Since you prefer ladies who are tall and dark."

Oliver groaned inwardly, but managed to keep a neutral expression. "Why do you want to learn to box?"

"I believe I was inspired by your display of skill," she said carefully.

Something in her eyes made him pause. "If you want me to teach you, Miss Fleming, you'll have to tell me the real reason."

Isabelle sighed. "I want to know how to defend myself," she confessed quietly.

"Against whom?" Oliver asked.

She chewed her lip and debated how to answer.

"Is it the man who has been sending you the poetry?" Oliver asked. "The Anonymous Admirer?"

"What?" Isabelle asked. "No. How did you know about that?"

"Lord Langley may have mentioned it," Oliver said carefully.

"Oh." Isabelle chewed her lip thoughtfully. "Does Lord Langley think I should be concerned about him?"

"Of course not," Oliver said quickly. "He thinks he's harmless."

"So why did he mention him to you? So you could laugh at the poetry?"

"No," Oliver said. "It's not amusing."

Isabelle fixed him with a stare. "So Lord Langley thinks the man is harmless, and he doesn't find the poetry amusing, but he still thought he should discuss it with you? I suppose he thought you should read it for its literary merit?"

Oliver sighed. "No. The truth is, Isabelle, he was worried the letter had upset you, and he asked my opinion on what to do if further letters came."

"I see," she said slowly. "What did you tell him?"

"His inclination was to give you the letters and trust in your judgment," Oliver explained. "I agreed with him."

"I suppose I should thank you," Isabelle said, although there was no gratitude in her voice.

Oliver could see she resented the fact that Langley had discussed it with him. "I know it's not my business, Isabelle."

"But you raised the subject."

"You asked me to teach you to fight, and you still haven't explained why you want to learn."

"I am friends with Miss Letitia Hunt," Isabelle explained. "I don't know if you were introduced when she came to visit last week?"

"We weren't introduced, but I know who you mean."

"Well. Shortly before we came to Stonecroft, we were at a ball in London. Letitia was there too, and she danced with a man named Lord Braden. He apparently put his hands on her in a way that made her uncomfortable."

Oliver knew Lord Braden by reputation, and his expression darkened.

"So when Mrs. Hunt wanted Letitia to dance with him again, she refused," Isabelle continued. "There was a scene, and I think it caused a minor scandal."

"Her mother wanted her to dance with him again?" Oliver repeated.

"Yes. Mrs. Hunt is hoping he'll make Letitia an offer of marriage."

"But isn't Braden nearly sixty?"

Isabelle didn't think to question how Oliver would know Braden's age. "Yes, but he has a title and fortune, so Mrs. Hunt thinks it would be a desirable match."

Oliver supposed he shouldn't be surprised. Society was full of mothers like Mrs. Hunt, who thought a title and fortune outweighed the fact that an elderly man's touch made a young lady uncomfortable.

"So will you teach me to box?" Isabelle asked again.

"I fail to see how Miss Hunt's situation relates to boxing," Oliver said.

Isabelle bit her lip. "I realized that if I were ever in a similar situation, and a man put his hands on me, I wouldn't know how to defend myself."

"But Miss Fleming, you would never be in that situation." The thought alone was distressing to Oliver. "If any man dared to treat you disrespectfully, your brother, or Lord Langley, would call him to account. If they didn't, I would."

Isabelle's looked at him in confusion. "How would you even know about it?"

Oliver realized he had spoken without thinking. "I meant I would if I knew about it."

Isabelle nodded thoughtfully. "But that's the problem. William and Lord Langley weren't at the ball, and they don't attend most of the balls that I do," she pointed out. "So if I had trouble, they wouldn't know about it until after the fact. I would like to be able to deal with the situation at the time. And it's not just about balls. Sometimes when we're in town Amelia and I walk in Hyde Park, or go to the shops, and we don't always have a footman with us."

Oliver had to admit she had a point. Most men were honourable, and most of the dishonourable ones had the sense to know it would be foolish to insult a lady like Isabelle. But he couldn't deny that some men were both dishonourable and foolish, and young ladies would be smart to learn how to defend themselves. Boxing was a more practical skill than needlepoint or watercolours, and Oliver decided that if he had daughters, he would want them to learn self-defence.

"If you really don't want to do it, I understand," Isabelle told him. "I imagine Adrian would teach me."

The thought of Adrian teaching Isabelle to box was too much for Oliver.

"I'll do it," he said with a sigh.

After they agreed to meet in the Old Cottage before breakfast the next day, Isabelle started back towards the house. She wanted some time alone with her thoughts, so she took a roundabout route down a little-used path that ran along the edge of the Stonecroft grounds. She was lost in a reverie when she heard a man call her name.

"Lord Malthaner," she said, trying to collect her wits. "I didn't know you were in the neighbourhood." She wondered if Amelia had invited him to Stonecroft in an attempt to play matchmaker, but she quickly dismissed the idea. Amelia was not above matchmaking, but she favoured a more direct approach, and she would have told Isabelle of her plans.

Malthaner gave her a satisfied smile. "I told you I make my own opportunities, Miss Fleming," he said proudly. "I am here at the invitation of the Hunts."

"Visiting the Hunts!" Isabelle exclaimed in surprise. "I wasn't aware you were acquainted with them."

"'Twas my mother's idea, actually. I wrote to Mrs. Hunt and told her I was interested in visiting Kent, and she was kind enough to invite me to stay. I didn't expect to see you when I walked in this direction, but I confess I hoped I would."

Isabelle realized Malthaner must be the surprise visitor that Mrs. Hunt had told them about, and her first thought was relief that it was him and not Lord Braden. "Does Mrs. Hunt take your visit to mean that you're interested in Letitia?" she asked.

"I believe so," Malthaner said. "But you have nothing to fear on that score. I have absolutely no interest in Miss Hunt.

"Then perhaps you shouldn't have implied that you did," Isabelle said tartly.

"I never implied an interest in Miss Hunt," he protested. "I merely implied an interest in Kent."

Isabelle sighed. "What reason did you give for this interest in Kent?"

"I wrote that I'd heard it was a beautiful county."

He had undoubtedly raised Mrs. Hunt's hopes, and likely Letitia's too. Given everything Letitia had endured, it seemed like a particularly cruel trick.

"How long are you planning to stay?" Isabelle asked abruptly.

"Why, Miss Fleming, aren't you going to tell me you're pleased to see me?"

"I am pleased to see you, Lord Malthaner," she said formally.

"Come, Miss Fleming," he teased. "I can see I've offended you, and I wish you would tell me how."

Isabelle decided to be honest. "Your visit implies an interest in Letitia," she told him.

"There's no need to be jealous, Miss Fleming," he said with a smile.

"I'm not jealous," Isabelle said stiffly. "But Letitia is under a great deal of pressure to marry, and her past Season was not a success. Regardless of the reason you gave for your visit, it implies a serious interest in her, and I fear you are setting her up for disappointment." She didn't add that if Malthaner then showed an interest in Isabelle, he would add insult to Letitia's injury.

"A serious interest—you don't think she expects an offer of marriage?" Malthaner asked, seeming shocked by the idea.

"I imagine she and her family are hoping for it, yes."

"But Miss Fleming, consider the situation. She is the daughter of an untitled country gentleman, and I have shown no particular interest in her before this visit. Surely it's a little presumptuous for her family to think I might marry her?"

"I don't think so," Isabelle said carefully.

"I see," Malthaner said thoughtfully. "My defence must be that I was so eager to see you, Miss Fleming, that I didn't think through the potential consequences of the visit."

He appeared truly contrite, and Isabelle softened.

"What do you think I should do?" Malthaner asked. "I'll do anything you suggest, so long as you don't suggest I leave immediately. It would be cruel to send me away when I have waited so long to see you again."

Isabelle's first thought had been that he should go away, as a short visit was less likely to be interpreted as a serious declaration of intent. She was silent as she considered the problem.

"Shall I be particularly kind to Miss Hunt?" Malthaner asked.

"No," Isabelle said firmly. "That would only raise her expectations."

"Particularly unkind, then?"

"Of course not," she said, but she couldn't help but smile at the teasing look in his eyes.

"Perhaps I should make a clean breast of the matter. I'll tell the Hunts that I angled for an invitation because I wanted to see their lovely neighbour, Miss Isabelle Fleming?"

Isabelle could well imagine Letitia's disappointment at being informed of his true motives.

"No," she said firmly. "Lord Malthaner, I don't think you must go away immediately, but I don't think you should stay too long. You might express an interest in some attractions in Kent, to give credence to the story that you came for that purpose."

"I will do whatever you advise," he said with a knowing smile. "Can I join you on your walk?"

Isabelle blushed. For some reason Malthaner seemed out of place at Stonecroft, and she realized she would prefer to walk by herself. "I don't think that's a good idea, Lord Malthaner. I should get back to the house before people start to wonder where I am."

"I'll escort you home," he suggested.

"But then the Hunts might wonder where you are," she demurred. "They might worry you had gotten lost."

"I'm weary of the Hunts already," Malthaner teased. "But you are quite right, and I will return before my hosts get up a search party." He bowed to her. "Farewell, Miss Fleming."

Isabelle curtsied, then turned to continue back to the house. When she looked back a few moments later, she saw that Malthaner remained where she had left him, and was watching her walk away.

Fourteen

Letter from Isabelle to her brother William

Dear William,

Mama and Mr. Garland left rather precipitously last week, after an argument with one of the neighbours. It wasn't clear where they were going next, so you may see them at Cliveden Manor if you haven't already.

Yesterday, I witnessed Mr. Oliver fight with one of the tenant farmers who was refusing to pay rent. I don't think Mr. Oliver wanted to fight, but the farmer struck him first, so Mr. Oliver had no choice but to knock him down. I never thought of Mr. Oliver as a fighter, but he fought very capably, and the farmer gave up after he received a second hit.

I think Mr. Oliver is getting used to life at Stonecroft. I have seen him smile several times in the past week, and his eyes crinkle at the corners when he does.

Yours, Isabelle

"Did you hear the screams from the servants' quarters last night, Miss?" Daisy asked Isabelle the next morning.

"What was that, Daisy?" Isabelle asked absently. She was about to slip out of the house to meet Mr. Oliver for her boxing lesson, and she was filled with nervous anticipation. She had wondered if Daisy would remark on her plan to go for a walk before breakfast, but it seemed her maid had other things on her mind.

"The screams in the servants' quarters, Miss," Daisy repeated. "Did you hear them?"

"No," Isabelle replied.

Daisy looked disappointed. "I think it was while you were still at dinner, and I suppose they weren't as loud as they seemed."

"Who screamed, Daisy?"

"Albert. He's one of the new footmen, and it seems he had been sneaking biscuits up to his room. You know the ones with the cheese?"

"I know the ones," Isabelle said, thinking that Daisy's style of storytelling left a great deal to be desired. "Why did Albert scream?"

"Well, would you believe, Miss, there was a rat! Just sitting in the middle of the room, eating a cheese biscuit, as bold as can be! We all ran in to see it," Daisy explained. "It was the first time I'd been to the men's quarters, because Mrs. Prescott said she'd have our heads if she found us in there. But she was there too, of course, and she seemed to understand. You don't see a rat like that every day, you know."

"I can see how that would have been startling," Isabelle said. "What happened to the rat?"

"Well, someone ran to get Mr. Matthews," Daisy explained. "He was still downstairs, talking to Mr. Oliver, so they both came up. And Mr. Oliver picked up the rat, as cool as you please, and took it away! Don't you think that was ever so brave?"

"Very courageous," Isabelle agreed.

"He took the cheese biscuit away too," Daisy added. "Which was clever, for even Albert wouldn't have wanted it after that."

"I imagine not," Isabelle said, biting her lip to keep from laughing.

"Poor Albert was very upset," Daisy continued. "He was worried Mr. Matthews would dismiss him for stealing biscuits. But apparently Mr. Matthews asked Mr. Oliver's opinion, and Mr. Oliver said he thought Albert had been punished enough."

When Isabelle arrived at the Old Cottage she found Oliver already there, sitting behind the desk and making careful entries into a record book.

"Good morning, Mr. Oliver," she said awkwardly.

"Good morning, Miss Fleming," he replied. Isabelle thought he looked just as awkward as she felt.

"I heard you're a hero among the staff," Isabelle said.

"What do you mean?"

"Daisy told me you rescued Albert from a rat."

Oliver grinned. "It was a mouse, Miss Fleming."

"Daisy said it was a rat," Isabelle insisted. "And she

thought you were clever to take away the cheese biscuit too, because even Albert wouldn't have wanted it after that."

Oliver's mouth quivered, but he managed to keep his composure. "It's not kind to laugh at the servants, Miss Fleming," he said, with mock severity.

"I'm sure they laugh at us."

"Not in my hearing," he said seriously.

"Oh," Isabelle said. She glanced around the cottage and noticed that the morning sunlight was shining through clean windows, and the dust and cobwebs were gone.

"You had the cottage cleaned," she observed.

"I cleaned it myself," Oliver replied gruffly. After he had found Isabelle writing in the Old Cottage, he had started cleaning it thoroughly at least twice a week.

"You must find it a more pleasant place to work."

"Oh, yes," he agreed. He supposed it was more pleasant to work in a clean office, but that wasn't really why he did it. It was irrational, but although he had told Isabelle not to come back to the Old Cottage, he had wanted it to be clean if she did.

There was a beat of silence before she remembered why she was there. "I wasn't sure what to wear," she said, as she pulled a folded piece of pink paper from the pocket of her skirt. She unfolded the paper to reveal a small packet of straight pins and started to pin up her skirts.

Oliver stiffened and turned away. "This isn't a social engagement," he said irritably. "Your opponent won't notice what you're wearing." It was a lie; he noticed everything Isabelle wore, and he had certainly noticed her blue cambric walking dress. He wished he hadn't agreed to teach her to fight.

"My opponent will certainly notice if I trip over my skirts," Isabelle replied. "Amelia used to wear a shirt and trousers around our family's estate because she found her skirts got in the way. I thought of asking to borrow them, but I don't think she brought them to Stonecroft."

"Your sister wore trousers around the estate?" Oliver asked in surprise.

"Oh, yes," Isabelle told him. "After Papa died, Amelia helped manage Cliveden Manor, and she preferred to wear trousers. But I'm not nearly as tall as she is, so I doubt her clothes would fit me."

"Likely not," Oliver agreed.

"And even if they fit, I wouldn't be able change in my bedchamber, because Daisy is a horrible gossip, and it wouldn't do for someone to see me walking here dressed in trousers. I would have to change here, and I have a hard time getting my dresses off by myself. Although I suppose you could help with the buttons," she mused.

Oliver wondered if she truly didn't realize the impropriety of the conversation or if she was deliberately trying to torture him. If she had set out to punish him for saying that he didn't admire her style of beauty, she couldn't have chosen a better method. He tried to focus on the only part of Isabelle's speech that didn't involve her changing her clothes in the Old Cottage with his assistance. "If Daisy is such a gossip, why don't you dismiss her?"

Isabelle sighed. "She's not really so bad. But I think I'm a disappointment to her, and she would rather be maid to someone like my mother, or even someone like Amelia."

"Do you care what Daisy thinks?"

"I know I shouldn't, but I can't help it," Isabelle confessed. "I think it's a reaction to growing up with my mother, who didn't care about anyone's opinion but her own. I don't want to behave like she does."

"No one could think you behave like your mother."

"No, but I think I might care too much," Isabelle reflected. "I suppose it's one argument in favour of marriage. My husband could help me dress, and I could dispense with a maid entirely. It would be economical, and I wouldn't have to worry about gossip."

"Your husband might encourage you to engage a maid you liked," Oliver pointed out.

"Yes, I suppose he would have better things to do than play lady's maid to me."

"I think you're wise to learn to fight in a gown," he told her. "If you do have to fight, that's likely what you'll be wearing."

"I suppose you're right," she said. "I thought of asking someone to teach me to shoot, but that skill would only be useful if I carried a pistol."

"Exactly," Oliver agreed.

"I'll need your help to do the back," Isabelle told him, and he turned to see that she had pinned up her dress so it fell just below the knee. The petticoat had been pinned separately and hung about an inch below the dress, leaving several inches of stocking visible above her boot.

She handed him the card of pins and turned to show him the back of the gown, which she hadn't been able to reach. "Pin the blue gown first and the petticoat second," she instructed. "It should only take a couple of pins in each."

Oliver gritted his teeth and pulled a pin from the card, then folded the cambric underneath itself. His hands were sweating, and he was convinced that either his fingers were too big or the pins were too small. He managed to stab his second pin into the pad of his thumb, and he bit back a curse.

Isabelle spun around and saw him examining his left thumb.

"Let me see it," she said, reaching for his hand.

He pulled his hand back. "It's only a scratch," he reassured her. His thumb was smarting badly, but it was a welcome distraction from the subject of her skirts. "Turn around and I'll finish pinning it up."

"How do we start?" Isabelle asked, once Oliver had completed his task.

Oliver pushed the desk and chair against the wall, creating an open space of about eight by six feet. "Stand over there," he instructed, pointing to the opposite side of the room. He had never taught anyone to box, but he vaguely remembered the lessons of his youth.

"We'll start with footwork," he announced, before taking a step back to put as much distance between them as possible.

"Footwork?" she asked dubiously.

"Yes, footwork," he said firmly. "The most important thing in boxing is getting yourself properly positioned. You need to be able to move out of the way of a hit, and your punch won't be effective if you don't start in the right place." He smiled at her. "That will be especially important in your case, since you'll have to rely on positioning over power."

"Aren't you going to take off your coat?" Isabelle asked. "You look hot, and it might restrict your movement."

"I'll be fine." As soon as he made it through this farce of a lesson he planned to jump in the river.

"All right," she said, looking at him expectantly.

"First, we'll warm up," Oliver said, and he demonstrated how to shuffle-step from one side of the room to the other. Isabelle was light on her feet, and she moved easily across the room.

"You're in good shape," he said, surprised.

She flushed. "I do a lot of walking."

Oliver taught her to make a proper fist, and how to hold her fists to protect her face. Next, he showed her how to move with her back foot gliding against the floor, so that she would have a chance to keep her balance if she were hit. After she had moved across the room several times with her fists up, he taught her to put her weight behind a punch.

Finally, he turned to face her and put his hands up.

"Try to hit me," he told her.

"What?" she asked.

"Try to hit me," he repeated. "You asked me to teach you to fight, and you need to get used to the feeling of throwing a punch."

Isabelle still hesitated.

"Pretend I'm Lord Braden, or someone else you really dislike," Oliver suggested. "It's all right, Miss Fleming, you won't hurt me."

That earned a small smile from Isabelle. "How do you know?"

"You won't hurt me with your fists, at least," he muttered under his breath.

"I beg your pardon?" Isabelle asked.

"I have experience, and I'm expecting the punch," he explained. "Go ahead, Miss Fleming."

Isabelle gathered her courage and threw a punch. Oliver caught her fist in his hand, and Isabelle's momentum carried her towards him.

He released her fist quickly and stepped back. "Not bad," he told her. "Try it again."

She punched again, and he still caught her hand easily, but he could tell her confidence was growing.

"Enough," Oliver finally said. Isabelle was flushed and sweaty, and he knew that he was too.

"When can we do this again?" Isabelle asked, as she bent over to pull the pins from her skirts.

"Again?" Oliver repeated blankly.

"I don't think this is the sort of skill that one masters in a day," Isabelle said. "I'll need to practice."

"Miss Fleming, I don't think–" he began.

"If you're busy, I could ask Adrian," she said.

Oliver sighed inwardly. "Tomorrow morning, then."

Isabelle smiled. "Until tomorrow, Mr. Oliver."

Isabelle was famished by the time she returned to the house, so she went straight to the breakfast room instead of going upstairs to change her dress. She found Amelia and Langley already eating.

"You look flushed, Isabelle," Amelia remarked. "Are you feeling well?"

"Oh yes," Isabelle assured her sister. "I've just been for a walk, and it's a warm day."

Amelia looked at her curiously, but since Adrian chose that moment to stroll in wearing his nightshirt and dressing gown, Isabelle was saved from further questioning.

"You don't think that dressing gown's a little loud for the breakfast table?" Langley asked his brother.

Adrian looked down at the dressing gown and grinned. "Isn't it splendid?" He turned slowly so everyone could see the full effect. The dressing gown was bright blue, with a gold peacock print and lemon yellow trim. "It's from a little shop on Bond Street that specializes in gentlemen's nightwear. The very height of fashion."

Langley chuckled. "If that's the height of fashion, I think I'll stay in the depths."

Adrian smiled good-naturedly. "I think you're jealous, Robert. I don't doubt that you've lost interest in fashion since your marriage, but if you decide you want to keep up with the mode, I'll give you the name of the shop."

"I'll keep it in mind," Langley said dryly.

"Miss Fleming, I appeal to your good taste," Adrian said. "What is your opinion of this dressing gown?"

Isabelle stopped on her way to the sideboard and surveyed the dressing gown thoughtfully. "It's very bright," she said diplomatically. She took a step closer and stared at the fabric. "Are those *peacocks*?"

Langley smirked. "I must ask you not to wear it to breakfast when we have houseguests, Adrian. I'd hate for you to frighten them away."

"I didn't think you liked houseguests, Robert," Adrian remarked.

"In general, I don't," his brother agreed. "But Lucas Kincaid is coming, and he's an exception. It seems he's having some trouble with his ward, so I invited them both to stay."

"My advice would be to take a firm hand with the boy," Adrian said.

"If he asks for your advice, I'll suggest that," Langley told him. "But it seems his ward is a girl. A Miss Felicity Taylor."

"Well, that puts a different complexion on the matter," Adrian admitted. "But I don't see how a girl could cause him much trouble. Surely he's hired a governess."

Langley glanced down at the letter. "Lucas writes that Felicity has a mischievous nature, and has caused trouble for a number of governesses. Apparently, though, the latest governess has the fortitude to ignore Felicity's pranks."

"But that should be a good thing," Amelia said. "I don't see the problem."

"The problem is that Felicity has started playing tricks on Lucas," Langley explained. "The back seam of his breeches split while he was riding in Hyde Park last week."

Adrian laughed. "His breeches were breached."

Langley smiled. "In effect, they were. His tailcoat covered the–er–area in question, but he heard them tear, and I gather the experience was unsettling. He had been riding with a young lady, but as you might imagine, he cut his outing short and returned home as quickly as he could. He was taking his valet to task when Felicity confessed that she had tampered with the seam."

"But that's brilliant!" Adrian exclaimed. "I wish I'd thought of a trick like that. I'd like to meet this girl."

"You will soon have the opportunity," Langley said. "Kincaid's coming tomorrow, with Miss Taylor and her governess. Hopefully, Miss Taylor won't get into as much mischief in the country as she does in town."

Adrian smiled. "If she's going after Kincaid's clothing, he'll be no less vulnerable here."

Langley's lips twitched. "I trust that no one here will encourage Felicity to misbehave."

Adrian gave his brother an innocent look. "I can't speak for the ladies, but I will be a model of decorum."

Fifteen

The following morning, Oliver arrived at the Old Cottage with Hermes at his heels, and explained to Isabelle that the dog had refused to be left behind. Hermes was instructed to sit in the corner to observe the boxing lesson, but he quickly made it clear that he wanted to participate. He frisked from one end of the cottage to the other while Isabelle practised footwork, and she had to be careful not to trip over him. The real problem arose when they tried to practise punching. After Oliver caught Isabelle's first punch, Hermes bared his teeth and growled at Isabelle.

"Hermes!" Oliver exclaimed. "Hermes, stand down!" The puppy continued to stare balefully at Isabelle, and only calmed down when Oliver picked him up and cradled him to his chest.

"Hermes seems to think I'm a threat," Isabelle joked.

"You are improving," Oliver admitted. "I think we've done all we can do for today."

Isabelle nodded. "Can you try to leave Hermes in your cottage tomorrow morning?"

Hermes gave Oliver a pleading look, and Oliver grinned. "He's a very jealous dog, Miss Fleming, but I can try."

Isabelle smiled. "Thank you, Mr. Oliver. I suppose I should leave you to your work."

"And I to yours," Oliver replied.

Isabelle looked at him in confusion. "I don't work, Mr. Oliver, so you'll be leaving me to my leisure."

"But Miss Fleming, you told me you were writing a novel," he pointed out. "Surely that's work."

Isabelle was touched by the fact that he took her writing seriously. "Right now it's frustrating," she admitted. "Some of the characters are refusing to behave rationally."

"I see," Oliver replied. "That might not be a bad thing, you know. If all of your characters behaved rationally, you would have a very dull book. Take *Emma*, for example. If Emma hadn't tried to meddle in her friends' affairs, she wouldn't have had a reason to fight with Mr. Knightley, and there wouldn't have been much of a story."

"You finished reading it?" Isabelle asked.

"I did."

"Did you enjoy it?"

"Very much. The characters had flaws, but it made them interesting. You can't write a book about a perfect hero who falls in love with a perfect heroine."

"You can't?"

Oliver shook his head. "Not only is it unbelievable, but there's nothing inspiring about a story like that.

What's inspiring is when two people see each other's flaws, but fall in love in spite of them."

"I've never thought of it that way," Isabelle admitted. She said goodbye to Mr. Oliver and walked back to the house, wondering if she would ever find a man who saw her flaws and loved her in spite of them.

∽

Isabelle spent the afternoon in the library, trying to work on her novel, but she was having trouble visualizing her characters. Although her Byronic hero was flawed, he didn't seem particularly inspiring, and her thoughts kept wandering to a man with dark blond hair and teasing hazel eyes. It was frustrating, but for some reason Isabelle was unable to banish the hazel-eyed man from the story. She stood and stretched her arms over her head in an effort to clear her mind.

"I've always thought you would know a true gentleman by his library," came a voice from the doorway. Isabelle turned and saw Lord Malthaner walking towards her.

"I've often thought the same," she replied.

"I have a splendid library at my estate," Malthaner told her. "I don't like to boast, but I think it's nearly as impressive as this one."

Isabelle smiled at him. "What do you like to read?"

"What? Miss Fleming, you don't suppose I actually read the books," Malthaner said with a chuckle. "I had enough of that at school."

"Oh," Isabelle said. "The books are decorative, then?"

"Exactly," he nodded. "If the shelves were empty, it wouldn't look nearly so much like a library."

"I suppose not."

"I must admit, there is one respect in which the Stonecroft library is far superior to my own," Malthaner mused.

"The windows?" Isabelle asked ironically.

"No," Malthaner said with a smile. "The Stonecroft library is currently honoured by the presence of the most beautiful lady in the country, Miss Isabelle Fleming."

Isabelle hardly knew how to reply, and she could feel her cheeks turning pink. Lord Malthaner was standing directly in front of her now, and the intensity of his expression made her nervous.

"I think Lord Langley is walking in the garden with my sister," she said shyly.

"I didn't come to see Langley," Malthaner told her. "Although that was the reason I gave the butler, and I think he's gone to tell Langley I'm waiting for him in the drawing room. So I suppose I should come to the point." He sank to his knees in front of Isabelle and took her hands in his.

"Marry me, Isabelle," he said.

"I beg your pardon?" Isabelle asked, thinking she had misheard him.

He smiled at her. "My dear Miss Fleming, would you do me the very great honour of becoming my wife?"

Isabelle realized she was gaping at him, and she made an effort to collect her wits. She supposed she shouldn't be surprised that Lord Malthaner wanted to marry her, since his decision to follow her to Kent suggested a serious interest. But she certainly hadn't expected him to declare himself so quickly, before they had the chance to become acquainted.

"Lord Malthaner," she said, trying to buy herself time. "I am flattered by your offer, but you have taken me by surprise. This is quite unexpected."

He seemed to enjoy her discomfiture. "Miss Fleming, surely this can't be a complete surprise. You are the beauty of the Season."

Isabelle blushed. "But you never showed an interest until the Somertons' ball. Lord Malthaner, are you sure you want to marry me? We barely know each other, and I was hoping to have a little more time to become acquainted."

"Isabelle–I hope you will let me call you Isabelle–I feel as though I know you very well."

"You do?"

"Certainly," he said confidently. "You're Cliveden's sister and Langley's sister-in-law."

Much as Isabelle liked her brother and brother-in-law, she wasn't pleased to be defined by her relationship to them.

"But you're so much more than that," Malthaner continued. "You are unquestionably a diamond of the first water. You look like a goddess, you dance divinely, and a man could drown in your eyes." He raised her hand to his lips and kissed it.

"Oh," Isabelle said weakly.

"I remember the day I met you," Malthaner continued. "It was at a rout party at the beginning of the Season. I told my mother I had met the girl I was going to marry."

"But you gave me no indication of it," said Isabelle, who was frantically trying to bring order to her thoughts.

There was something endearing about the fact that he had discussed her with his mother.

"That was strategic," Malthaner said proudly. "My mother's suggestion, actually. By appearing indifferent to you, I would excite your interest and distinguish myself from the other men who were vying for your hand."

"I see," Isabelle said, reflecting that his strategy had also ensured that they had very few opportunities to get to know each other. Malthaner was undoubtedly eligible, and a month ago she would have said he was the most fascinating man on the *ton*. If Isabelle accepted him she would be a viscountess, and the mistress of her own establishment. She could be the wife of Lord Malthaner, rather than the sister of Lord Cliveden and the sister-in-law of Lord Langley.

Somehow, the prospect left her unmoved.

"Thank you for your offer, Lord Malthaner, but I'm afraid I must decline it," Isabelle said.

"Decline it?" Malthaner asked incredulously.

"We don't know each other well enough to know if we would suit, and I have no intention of entering into an engagement this Season."

"No intention of entering into an engagement?" he repeated in disbelief.

"That's right," Isabelle affirmed.

"But why did you go to balls if you don't wish to enter into an engagement?"

"For entertainment," Isabelle replied.

"Are you betrothed to someone else?" Malthaner asked abruptly.

"No."

"Then I don't understand," Malthaner said, as though

a prior engagement was the only conceivable reason why a young lady might reject his proposal. "Perhaps you think I should have spoken to your brother first?"

"No," Isabelle said vehemently. If Malthaner went to see William her mother would likely hear about it, and she would be forced to explain why she had declined such an eligible offer. She could still hear her mother's voice, telling her she was almost on the shelf, and she wondered if her expectations were too high. "Please, Lord Malthaner, I don't think–"

"I understand, Miss Fleming," Malthaner interrupted with a knowing smile. "I have caught you by surprise. Perhaps we should discuss this further next week? The Hunts have been invited to dine at Stonecroft on Tuesday, and your sister has kindly included me in the invitation."

"I'm not sure that will be the best time to discuss it. I will need more time," she improvised. If she could put him off, he might fall in love with another young lady, and then her family would never need to know about his proposal. Isabelle blushed and lowered her voice. "My sister is with child, and I am determined not to enter into an engagement until after her confinement."

"I can understand why you might not want to marry before her confinement, but surely an engagement–"

"No," Isabelle said firmly. "Amelia would want to host an engagement party, and the stress of planning an event might compromise her health."

"I can set your mind to rest on that point," Malthaner said confidently. "My mother would be delighted to host an engagement party. Neither you nor your sister will have to lift a finger."

"That's very generous, Lord Malthaner, but I'm afraid

it won't do. Amelia has an anxious disposition, and the doctor has said she is at risk of a nervous crisis."

Malthaner frowned. "She appeared to be excellent health at the Somertons' ball."

"She takes great pains to hide it," Isabelle said. "My sister suffers in silence. In fact, she would be shocked to learn that we were having this conversation. But you must understand why I am determined not to do anything to distress her."

Malthaner smiled. "But surely the news of our engagement would delight Lady Langley, not distress her?"

"The illness can be unpredictable."

"You are very devoted to your sister."

"Yes," Isabelle agreed. "And she is very devoted to me."

"I see," Malthaner said. "I confess I am disappointed, Miss Fleming, but I assure you I can be patient." He bowed. "I suppose I should return to the drawing room before your sister and Lord Langley return."

Malthaner took her face in his hands, gazed into her eyes, and pressed a kiss to her lips. It was the first time that Isabelle had been kissed, and it left her disappointed. It seemed to please Malthaner, though, for he gave her a satisfied smile before bowing again and turning to leave.

Isabelle watched him walk away and reflected that she hadn't handled the situation very well. She didn't know if Malthaner thought they had some sort of understanding, and she wished she had been more resolute in her refusal. For a moment she wondered if she should have said yes. She knew many girls would be overjoyed to receive a proposal from Malthaner, and she wondered if there was something wrong with her.

But she remembered what Mr. Oliver had said that morning, that it was inspiring when two people saw each other's flaws and fell in love in spite of them. Malthaner hadn't seen her flaws, and Isabelle suspected his admiration was based on nothing more than her looks, her connections, and the way she danced. In effect, he had told her that it was. Malthaner didn't know that she was timid and inclined to daydream, or that she was trying to write a novel.

Isabelle wondered if Malthaner would still admire her if he knew her true character, but she suspected that if she married him, he would never see her as anything more than the beauty of the Season. He might not see her flaws, but a man who wasn't perceptive enough to see her flaws was unlikely to appreciate her strengths.

Isabelle stood and collected her papers, and resolved to find somewhere else to write. She had now received two unexpected proposals of marriage in the Stonecroft library, and she had no wish to receive another.

Langley was not pleased when Matthews interrupted his walk with Amelia to tell him that Lord Malthaner had called, but he returned to the house to welcome the viscount to the neighbourhood. To Langley's relief, Malthaner left within half an hour, so he asked Mr. Oliver to join him in his study to review a set of accounts. They had barely begun when Matthews announced the arrival of Mr. Kincaid, and Langley laid down his pen with a smile.

"At last we have received a visitor whom I actually want to see," he said to Oliver. "Come and meet one of my oldest friends."

"I should get back to work," Oliver demurred. Whenever Langley treated him like an equal he wondered if the earl had guessed his true identity, but he was convinced it was impossible. He was sure that if Langley had recognized him as Oliver St. Clair, he would have said something.

"I think you've done enough work for today," Langley said as they walked to the entrance hall.

Amelia and Isabelle were already there, talking to a young lady in a fashionable pink travelling dress with a matching bonnet. She was tall, with chestnut hair and mischievous brown eyes, and looked to be about Isabelle's age. Several feet away, a young gentleman stood next to a middle-aged woman in a plain brown gown.

"Robert!" Amelia exclaimed. "Come and meet Miss Felicity Taylor. Can you believe she is Mr. Kincaid's ward?"

Langley bowed to Miss Taylor. "What my wife means to say, Miss Taylor, is welcome to Stonecroft," he said, with a twinkle in his eye. "I am Lord Langley."

Miss Taylor curtsied. "I'm pleased to make your acquaintance, my lord."

Langley turned to the lady in the drab gown, then looked inquiringly at his wife.

"Oh, this is Miss Flint," Amelia said quickly. "She is Miss Taylor's companion." Miss Flint was of medium height and build, with soft brown eyes and a bovine expression. Langley bowed to her politely, greeted Kincaid, and introduced Oliver to the newcomers.

Oliver wondered if the earl and countess considered Kincaid a prospective husband for Isabelle, and tried to study the man without appearing to do so. Kincaid was tall, with brown hair and blue eyes, and Oliver supposed he had the sort of features women found attractive. As Oliver watched, Kincaid greeted Isabelle politely but with no particular interest, and he didn't seem affected by her beauty. Oliver questioned his eyesight and liked him immediately.

"Come into the drawing room, and I'll ring for tea," Amelia suggested. "You must join us, Mr. Oliver," she said politely, when she saw him heading for the front door instead of the drawing room.

"It's good to see you, Lucas," Langley said to Kincaid.

"It's good to be here, Robert," Kincaid replied with a sigh.

"Was it a tiresome journey?" Langley asked, looking surprised. Stonecroft was only forty miles from London and the weather was fair, so the trip should not have been difficult.

"You could say that. Felicity was in one of her miffs because I forbade her to ride beside the carriage."

Amelia overheard and turned to Felicity. "Are you a horsewoman, Miss Taylor?"

Felicity smiled. "Oh, please call me Felicity, and yes, I ride whenever I can. I have the most delightful little mare, Sugarplum, and I confess I miss her already."

"You should have brought her with you," Amelia said.

Felicity shot a look at Kincaid. "I wanted to, but Mr. Kincaid thought it would be an imposition."

"Oh no," Amelia said. "We have so many horses that one more would hardly be noticed. I would have liked to meet Sugarplum." She looked down at her rounded stomach and smiled. "As you can see, I'm not riding right now, so you can ride my horse while you're here."

"When do you expect to be confined?" Felicity asked.

"Felicity!" Kincaid exclaimed. "You can't ask her that!"

"Why not?" Felicity asked. "Lady Langley raised the subject."

"She made an oblique reference to it, but that's very different from discussing it outright," Kincaid said.

"It was hardly oblique, Mr. Kincaid," Felicity argued. "Only a child or a simpleton would have missed her meaning, and I am neither."

"But it's still not proper to speak of it," Kincaid insisted.

"To speak of what?" Felicity asked mischievously.

Kincaid had no experience in discussing pregnancy with innocent young ladies, or even with young ladies who were supposed to be innocent but seemed to know far too much. He searched his mind for a proper euphemism, but couldn't come up with one. He turned to Miss Flint, hoping for a rescue, but she had occupied herself with some needlework and seemed oblivious to his predicament.

"Of her condition," Kincaid said weakly.

"I don't see why it's such a secret," Felicity said unrepentantly. "I imagine Lord Langley knows that his wife expects to be confined–"

"I do," Langley cut in. Although his tone was serious, his dark eyes were full of amusement, and Kincaid could tell his friend was enjoying the conversation immensely.

"He may even be pleased about it," Felicity continued.

"He is, but I think he's a little nervous," Amelia said, smiling at her husband. "The midwife thinks it will be at least another month, but Robert has arranged for a physician to come from London next week, and stay until the baby arrives."

"Nervous? You, Robert?" Kincaid said.

"Your turn will come," Langley told his friend good-naturedly.

A maid entered with the tea, and Amelia poured. Felicity moved to a chair opposite Mr. Oliver, and within minutes, they were engaged in a lively conversation. Isabelle was too far away to hear what they were saying, and she couldn't think of a reason to move closer. She realized that Felicity's dark beauty was in exactly the style that Mr. Oliver claimed to admire.

"When you said you had a ward, Lucas, I assumed she was a child," Langley remarked.

"I assure you, she behaves like one," Kincaid muttered.

Although the men had lowered their voices, Felicity overheard them, and turned to address Kincaid. "I try very hard to meet your expectations. Since you treat me like a child, I behave like one."

Kincaid sighed. "As you see, we are at an impasse."

"You certainly seem to be," Langley agreed. "Can I get you something stronger to drink, Lucas?"

Sixteen

Letter from Isabelle to her brother William

Dear William,

Lord Langley's friend, Mr. Kincaid, has come to visit with his ward, Miss Felicity Taylor. Miss Taylor is my age, or perhaps a year older, but we have very little in common. For one thing, she is mad about horses. For another—well, I don't like to speak ill of another lady, but Mr. Kincaid said she behaves like a child, and I fear he is right. Yesterday Mr. Oliver joined us for tea, and Miss Taylor flirted quite shamelessly with him. I suppose she is pretty enough, for a dark-haired girl, but the situation was still awkward, and poor Mr. Oliver looked very uncomfortable.

Mr. Oliver likes to read, so I recommended he read *Emma*, and he said he enjoyed it. He observed that flawed characters make for a more interesting story, and I think he's right. I suggested he read *Pride and Prejudice* next.

Yours,
Isabelle

~

When Isabelle tried to slip out to meet Oliver the following morning, she encountered Felicity Taylor at the top of the stairs.

"Another early riser," Felicity said cheerfully. "Travelling makes me dreadfully hungry, so I'm going down to the kitchen to look for something to carry me through until breakfast. Will you join me?"

"I'm actually going for a walk," Isabelle said quickly. "I like to get out before it's too hot."

"In that case, I will join you," Felicity said brightly.

"Oh," Isabelle replied, trying to hide her disappointment. "But I thought you were dreadfully hungry?"

"Not so very dreadfully," Felicity assured her. "I spent all of yesterday in a travelling carriage, so I need to stretch my legs."

"That sounds lovely," Isabelle lied.

Felicity changed into her walking boots, and the two of them set out across the fields. Isabelle led them towards the Old Cottage, hoping Mr. Oliver would see her with Felicity and understand why she couldn't meet him as planned.

"It's beautiful here," Felicity remarked. "When Mr. Kincaid told me we were going to the country and I couldn't bring my horse, I thought I would be dreadfully bored. But I think I may enjoy myself after all."

"I'm pleased to hear it," Isabelle said.

Felicity caught the ironic note in Isabelle's tone. "I'm

sorry, I didn't mean to be rude," she said easily. "I'm in the habit of saying what I think. Mr. Kincaid says that if I don't learn to control my tongue before I make my debut, I'll never get vouchers for Almack's. He seems to think Almack's is very important, but I think it sounds rather dull."

Isabelle laughed. "It is dull."

Felicity nodded. "It's a relief to hear that, because there's a very good chance I'll offend one of the patronesses and never be allowed inside. It's hard to be a meek young lady when you're used to speaking your mind."

Isabelle reflected that the opposite was also true.

"Lord Langley is very handsome," Felicity continued. "Your sister is very fortunate."

"Lord Langley is fortunate to have Amelia," Isabelle said staunchly.

Felicity nodded. "I'm sure he is."

As they approached the Old Cottage, Isabelle saw Mr. Oliver walk up to the door. He caught her eye and lifted his hat before disappearing into the cottage.

"Was that Mr. Oliver?" Felicity asked. "He's very attractive too, don't you think?"

"I never really thought about him," Isabelle replied.

The following morning, Isabelle made it out of the house unobserved, and walked down to the Old Cottage to meet the man she never really thought about. They hadn't discussed further boxing lessons, so she wasn't sure that Mr. Oliver would come, but he arrived five minutes after she did. Isabelle couldn't keep the smile from her face when she saw him.

"I'm sorry I couldn't meet you yesterday," she told him. "I was walking with Felicity."

"I gathered as much when I saw you walking with Felicity," Oliver said dryly.

"I assumed that since we couldn't practise yesterday, we would today," Isabelle said, smiling at him shyly. "I'm glad you thought the same."

"Yes," he told her. "But this must be our last session, Miss Fleming."

Isabelle frowned. "Why?"

"Because after today, you will have learned enough to defend yourself creditably, and we will have achieved our objective." This was certainly true; Isabelle was quick on her feet, and she had good judgment. But the real reason Oliver didn't want to continue the boxing lessons was that Isabelle was consuming his thoughts, and he didn't want his happiness to depend on a girl who could never be his.

"I suppose you're right," Isabelle agreed reluctantly. "But I haven't practised dodging blows, and if this is to be our last session, perhaps we should do that today?"

"What do you mean?" Oliver asked, although he had a fairly good idea of what she meant.

"Well, I've practised trying to punch you, but you haven't tried to punch me."

"I'm not going to punch you, Miss Fleming," Oliver said matter-of-factly.

Isabelle looked disappointed. "Then how will I learn how to avoid a punch?"

"You won't," Oliver said unapologetically. "I'm not going to pretend to hit you." She looked like she wanted to argue the point, so Oliver continued. "Let's begin with footwork."

When they finished their session an hour later, Oliver told Isabelle she had made great progress.

"Thank you," Isabelle said. "And thank you for teaching me." She wished they could continue the boxing lessons, but she knew Mr. Oliver was busy, and she had no claim upon his time.

Oliver nodded. "It was my pleasure, Miss Fleming."

"I understand Lord Langley invited you to dinner tomorrow?" she asked shyly. She had no claim upon his time, but that didn't stop her from wanting more of it.

"He did," Oliver confirmed. The Hunts and Lord Malthaner had been invited to dinner, but Oliver had politely declined the earl's invitation to join them.

"I was hoping you would come," Isabelle said.

"You were?"

Isabelle met his eye. "I was."

"To be clear, Miss Fleming, you are not suggesting I come to dinner to make up the numbers, or because another member of your family requested my presence?"

"No," she said simply.

"Then I will come."

When Oliver entered the drawing room the following evening, the first person he saw was Isabelle. She was wearing a buttercup yellow dress with an empire waist and flowing skirts, trimmed with *broderie anglaise* at the neckline and hem. Oliver was no connoisseur of fashion, but he knew a yellow dress should have been wrong for a blonde; on Isabelle, though, it was entirely right. Her blue eyes and red lips stood out against a backdrop of honey hair, creamy skin, and yellow satin. He forced himself to look away from Isabelle and approached Miss Flint, who was sitting on a sofa by herself.

"Good evening, Miss Flint," he said politely.

Miss Flint gave him a nod before returning her attention to her lap, and Oliver realized she was occupied with needlework. He couldn't think of a single thing to say about needlework, so he offered to get her a drink.

"No thank you," she replied, without looking up from her stitching. Oliver abandoned his efforts at conversation and gave in to the temptation to watch Isabelle, who was talking to Felicity.

Mrs. Hunt arrived a short time later, accompanied by Letitia and Lord Malthaner. Malthaner's eyes went directly to Isabelle, and after making a perfunctory bow to Amelia, he crossed the room to join her. Mrs. Hunt watched in vexation as he drew Isabelle and Felicity into a spirited conversation.

"Mr. Hunt was unable to join us tonight?" Amelia asked Mrs. Hunt.

Mrs. Hunt smiled apologetically. "He sends his apologies, Lady Langley. He is suffering from indigestion."

Adrian had wandered over to stand beside Oliver. "Hunt's more likely suffering from too much time with his wife," he muttered under his breath. "I don't know how married men survive in the country. At least when they're in town, they can go to their clubs."

"Some men enjoy the company of ladies," Oliver replied, trying to keep his eyes off Isabelle.

"Oh, undoubtedly," Adrian agreed. "But in the country, a man is stuck with his wife."

Amelia introduced Oliver to Mrs. Hunt and Letitia before excusing herself to speak to Miss Flint, who was still sitting by herself.

"Are you enjoying your time in the country, Miss Hunt?" Oliver asked. His interest in Letitia had increased since he had learned that she and Isabelle were close friends.

"Yes, very much," Letitia replied, with a nervous glance at her mother.

Mrs. Hunt cast an appraising eye over Oliver. "Are you new to the neighbourhood, Mr. Oliver?"

"I am, Mrs. Hunt," he said. "I'm the new land agent at Stonecroft."

"Indeed. How fascinating," Mrs. Hunt remarked, although her tone suggested it was anything but. She turned to her daughter. "Letitia, I forgot to ask Lord Malthaner if he would prefer chicken fricassee or lamb cutlets for dinner tomorrow. Go and ask him, my dear."

Letitia's cheeks turned pink with embarrassment. "Surely you can ask him later, Mama," she protested.

"But it's come to mind now, and I might forget later," Mrs. Hunt said stubbornly.

Letitia lifted her eyes to Oliver in a silent apology, and he smiled to show he understood.

Mrs. Hunt watched Letitia cross the room to join Lord Malthaner before turning back to Oliver. "Where are you from, Mr. Oliver?"

"Before I came to Stonecroft, I was a soldier, ma'am."

"Yes, but who are your family?" Mrs. Hunt persisted. "Have I heard of them?"

Oliver chose to ignore the first question and reply to the second. "Surely you would know the answer to that better than I would, Mrs. Hunt."

Mrs. Hunt narrowed her eyes, but Oliver was spared further interrogation when Matthews arrived to announce that dinner was ready.

"What brings you to Kent, Lord Malthaner?" Amelia asked politely, once they were all seated at the table.

"I heard that Kent is home to the most beautiful sights in England." Malthaner was staring at Isabelle as he spoke, and there was no mistaking his meaning.

"Are there any sights in particular that you want to see?" Langley asked.

Malthaner took a sip of wine. "There are so many that it's hard to recall the specifics."

"Surely your memory can't be so poor as that," Langley said gently.

"I distinctly recall hearing of a church," Malthaner tried.

Langley smiled. "You must mean the Norman church at Cheltham. It's certainly worth a visit."

Adrian looked at Malthaner skeptically. "You don't expect us to believe you came to Kent to see a church?"

"Perhaps Lord Malthaner is interested in Norman architecture," Langley suggested.

"Yes, I am," Malthaner agreed. "How far away is this church?"

"No more than ten miles away," Langley replied.

"Then we should get up a riding party," Malthaner proposed. "Perhaps Miss Fleming, Miss Hunt, and Miss Taylor will join me."

"Oh yes," Felicity said enthusiastically. "That is, if we

can borrow horses. You will come to chaperone, won't you, Miss Flint?"

Miss Flint looked up for just long enough to nod at Felicity, then returned her attention to her white soup.

"Will you join us, Miss Fleming?" Lord Malthaner asked.

The prospect of a riding expedition filled Isabelle with dread. "Perhaps," she said cautiously, trying to think of an excuse to avoid it.

"It wouldn't be the same without you, Miss Fleming," Malthaner said with a teasing smile.

Malthaner's pointed interest in Isabelle was irritating Mrs. Hunt, and she inexplicably chose to vent her frustration by attacking Felicity Taylor.

"I'm surprised we haven't encountered you in London, Miss Taylor," Mrs. Hunt remarked. "Although I suppose the events we attend are quite exclusive."

"There's nothing surprising about it, Mrs. Hunt. I haven't made my debut yet," Felicity replied calmly.

Mrs. Hunt raised her eyebrows. "How old are you, Miss Taylor?" she asked bluntly.

"I was twenty last month," Felicity said matter-of-factly. "How old are you?"

Mrs. Hunt coloured. "I would think that at twenty you would know better than to ask," she said acidly.

"I'm terribly sorry. I didn't know it was impolite to ask a lady her age at the dinner table," Felicity said sweetly.

"It is a perfectly acceptable question to ask a young girl, but not an older lady," Mrs. Hunt said through gritted teeth.

"Do you consider yourself an older lady, Mrs. Hunt?" Felicity asked. Everyone at the table was focused on their exchange, except for Miss Flint, who was focused on her chicken cutlets.

"Felicity," Kincaid said, in a tone that was half reproachful and half pleading.

Mrs. Hunt's eyes narrowed. "I find it unusual that at twenty, you haven't had a Season," she remarked.

Felicity smiled. "I've chosen to wait until next year, when I come of age."

Mrs. Hunt feigned a look of concern. "If you're not careful, you'll be on the shelf before you've left the schoolroom."

If anyone thought this was a strange comment from a lady whose daughter had not received an offer of marriage after two Seasons, no one remarked upon it.

"Perhaps I'm hoping to find a man who will love me when the bloom of youth has faded," Felicity replied.

"And what if you can't find one?" Mrs. Hunt asked.

Felicity smiled mischievously. "I'm an heiress, ma'am. I expect the men will find me, and if they don't, I'll have the resources to entertain myself."

Although Mrs. Hunt should have been relieved to learn that her concerns for Felicity's future were unfounded, she did not appear pleased.

Adrian looked at Felicity with interest. "Kincaid never told us you were an heiress." He turned an accusing eye on Kincaid. "You might have mentioned that."

Kincaid glowered at him. "If you had a ward who was an heiress, I doubt you would advertise the fact."

"Well, of course I wouldn't! I'd probably want her for myself," Adrian replied.

Kincaid choked on a sip of his wine.

"There's certainly no fear of that in our situation,"

Felicity said blandly, while Kincaid caught his breath. "I'm afraid I've been quite a trial for Mr. Kincaid. When I think about it, I'm surprised he didn't marry me to the first fortune hunter who expressed an interest!"

"If you're not careful, I might," Kincaid muttered.

"Poor Mr. Kincaid has had to spend an extraordinary amount of time interviewing governesses for me," Felicity continued. "In the six years that I've been his ward, I don't think I've had a governess stay for more than six months! Until we found our dear Miss Flint, of course. She's been with us for almost a year."

All eyes turned towards Miss Flint, who seemed oblivious to the attention and continued to focus on her dinner.

"I don't think your governesses left because of me, Felicity," Kincaid said with irritation.

"I would hope not," Felicity said, with a look of surprise. "I never thought of you as the sort of man who would pester a governess."

Kincaid made a choking sound again.

"Something in your throat, Lucas?" Langley asked with a smirk.

Kincaid cleared his throat. "The wine went down the wrong way."

"Do you know, we have employed the same governess for fifteen years?" Mrs. Hunt remarked, with a smile at Letitia. "Letitia no longer needs a governess, of course, but dear Miss Winthrop still looks after the younger girls. She frequently tells me that our daughters are the best behaved girls she has ever met."

The table fell silent, and Letitia flushed crimson.

"It sounds like a fortunate situation for all concerned," Oliver finally said.

Mrs. Hunt nodded. "Miss Winthrop says that the day I hired her to be governess to my children was the best day of her life. Can you imagine?"

"It's almost unbelievable," Langley remarked.

Felicity turned to Mrs. Hunt. "It's unfortunate that we weren't acquainted with you when Mr. Kincaid was having such difficulty finding me a suitable governess. I'm sure he would have benefited from your advice."

"Felicity, you know very well that the governesses were driven away by your behaviour," Kincaid said in frustration.

"I know nothing of the sort!" Felicity protested. "The problem was your lack of skill in selecting them. It's no surprise, since you had no experience with the task. To your credit, you improved with practice, as evidenced by our dear Miss Flint. Although she's more of a companion than a governess. Like Miss Hunt, I'm beyond the stage of needing a governess."

"Some might disagree with you on that point," Kincaid said.

Felicity smiled at Mrs. Hunt. "As you can see, Mr. Kincaid and I have different opinions on so many things, there's no question of us making a match of it," she said candidly. "There's also the problem of his age."

"What about my age?" asked Kincaid, who was thirty.

"Why, you heard Mrs. Hunt. It's much easier to find a marriage partner when one is young," Felicity said innocently. "If you're not careful, you'll end up on the shelf."

"Do you prefer men closer to your own age, Miss Taylor?" Adrian asked hopefully.

Felicity smiled mischievously. "I prefer men closer to my own intelligence." She looked to Kincaid for a reply, but he didn't rise to the bait.

"I think you're clever to wait to have your Season, Felicity," Isabelle said diplomatically. "The balls can be rather overwhelming."

"Oh, I'm not intimidated by the thought of going to balls," Felicity said. "I can dance tolerably well, and I'm not afraid to talk to people. The real problem is that until I turn twenty-one, I can't marry without Mr. Kincaid's approval or I'll lose my inheritance. It will all go to an odious cousin, and he's unworthy of it."

"But how do you know Mr. Kincaid wouldn't approve of your choice?" Amelia asked. "Unless you've already formed an attachment? Are you hoping to marry someone completely ineligible?"

Langley laughed. "If she were, she would hardly tell you, especially with Kincaid at the table."

Felicity smiled. "Nothing so scandalous, I assure you. I have had no opportunity to form an attachment, for Mr. Kincaid growls like a bear whenever a man so much as looks at me."

Adrian frowned. "Do bears actually growl?"

Miss Flint finally looked up from her dinner. "You know, I don't think they do. Dogs growl, and cats of course, but bears rarely do. They sometimes moan, which can be mistaken for a growl, but it's actually a sign of fear."

The table was quiet for a moment while everyone considered this.

Langley finally broke the silence. "Perhaps Lucas wasn't growling, but moaning in fear."

Even Kincaid laughed at that. "If you saw some of the men who look at Felicity, Robert, you'd be afraid, too."

Felicity smiled. "Yes, we met a middle-aged vicar last month who was particularly terrifying. I had to offer Mr. Kincaid my smelling salts."

Kincaid rolled his eyes. "Felicity, I just thought he was standing needlessly close to you."

"I'm afraid I'm not confident in Mr. Kincaid's ability to judge whether a man would be suitable for me," Felicity remarked. "Why, he had such a difficult time finding a governess who would stay for more than a few months! He might give his approval to a man who would disappear in a similar manner." She sighed. "I think a husband would be far more difficult to replace than a governess. And unlike the governesses, a husband might take my fortune with him when he left."

"If it would make your life easier, I could arrange to lose your fortune on the stock exchange," Kincaid offered. "Or better yet, I could embezzle it. Then you could be confident your suitors weren't interested in your fortune."

Felicity gave him a look of feigned gratitude. "You would do that? For me?"

Kincaid rolled his eyes. "With pleasure."

"I doubt you would like it if I had the power to veto your choice of marriage partner," Felicity said.

"You essentially do," Kincaid muttered. "Once a young lady learns that I'm responsible for you, she'll run in the opposite direction."

The table fell silent. Felicity's lower lip trembled, and she stared down at her plate.

"I never thought of it like that, but I can see how it

would be awkward for you," Felicity finally said in a small voice.

"Felicity," Kincaid began remorsefully. "You know I didn't mean it that way."

Felicity looked up and gave her guardian a bright smile, and Kincaid let out a sigh of exasperation as he realized she had been shamming it.

"This is excellent beef," Miss Flint remarked.

"Tell me about your family, Mr. Kincaid," Mrs. Hunt said. "Do you have noble relations?"

"I do, but I don't like to boast of them," Kincaid said, with a gleam of amusement in his eye.

"Oh, come now, Mr. Kincaid, I'm sure there's no need to be ashamed of your family," Mrs. Hunt said archly.

"Oh, I'm not ashamed of my family, but I would be ashamed to boast."

"That's nonsense," Mrs. Hunt said dismissively. "If I had noble relatives, I would not hesitate to speak of them. To whom are you related, Mr. Kincaid?"

"My brother is the Earl of Brentwood."

Mrs. Hunt's face fell at the news that he was a younger son. "Does your brother ever accompany you on your visits to Stonecroft? I always say that there's no finer county than Kent."

"It must be years since Archie's been to Stonecroft. He's busy with the estate, of course, and he has three sons in the nursery."

"Three sons?" Mrs. Hunt said, unable to hide her disappointment.

"Yes," Kincaid confirmed with a smile. "The younger two are twins, and I'm told they keep their nurse very busy. I've never seen such healthy boys. So you see, Mrs. Hunt, there is little risk that I will inherit the title."

"One never knows what will happen," Mrs. Hunt said optimistically. "Why, I recently learned that the Duke of Edgeworth's heir, Lord Rupert St. Clair, died last month. He was in the pink of health, too, until he fell from his horse and broke his neck. He had no sons, so the title will go to his brother."

The clatter of a knife against a plate silenced Mrs. Hunt. Isabelle turned towards the sound and saw Oliver's stricken expression. A footman moved to replace his knife, which had rolled off his plate and onto the floor.

"I beg your pardon," Oliver said stiffly.

"Are you unwell, Mr. Oliver?" Amelia asked, looking at him with concern. "You are very pale."

"I'm quite well, thank you, Lady Langley," Oliver lied. He could hardly explain that he was in shock because he had just learned of his brother's death.

"He's only suffering from the inability to hold a knife," Malthaner muttered.

Isabelle took a sip of wine and carefully set down her glass near the edge of the table. She turned towards Lord Malthaner and managed to knock her wineglass onto his lap.

"Oh, Lord Malthaner, I'm so sorry!" Isabelle exclaimed. "I can't imagine how I could be so clumsy. I'm afraid the wine is on both your waistcoat and your pantaloons. It's a shame that I was drinking burgundy, since I usually prefer white wine."

"White wine would have been wrong with this beef," Miss Flint said matter-of-factly. "And that would have been a shame, since this is excellent beef."

"I suppose you're right, Miss Flint, but oh, Lord Malthaner, I wouldn't have had this happen for the world!" Isabelle said. "I've read that lemon juice is often effective for wine stains, so perhaps the stains could be removed."

Isabelle made such a charming picture of flustered innocence that Malthaner couldn't be angry with her. "Please don't distress yourself, Miss Fleming," he said kindly. "It's the sort of thing that could happen to anyone."

"You are too kind, Lord Malthaner," Isabelle said.

He smiled. "Nonsense. I have plenty of waistcoats, but there is only one Miss Fleming."

Langley cleared his throat. "Malthaner, I'll send someone to fetch my valet."

Malthaner bowed. "Thank you, my lord."

Langley's valet led Malthaner away with the assurance that the waistcoat could be saved by the prompt application of bicarbonate. Unlike the waistcoat, the dinner party could not be saved, and there was very little conversation for the rest of the meal. When Malthaner returned, wearing one of Langley's waistcoats, he found that Isabelle could barely meet his eye. He attributed this to her embarrassment at having spilled her wine.

In a display of uncharacteristic insight, Mrs. Hunt called for her carriage as soon as the last course was complete, and departed with Letitia and Lord Malthaner. As soon as their carriage drove away, Oliver quietly took his leave and made his way back to his cottage.

Seventeen

Oliver hadn't spent an evening drinking since Hermes had come into his life, but as soon as he returned to his cottage, he poured himself a glass of whisky and gave in to his grief. He mourned his brother, dead before his thirty-first birthday, and regretted that his fight with his father had led to an estrangement from his entire family.

Oliver found himself regretting many of his decisions. He could argue that joining the army had been courageous; however, his failure to seek out his family after his return to England seemed cowardly. The reasons for his quarrel with his father no longer seemed important, and for all he knew, his father might have been interested in a reconciliation. But instead of facing his father, Oliver had chosen to hide on another man's estate, where he had learned of his brother's death from a gossiping busybody.

He was just beginning to enjoy the effects of the whisky when Isabelle knocked on his door an hour later. Her candle gave just enough light for Oliver to see that she still wore her yellow satin dress, and for a minute Oliver wondered if he was hallucinating. But Hermes was expressing his delight at her visit by barking at her feet, and Oliver thought it was unlikely that both he and his dog were victims of a delusion.

"You shouldn't be here, Miss Fleming," he told her harshly. He stepped outside and closed the door behind him, for he had enough sense left to know that letting her into his cottage could be disastrous.

Isabelle was silent for a moment, and then she surprised him by sitting down on the shallow step that led to his front door.

"You'll ruin your dress," Oliver protested as he sat down next to her.

She shrugged. "The step is dry, so I don't think it will stain, but if it does, I have other dresses."

"None quite like that one, though," Oliver remarked, before he could stop himself.

Isabelle gave him a strange look, and Oliver mentally castigated himself for thinking of her dress hours after learning that his brother was dead.

"Are you warm enough?" he asked. She wasn't wearing gloves, and her dress's little puffed sleeves left her arms bare.

"Yes, I'm quite comfortable." There was a softness to the summer air, and Isabelle thought that under different circumstances she might be enjoying the evening immensely. "I've dropped cutlery often," she said kindly, "and I don't think Lord Malthaner meant to be insulting."

"What?" Oliver asked. Even in the candlelight, Isabelle could see that he looked confused, and she wondered if she had misinterpreted his reaction at the dinner table.

"When you dropped the knife," she explained. "No one thought anything of it, really. Except perhaps Lord Malthaner, who tried to be clever but didn't succeed."

"It doesn't matter, Isabelle," Oliver said honestly.

"That's not what upset you," Isabelle said slowly. She tried to remember what they had been discussing before Oliver dropped his knife. "Are you unwell?"

Oliver could see the concern on her face, and he decided to tell her part of the truth.

"Mrs. Hunt mentioned a man who died," he explained. "Lord Rupert St. Clair. I knew him when I was a boy. I grew up close to his father's estate, and we played together growing up. I didn't know he was dead."

Isabelle's eyes widened. "Oh Mr. Oliver, I'm so sorry."

"I didn't know him well," he admitted. That was a large part of the problem; he and his brother hadn't been close, but they should have been. Oliver wanted to blame his father for raising his sons in a way that made it impossible for them to be friends, but he knew that wasn't entirely fair. He should have tried to befriend Rupert in spite of his father.

"Regardless, you knew him, and he died young," Isabelle said. "It's not surprising that you're upset after hearing that news. It would be more alarming if you weren't."

"Yes, perhaps," he agreed. "But I'm all right now. You should go back to the house, Miss Fleming. If anyone knew you were here–"

"But no one does."

"Your maid?" he persisted. "She's not waiting to help you change?"

"No," Isabelle said. "I let Daisy get me ready for bed, then I changed back into this gown. I can get it on and off without help, if I leave the top three buttons undone."

The knowledge that three of her buttons were undone did not help Oliver's mental state. "I'm not fit company for you tonight, Isabelle," he said, unconsciously using her Christian name.

She frowned. "Because you've been drinking?"

He smiled ruefully. "I didn't think I was drunk yet, but if you've remarked upon it, I may be farther along than I thought. But I wouldn't be fit company for you any night. It's a damned shame, but there it is."

"Why not?" she asked curiously.

"This isn't the first evening I've spent drinking."

Isabelle stared at him. "I would be very surprised if it was. I'm not a complete innocent, you know."

Oliver burst out laughing. "Oh, Isabelle," he finally said. "That's exactly what you are."

"Perhaps I am," she agreed defensively, and Oliver could tell she was insulted. "Many people would consider it a virtue."

"It is a virtue," he agreed. "It seems that you have all the virtues, while I have all the vices."

Her brow furrowed. "Why do you say that?"

"Well, as you so cleverly pointed out, I'm drunk. At least, I was well on my way there when you showed up."

"Yes, but you just learned that your friend had died," she pointed out. "I'm sure many men would drink after hearing news like that. It's normal to want to forget."

"The problem is that there are a lot of things I want to forget." Five years in the army had made sure of that.

"Memories from the war?"

"Yes."

"Does it help to talk about them?"

"No."

"I see," she said. She wore her emotions on her face, and he could tell she was hurt that he didn't confide in her. He considered telling her he was haunted by the faces of the soldiers he had seen die in battle, both French and English. Worse, he was haunted by the knowledge that he had left his best friend, Major Francis Coates, to die on a field at Waterloo.

In one of the British Army's few reverses at Waterloo, a cavalry charge had pressed forward too far. The British had found themselves stuck in a muddy field, surrounded on three sides by the French, and Oliver would never forget the chaos of the retreat. Major Coates had been riding ahead of him, and Oliver had watched his friend take a shot to his back that had knocked him off his horse. Coates had landed on his side, and his eyes had met Oliver's in a look of silent entreaty.

Oliver hardly knew how he had made the decision. He liked to think it had been clear that Coates' wound was fatal, and that if Oliver had stopped, they would both have died. But the fact remained that Coates had called his name, and Oliver had left him behind. Coates' body had been among those recovered the following day.

Oliver was tempted to unburden himself to Isabelle, but he couldn't bring himself to do it. He thought she respected him, and he feared that if she knew his secrets, she would revise her opinion.

"I've done some unforgivable things, Isabelle."

"And they haunt you." She said it matter-of-factly, as though there was nothing unusual about being haunted by memories of past failures. There was curiosity and sympathy in her eyes, but fortunately, no pity. Oliver didn't think he could tolerate being the object of Isabelle's pity.

"They haunt me," he confirmed.

"And there's no way to make amends?"

"No." Francis Coates was dead. Oliver had had the opportunity to save him and had failed to do so, and there was no way to make amends for that.

"And liquor is the only thing that will chase the memories away?"

"Yes," he said simply. It was a lie, because Isabelle was a more effective distraction than liquor. More intoxicating, more dangerous, and not an idea that he should pursue.

"I don't think anything is truly unforgivable," she said earnestly. "Sometimes we do harm despite having good intentions."

"I'm sure nothing you've done is unforgivable," Oliver said, with a note of condescension in his voice. "I expect your greatest transgression has been something like speaking sharply to your maid."

"I've never spoken sharply to my maid," Isabelle said simply.

"Taken more than your fair share of the pudding, then."

The suggestion raised Isabelle's ire. "*More than my fair share of the pudding?*" she repeated incredulously. "Is that really how you see me? A girl in the schoolroom, fighting with her siblings over pudding?"

Oliver realized he had been insensitive. "No. Isabelle, I didn't mean–"

"I think you did," she said. "You think that because I haven't been to war, I can't imagine the things you endured, and I wouldn't understand if you told me about them."

Oliver knew better than to reply to that. He didn't know if she would understand, but he didn't have the courage to tell her about his cowardice on the battlefield.

"And you think that just because I haven't been to war, I haven't been tested," Isabelle continued. "And that the challenges you faced were more difficult than mine. But I've been tested, Mr. Oliver. Do you know how my father died?"

Oliver shook his head. "No."

"He lost a fortune to Lord Langley at cards and then drowned in the Thames," she said succinctly. "It's not clear if his death was an accident or he threw himself in the river, but either way, he left us deeply in debt. Amelia rose to the challenge; she confronted Lord Langley, and she was prepared to marry Mr. Garland in exchange for a marriage settlement."

"*Amelia* was going to marry Mr. Garland?" Oliver asked in disbelief.

"Oh, yes," Isabelle said. "Mama was very angry when she heard they were betrothed. She thought Mr. Garland was beneath us because his family made their fortune in textiles."

"And yet your mother ended up married to him?"

Isabelle smiled. "Mama visited Mr. Garland several times to express her disapproval of the match," she explained. "Somehow, she decided that although marriage to a mill owner wasn't good enough for her daughter, it was perfectly acceptable for her, provided there was enough money to distract her from the smell of the factory."

"I see."

"I couldn't have married him," Isabelle said abruptly. "Not even to save the family from ruin. I suppose if we were dying of starvation, I would have considered it, but–"

"Isabelle, you were a child," Oliver interrupted harshly, revolted by the thought of her married to Garland.

"I was almost eighteen. Two years younger than Amelia. And I know that if our ages had been reversed, and Amelia had been the younger sister, she would still have been the one to save the family."

"You don't know that," Oliver pointed out. "You'll never know what you would have done if you were the elder sister."

"I know," Isabelle insisted. "Amelia was born brave, and I was born timid. And sometimes, although I'm grateful for all that she's done for me, I'm jealous of her strength."

Oliver realized the courage it must have taken for her to admit that.

"But I can't change the past, and it does me no good to dwell on it," Isabelle continued. "All I can do is look to the future and try to do better. But there are times when my mind seems to get stuck on memories of my past mistakes, and when that happens, I try to think of other things."

"What other things?"

Isabelle took a deep breath. "Things like watching the sunset here at Stonecroft, or the satisfaction I get when I write a sentence that perfectly expresses how I feel. The look in–" she paused. She had been about to say, "the look in your eyes when I make you laugh," but she lost her nerve.

"What?" he asked.

"The look in Amelia's eyes when I make her laugh."

"That's a good list," Oliver said lightly.

Isabelle looked at him earnestly. "Perhaps you should think of things that make you happy."

"I can't, Isabelle. It's not that simple."

"Why not?"

Oliver had the wild impulse to tell Isabelle that the thing that would make him happiest was not a thing, but a young lady, and she was sitting next to him. Before Rupert's death, she had been safely out of his reach, since a lady like Isabelle would never consider marriage to her brother-in-law's land agent. But now Oliver was heir to a dukedom, and he had no doubt that society would consider Lord Oliver James Montgomery St. Clair a very eligible match for Miss Isabelle Fleming.

And Oliver knew that Isabelle deserved better. She should marry someone like Malthaner; preferably not Malthaner himself, for an evening's acquaintance had been enough to convince Oliver that the man was an idiot. But she deserved a man who hadn't known the horrors of the war, and who hadn't left his honour on a battlefield in Belgium.

He hardened his heart. "I'm not a child in the schoolroom, Isabelle," he said derisively. "I can't simply trick my brain to think of good things."

His reference to a child in the schoolroom cut her to the quick. She wondered if he saw her as one of the duties of his position; along with managing the tenants and keeping the accounts, he was responsible for entertaining the countess's younger sister. Perhaps he saw her in the same light as her mother and Mr. Garland, which was a very lowering thought.

"I didn't say it was easy," she said carefully. "I'll probably never have Amelia's courage, but that doesn't mean it's not worth trying to be better."

"I don't think you can be much better," Oliver said, without thinking. She was already his idea of perfection.

He saw the hurt in Isabelle's eyes before she got control of her expression, and realized how she had interpreted his remark. He debated whether to explain, but he decided it was safer to let her believe he meant it as an insult.

Isabelle lifted her chin. "Perhaps I can't, but I don't choose to be defined by my past failures," she said coolly.

There was a bitter note in Oliver's laugh. "I don't think you know what failure is, Isabelle."

She met his eye. "If I didn't know before this evening, I certainly do now." She picked up her candle and stood. "I'm sorry to have kept you from your drink, Mr. Oliver."

Oliver stood too, and escorted her silently back to the house. Isabelle wished she could tell him that she didn't need his protection, but the night was dark, and she was grateful he was there. After he had seen her safely to the kitchen door he walked slowly back to his cottage, lost in his thoughts. Now that he knew that Rupert was dead, he couldn't ignore his duty to visit his father, but he hated the idea of it. He wasn't afraid to face the duke, but he knew that when he left Stonecroft, he was unlikely to return. Even though he couldn't have Isabelle, he couldn't bring himself to leave her.

Eighteen

The week that followed brought glorious weather, and Isabelle spent hours walking around the Stonecroft grounds. She was frequently accompanied by Felicity Taylor, and she was grateful for her company. Stonecroft would have been very dull without Felicity; now that Amelia was in the last month of her pregnancy, her conversation was limited to the subject of how impatient she was for her baby to arrive, and Adrian had gone to visit a friend in Essex. Isabelle had no desire to work on her novel, and at night she was too restless to sleep well. She always had an eye out for Mr. Oliver, but instead of hoping to contrive a meeting, she now hoped to avoid one.

Isabelle desperately needed a distraction, so when Lord Malthaner sent a note proposing a riding expedition to see the famous Norman church in Cheltham, she decided to go. Miss Flint agreed to come as chaperone, and Isabelle reassured herself that they could hardly set a reckless pace when Felicity's middle-aged companion was one of the party.

"I abhor lateness in others," Felicity remarked on the morning of the outing. She, Isabelle, and Kincaid were sitting on the front steps of the house, waiting for Lord Malthaner and Letitia. Miss Flint had decided that she preferred the comfort of the sofa to that of the stone step, and was waiting in the drawing room.

"Only in others?" Isabelle asked.

Felicity's eyes twinkled mischievously. "I have been known to be late myself, but never without a good reason. Perhaps we could ride around the estate while we wait."

"I think the horses will get more than enough exercise on the ride to Cheltham," Kincaid said. "We don't want to overtire them."

"I suppose not," Felicity agreed, but her disappointment was obvious. "But we could walk down to the stables and help the grooms get the horses ready."

"Or we could stay here and enjoy this lovely spring morning," Kincaid countered. "The grooms don't need you telling them what to do."

Felicity looked insulted. "I would never tell them what to do," she said defensively. "I might make *suggestions*, but you must admit that I know more about horses than most grooms."

"It's not your knowledge that's in question," Kincaid replied. "It's your judgment. It's not polite to tell another man's staff how to go on."

Felicity smiled. "Do you know, Mr. Kincaid, I think that is one of the strongest arguments for marriage that I've heard? If I had my own household, no one could complain about my interference in the stables."

"Except, perhaps, your husband," Kincaid pointed out dryly.

"Yes," Felicity said with a frown. "Of course, I would try to come to an agreement with him before our marriage, but I don't suppose I would have any recourse if he didn't hold to it. It seems terribly unfair." She sighed. "What do you think, Isabelle?"

Isabelle smiled. "I have no desire to interfere in the management of the stables." She was already regretting her decision to join the riding party. When the idea was proposed, she had been determined to face her fear of horses, but as the moment of reckoning drew near, she felt her courage ebbing away.

"I don't suppose many women do, but it's the principle of the thing," Felicity said. She paused as she saw Mr. Oliver come around the corner of the house, walking briskly towards his cottage.

"Mr. Oliver!" Felicity called loudly.

Oliver turned and came towards them, smiling politely.

"Good morning, Miss Taylor," he said, sketching a bow. He bowed to Isabelle next, but didn't meet her eye.

"Are you feeling better, Mr. Oliver?" Felicity asked. She and Isabelle had encountered him on their walk the previous day, and Felicity had invited him to join them for a turn through the garden. Oliver had declined on the grounds he had a headache, and was on his way back to his cottage to rest.

"Much better, thank you," Oliver replied. This was a lie; after a night of too much liquor and too little sleep, he wasn't feeling well at all.

"I am pleased to hear it," Felicity said. She sneaked a

EMMA MELBOURNE

glanced at Kincaid, who was glowering at her, before giving Oliver a flirtatious smile. "I was worried about you, you know."

"You look like you're plotting mischief, Miss Taylor," Oliver said.

"Not at all," Felicity said innocently. "If you must know, we were in the midst of a debate."

"And what were you debating?"

"Marriage," Felicity replied.

"I see. Its merits in general, or one aspect in particular?"

"I think it's unfair that a husband could prevent his wife from pursuing an interest simply on a whim," Felicity said, with a glance at Kincaid. "Say, because he was concerned she might do it better than he did, and make him look foolish."

Kincaid snorted. "You give yourself a lot of credit."

"We are speaking of generalities, Mr. Kincaid," Felicity said innocently. "What do you think, Isabelle?"

"I agree it's unfair," Isabelle said carefully. "But I think that if you loved your husband, you wouldn't want to make him look foolish, and if he loved you, he wouldn't care if you did."

"Until you had a fight," said Felicity cynically. "Then your husband might not be so tolerant of your interests, especially if your talents were superior to his own."

"If you truly loved each other, you wouldn't fight," Isabelle said. "Or, if you did, you would realize the error and reconcile quickly."

"You have a very optimistic view of men," Felicity said.

"I like to think I have an optimistic view of love," Isabelle replied.

"What do you think, Mr. Oliver?" Felicity asked.

"Really, Felicity, it's not fair to ask him a question like that so early in the day," Kincaid protested.

"I think you're both right," Oliver said lightly.

"We can't both be right," Felicity protested. "You're trying to avoid the question."

"I think that if a man truly loved a woman, he would never fall out of love with her," Oliver said quietly. He still hadn't looked at Isabelle, but she felt as though he was speaking directly to her. "But that doesn't mean he would never fight with her. Circumstances might force him to make decisions he couldn't explain."

Felicity laughed. "You speak as though you have experience, Mr. Oliver," she said archly.

"Not at all," he replied. "Just a theory."

"You must join us on our riding expedition and entertain us with your theories," Felicity suggested.

Mr. Oliver finally looked at Isabelle and noticed she was wearing a riding habit. It was a flattering outfit of royal blue, a shade darker than her eyes, but he surveyed it with a frown.

"You're going riding?" he asked her abruptly.

"Yes," Felicity answered, when Isabelle didn't. "Lord Malthaner and Letitia are joining us, and we're going to ride to Cheltham. If you recall, Lord Langley suggested we visit the Norman church there."

Oliver didn't take his eyes off Isabelle. "Are you sure that's a good idea?"

"Why wouldn't it be a good idea?" Isabelle asked.

Something in her expression told Oliver that Felicity and Kincaid didn't know about her fear of riding.

"Because you don't enjoy the hot weather," he answered.

Isabelle laughed. "I'm not as delicate as I look. And even if I were, it's a beautiful day. I don't expect it will be terribly hot."

"Yes, it's one of the nicest days we've had all year," Felicity said enthusiastically. "Do say you'll come, Mr. Oliver. As it stands, our party is unbalanced, with four ladies and only two gentlemen."

"Who are the other ladies?" Oliver asked.

"Miss Hunt is coming, and Miss Flint, of course," Felicity replied.

"Oh, of course," nodded Oliver. Like Isabelle, he took comfort in the thought that Miss Flint was unlikely to be much of a horsewoman, and she would hold the group to a plodding pace.

"So you see why you must join us," Felicity said, with a persuasive smile for Oliver.

"Don't harass him, Felicity," Kincaid said reprovingly. "I'm sure he has things to do, and even if he doesn't, he might not want to spend the day listening to you prattle."

"Well, I don't see why he wouldn't," Felicity said flirtatiously. "Many people find me entertaining."

"Felicity," Kincaid repeated, with a warning in his tone.

Isabelle, who had been studying her boots, raised her eyes to find Oliver staring at her.

"I would like to join you," Oliver said curtly. "I'll need to return to my cottage to change, but I won't delay you long."

Felicity was the only person who appeared pleased by this announcement.

In the end, Oliver didn't delay them at all, since Lord Malthaner and Letitia still hadn't arrived when he rejoined the group on the front steps. Half an hour later, Malthaner finally arrived on a beautiful bay horse, nattily attired and full of apologies for his lateness. He explained that Letitia feared she was developing a sore throat, and had decided not to join them.

The Stonecroft grooms brought the horses around, Miss Flint was fetched from the sofa, and the party set off at last. Felicity and Kincaid took the lead, and Isabelle followed next to Malthaner, leaving Oliver and Miss Flint to bring up the rear. To Oliver's surprise, Miss Flint appeared to be a capable horsewoman.

"Lovely weather we're having," Oliver tried.

"Yes," Miss Flint agreed.

"This sort of outing would be miserable in the rain."

"Yes."

Oliver gave up and allowed his mind to wander. Not surprisingly, his mind and his eyes wandered to Isabelle, who was riding ten feet ahead of him beside Malthaner. From what he could tell, Malthaner wasn't having much more success in engaging Isabelle in conversation than Oliver had had with Miss Flint. Unlike Felicity, who rode as though she were an extension of her spirited brown mare, Isabelle was clearly uncomfortable. There was nothing wrong with her position in the saddle, or the way she held the reins, and someone who didn't know her well might not have noticed that anything was amiss. But whenever a bend in the road gave Oliver a glimpse of her profile, he could see the tension in her shoulders and the anxiety in her face.

There was very little traffic, but after half an hour they were forced to move to the side of the road to allow a coach to go past. When they returned to the road, Felicity and Isabelle took the lead, Lord Malthaner rode next to Mr. Oliver, and Kincaid fell back next to Miss Flint.

"I've had enough of Mr. Kincaid's conversation," Felicity remarked to Isabelle.

"Felicity, he might hear you," Isabelle protested.

"Nonsense," Felicity said, turning around to look behind them. "He and Miss Flint are a good twenty feet behind us, and although his vision is excellent, I don't think his hearing is particularly acute. In any case, I'm sure he will be too distracted by his charming companion to pay any attention to us."

Isabelle smiled. "Perhaps," she acknowledged.

"But I don't mind if he does hear me," Felicity continued. "If you can believe it, Mr. Kincaid accused me of flirting with Mr. Oliver."

"I see," said Isabelle slowly. "Well, I think Mr. Kincaid might have a point."

"Yes, I may have been flirting with Mr. Oliver," Felicity admitted. "But there was no need for Mr. Kincaid to make such a fuss about it. Why, I'm tempted to elope with Mr. Oliver just to see the look on Kincaid's face!"

"Has Mr. Oliver suggested an elopement?" Isabelle asked coolly.

"What?" Felicity asked in surprise. "No, of course not."

"It's not kind of you to flirt with him, Felicity," Isabelle said. "It would be cruel to raise his expectations."

"How do you know I'm not serious?"

Isabelle's heart sank as she realized that a match between Felicity and Mr. Oliver might indeed be possible. Society would see it as an unequal marriage, but perhaps not a laughable one. Mr. Oliver was the son of landed gentry, and had served in the army after going to Cambridge. Furthermore, he was Mr. Oliver, and Isabelle was convinced that any woman who met him would understand why Felicity wanted to marry him.

"Are you in earnest?" Isabelle asked carefully.

"No," Felicity admitted.

"Well, I hope you know what you're about."

Felicity smiled mischievously. "Mr. Oliver knows very well that I'm not in earnest."

"Then you're making a mockery of him," Isabelle said angrily. "As though the idea of a match between the two of you is so ludicrous that you couldn't be serious."

"That wasn't what I meant either," Felicity said. "I should have said that Mr. Oliver and I understand each other."

Isabelle wasn't sure she liked that answer any better.

Nineteen

As Oliver rode, he kept his eyes fixed on Isabelle, who was riding ahead of him next to Felicity.

"She's beautiful, isn't she?" Malthaner remarked.

"Miss Taylor is very attractive," Oliver said carefully.

"What? Oh, she's fine, but I don't consider her anything out of the ordinary." Malthaner lowered his voice. "And I don't need to marry for money. My mother advised me that when you have a fortune of your own, you should never marry an heiress."

"Does she believe you should leave the heiresses for the less fortunate?"

Malthaner laughed. "No, but when a lady brings money to a marriage, she may expect to have a say on how it's spent."

"I see." Oliver's expression was inscrutable.

"Your situation's different, of course," Malthaner pointed out. "If you can persuade Miss Taylor to look at you, you should take your chance."

"I'll keep that in mind."

"I was referring to Miss Isabelle Fleming," Malthaner continued. "I think she's the loveliest young lady I've ever seen. The blonde hair, the blue eyes; she's the diamond of the Season."

Oliver hadn't seen any of the other young ladies who were currently out, but he had no doubt that Malthaner's assessment was accurate.

"I'm going to marry her, you know," Malthaner said casually.

Malthaner's admiration for Isabelle was obvious, so this wasn't entirely a surprise, but it still struck Oliver like a blow. He fought to keep his expression neutral. "Congratulations. Has the betrothal been announced?"

"Oh, there hasn't been an announcement yet. Because of her sister's situation, of course."

Oliver looked at him blankly. "What situation?"

"Lady Langley suffers from a nervous condition," Malthaner explained.

"A nervous condition?" Oliver repeated incredulously.

"Yes," Malthaner affirmed. "And Miss Fleming does not want to announce our engagement until after Lady Langley has given birth to her child."

"I see," Oliver said carefully. The idea that Lady Langley suffered from a nervous disorder was laughable, and the fact that Isabelle had given Malthaner such an excuse gave Oliver hope.

"The delay is rather a nuisance, but a girl like Miss Fleming is worth waiting for," Malthaner explained.

"Indeed," Oliver agreed.

"You seem to have found yourself a good situation at Stonecroft," Malthaner remarked.

"Yes."

"I mean, riding parties, dinners with the family; it must be a big change from the army."

"Yes." Oliver realized he was starting to sound like Miss Flint. "Although I do occasionally have to work."

Malthaner laughed. "You didn't consider staying in the army?"

"No."

"You were an officer?"

"Yes. A cornet."

"I wish I had been able to join the army. I'd have shown Napoleon what was what."

"Why didn't you?"

Malthaner laughed again. "I'm a viscount."

Oliver feigned confusion. "Are noblemen unable to enlist?"

Malthaner frowned. "Well technically I could have, but I had no reason to. I have a title and a fortune, so I don't need a profession."

"But you said you would have liked to join the army," Oliver pointed out.

"Oh yes, in theory," Malthaner agreed. "I think it would have been exciting. But I can't imagine what my mother would have said. I don't have any brothers, you see."

"I see. In effect, you're irreplaceable."

Malthaner laughed. "I wouldn't have put it quite like that, but I suppose I am. If I die without an heir, the title will go to a second cousin. He's a nice enough fellow, but the thing is, he's a country vicar."

"And you don't think he would want to abandon his parishioners?" Oliver looked pensive. "Surely a replacement vicar could be found."

Malthaner laughed. "I'm sure he would abandon his parishioners quickly enough if he inherited a title, but he wouldn't have any idea how to go on. He wasn't born to it, and birth tells." He smiled at Oliver. "It would be as though you inherited a title."

"Quite," Oliver said, trying to suppress a smile. "Ridiculous."

"My mother always says a true nobleman can recognize another within minutes of meeting him."

Oliver feigned confusion again. "I don't see the difficulty there. Presumably when they are introduced to each other, they will realize they both hold titles?"

Malthaner's smile was condescending. "Even without an introduction, a nobleman would know another by his behaviour and conversation."

"But would a nobleman converse with a man to whom he had not been introduced?"

Malthaner was starting to look annoyed. "Of course not. I mean you can tell a man's birth by his behaviour."

Oliver nodded. "And your second cousin, the vicar, doesn't know how to behave?"

Malthaner shook his head. "Not his fault, of course."

"Of course not," Oliver agreed sympathetically. "Given your situation, I'm surprised you came on this riding expedition."

Now Malthaner looked confused. "What do you mean?"

"Well, think of the risks. You could be thrown from your horse, or we could be set upon by highwaymen. I didn't think to bring a pistol."

Malthaner looked at him suspiciously, and Oliver

wondered if he had pushed the jest too far. But Malthaner's expression relaxed.

"I think I can look after myself, even without a pistol," he said, with the confidence of a man who has never been tested.

"I'm relieved to hear it."

"You're only at Stonecroft on a temporary basis, is that right?"

"Yes. The usual man, Mr. Pettigrew, is expected to return next month."

"Ah," Malthaner nodded. "What do you plan to do next?"

Oliver forced himself to smile at the man. "I'm considering several opportunities."

Malthaner nodded. "Well, if you find yourself at a loss, I'm sure I could find a position for you on my estate. I already have a land agent, of course, but perhaps another outdoor position."

"Perhaps you have need of another undergardener," Oliver suggested dryly.

"Very likely," Malthaner said seriously. He chuckled. "I'm not as liberal as Langley, so you wouldn't be dining with us, but I think my staff are happy nonetheless."

"I'll keep it in mind."

"Do."

A curve in the road gave Oliver a look at Isabelle's profile, and he thought she was drooping in the saddle. He turned to Malthaner. "Do you think it's wise to have the ladies riding in front?"

"What do you mean?" Malthaner asked.

"If we were set upon by highwaymen, or if an animal wandered into the road, Miss Taylor and Miss Fleming would be unprotected." Oliver knew it was a weak argument, but it was the best he could come up with.

"Do you think we should go ahead of them?"

"I think at least one of us should ride up front with them," Oliver said.

"I can do it," Malthaner offered. As Oliver had hoped, Malthaner nudged his horse into a canter, and drew up beside Felicity. He, Felicity and Isabelle rode side by side for a short distance before Isabelle fell back and ended up next to Oliver.

"Your riding habit is almost the exact colour of your eyes," Oliver commented casually. "The habit is a little darker, but they're very close."

Isabelle smiled. "The modiste said the same thing when I was choosing the colour."

"It looks brand new."

"Are you a connoisseur of riding habits, Mr. Oliver?" she said lightly. He was right; although she had bought the outfit the previous autumn, this was the first time she had worn it.

"When was the last time you rode before today?" he asked bluntly.

"Several weeks ago, when I twisted my ankle and you let me ride your horse."

"Come, Miss Fleming, you know that's not what I meant."

Isabelle couldn't lie to him. "I don't remember when I last rode."

Oliver nodded. "So unless your memory is remarkably poor, you haven't ridden for quite some time."

"Yes," Isabelle admitted.

"And you thought that an all-day riding excursion was

a good idea? You didn't think that a few easy rides around Stonecroft might have been a better way to start?"

"I did a great deal of riding when I was younger," Isabelle said defensively. "It's not a skill one forgets."

"Your mind might not have forgotten, but your muscles almost certainly have."

Isabelle knew he was right. Although she was far more physically fit than she had been when she arrived at Stonecroft, riding used muscles she hadn't known she possessed. She was certainly aware of them now.

Her misery must have shown on her face, for Oliver's expression softened. "We can turn around now," he suggested. "It was an overly ambitious plan."

"No," Isabelle protested. "I don't want to spoil the outing."

"The others are probably tired too, and just too proud to say so," he told her. "I know I'll be glad to get out of the saddle."

She looked at him skeptically. She didn't know much about his time in the army, but she imagined he was used to riding for more than two hours at a time.

Up ahead, the road curved sharply to the left. Felicity checked her horse and appeared to survey a grassy field straight ahead of them.

"I think Bluebell wants to jump that fence," she announced gaily. "We'll shake the fidgets out." The wooden fence was about three feet high and enclosed a grassy field.

Before Kincaid could comment, Felicity took off at a gallop, appearing perfectly at ease on her horse. They flew over the fence, clearing it with over a foot to spare.

"Well done, Miss Taylor," Malthaner called.

"Of all the reckless ideas," Oliver muttered.

"I'm going next," Isabelle announced.

"You are not!" Oliver exclaimed. "Isabelle, you can't–you mustn't."

Isabelle was determined to show him that she could. She dropped her hands and nudged her horse, Cressida, to a canter. The horse seemed surprised, but obeyed, and all of a sudden Isabelle found herself flying towards the fence. Time seemed to slow down and stretch out. The scenery passed by in a blur of green, the wind whipped her cheeks, and Isabelle felt as though she were invincible. She closed her eyes.

If she had kept her eyes closed, she probably would have been fine, and Cressida would have carried them over the fence without difficulty. But seconds before Cressida would have jumped, Isabelle opened her eyes, panicked, and pulled up on the reins. Cressida obediently turned away from the fence, but Isabelle was thrown. She sailed over the fence and landed hard on the grass.

The sight of Isabelle lying on the ground almost undid Oliver. He remembered that his brother had died after a fall from a horse, and he couldn't bear the thought of losing Isabelle the same way. He steered his horse towards the fence at a point about a hundred feet away from her, so he wouldn't disturb her with the force of his landing. His horse cleared the jump easily, and Oliver dismounted and ran towards her.

By the time he reached Isabelle, she was sitting up and talking to Felicity, who looked more distressed than she did.

"I'm all right," Isabelle said, with a rueful smile. "I

suppose you were right, Mr. Oliver. I shouldn't have tried to jump it."

Oliver wanted to take her in his arms and kiss her until they were both out of their senses, or at least until he forgot the terror he had felt when he saw her fly off her horse. But he had no right to hold her or to kiss her, and since he had no other outlet for his emotions, he took her roundly to task.

"What were you thinking, Miss Fleming? Of all the reckless, irresponsible, idiotic things to do! Were you trying to get yourself killed?"

Isabelle's expression changed. "Is it any business of yours if I was?" she asked coolly.

Oliver forced himself to take a deep breath. "You're right," he said stiffly. "It isn't my concern."

Malthaner and Kincaid rode up and dismounted, and Malthaner rushed to Isabelle.

"You gave us quite a scare, Miss Fleming," he told her. "No, don't try to stand, we'll bring a carriage." He turned to Oliver. "Ride back to Stonecroft and fetch a carriage for Miss Fleming."

Oliver hardly knew what to say. He resented taking orders from Malthaner, and he didn't want to leave Isabelle. But it was clear that she was in no condition to ride, and he didn't trust himself to control his emotions if he stayed.

"I'll fetch the gig," Oliver finally said.

"There's no need for the gig," Isabelle protested, as she rose to her feet. "I can ride, provided that Cressida isn't injured." She looked across to the other side of the fence, and was relieved to see that Miss Flint was holding Cressida's reins and Cressida appeared unharmed.

"I don't think you can ride," Oliver said, without thinking. "I'll fetch the gig."

"I may not ride as well as Miss Taylor, but I can ride well enough to get home," Isabelle said with dignity.

"Isabelle, you know that's not what I meant," Oliver replied. "You've taken a bad fall, so I don't think you should."

She ignored him and turned to study the fence, which came to about the height of her hip. "Now I just need to get back over the fence," she said thoughtfully. "I think I could climb over it–"

"No need, Miss Fleming," Lord Malthaner said gallantly. "If you will allow me, I would be honoured to lift you over the fence."

"Thank you, Lord Malthaner," Isabelle said shyly. Oliver gritted his teeth as he watched Malthaner pick her up and set her gently down on the other side of the fence.

Felicity, Kincaid, Malthaner, and Oliver mounted their horses and jumped back over the fence to join Isabelle and Miss Flint. Malthaner dismounted again to help Isabelle, and she gathered her courage as he threw her up into the saddle. Oliver could see the terror in her eyes as she settled herself on the horse.

"You're very brave, Miss Fleming," Malthaner said with admiration.

Oliver took the lead on the journey home so he wouldn't have to watch Isabelle ride next to Lord Malthaner. Felicity and Kincaid fell behind, and Kincaid took the opportunity to tell Felicity what he thought of her decision to jump the fence.

"That was a shameful display," he told her. "You are unquestionably the best horsewoman in the party, and there was no need to prove it with a reckless display of skill. Did you not consider that others might feel inspired to imitate you?"

Felicity thought of saying that the fence wouldn't have posed a challenge for most riders, or that no one had forced Isabelle to try the jump. But she didn't argue, because she knew Kincaid was right. It had been clear from the time they set out that Isabelle was nervous in the saddle.

"You're right, Mr. Kincaid," she said contritely. "I'm sorry."

His expression softened a little when he realized she wasn't going to try to justify her actions. "I suppose it wasn't a very high fence," he said grudgingly.

When they arrived back at Stonecroft, Lord Malthaner helped Isabelle dismount and offered her his arm to help her into the house. Oliver returned to his cottage without a word to anyone, and the next day, he informed Lord Langley that was leaving Stonecroft. An urgent family matter had arisen, and he would not be able to return. Langley was so understanding that Oliver was bold enough to ask if he could leave Hermes at Stonecroft, since he didn't want to travel with a dog.

Twenty

Letter from Isabelle to her brother William

Dear William,

Tonight I'm going to a dance at the Maidstone Assembly Rooms with Felicity, Miss Flint, and Mr. Kincaid. Letitia Hunt is going too, with her mother and Lord Malthaner. When I left London, I was heartily sick of dancing, but I think tonight should be enjoyable.

Amelia is very impatient for the baby to arrive. A doctor arrived from London yesterday, and will stay at Stonecroft until the child is born. At first he said the babe wouldn't arrive for at least a fortnight, but when Amelia insisted the birth would take place within a week he was clever enough to agree with her. He also professed himself delighted to work with the midwife, so I don't expect trouble there.

Oh, and Mr. Oliver left rather unexpectedly last week. He told Lord Langley he had to attend to an urgent personal matter, and I don't think he plans to return. He left Hermes *behind, and I spent two days trying to coax the poor dog out of the sulks. But Hermes came for a walk with me today, and he seems to be resigned to the situation. Fortunately Mr. Pettigrew should be back next week, so Mr. Oliver will hardly be missed.*

Yours,
Isabelle

∼

As the carriage bounced along the road to Maidstone, Isabelle wished they were heading home instead of to the Assembly Rooms. Despite what she had written to her brother, she was not looking forward to the dance. She hadn't slept well for several days, her head ached, and the whole affair seemed like a frivolous waste of time. Isabelle leaned her head against the side of the coach and tried to ignore the argument taking place between Felicity and Mr. Kincaid.

"I suppose that since I'm not yet out in society, you won't allow me to stand up with anyone but you," Felicity said crossly.

"On the contrary, Felicity, I don't see how you can come to any harm at a county assembly. In fact, I'll encourage you to stand up with anyone but me. You seem to be in a particularly quarrelsome mood tonight, and I prefer to dance with more agreeable partners."

Felicity flushed. "I'll have you know, Mr. Kincaid, that I only quarrel with you," she said hotly. "Other men find my company perfectly agreeable."

Kincaid smiled. "Why, Felicity, you recently accused

me of forbidding you to speak to men. How would you know if they find your company agreeable or not?"

Felicity sighed. "You can't blame me for being quarrelsome when you deliberately try to provoke me."

"That sounds like the rebuttal of someone who has no logical counter-argument."

"If I'm unable to form a logical argument, I have no one to blame but you," Felicity retorted. "A responsible guardian would have ensured I was educated in the arts of logic and rhetoric."

"I don't think many young ladies are educated in logic and rhetoric," Kincaid replied.

Felicity raised an eyebrow. "Are you saying you don't believe in education for women?"

Kincaid sighed. "You know that's not what I'm saying, Felicity."

"That sounds like the rebuttal of someone who has no logical counter-argument," Felicity said sweetly.

Kincaid smiled appreciatively. "You don't seem to need further instruction in the art of logic, Felicity. Perhaps I haven't been such a negligent guardian after all." He leaned back and watched with satisfaction as Felicity realized that a clever reply would only prove his point.

Felicity snorted and turned to Isabelle. "Do you think Lord Malthaner will come to the assembly, Isabelle?"

"What?" Isabelle asked. Her head was aching, and she had stopped paying attention to Felicity's quarrel with Kincaid. "Oh. Perhaps."

"It's such a shame that Mr. Oliver left," Felicity continued. "I'm sure he would have been a most agreeable dancing partner. Do you know where he went?"

"Lord Langley said that Mr. Oliver had to leave to attend to a family matter," Isabelle said listlessly.

"When will he return?" Felicity asked.

"I don't think he intends to return."

"It's strange that Mr. Oliver didn't take Hermes," Felicity remarked. "He seemed very attached to him, and he doesn't seem like the type of man who would abandon a dog." She shrugged. "Perhaps he found another position, and his new employer wouldn't allow him to bring Hermes."

"Perhaps," Isabelle agreed. She had wondered the same thing herself.

"Well, I'm sure you will miss him at Stonecroft," Felicity said. "I would be pleased to meet him again after I come of age." She cut a glance towards Kincaid, who had leaned back against the squabs and closed his eyes.

When the coach finally came to a halt outside the Assembly Rooms, Kincaid helped the ladies to descend, and Isabelle was relieved to stand and stretch her legs.

"Try not to fall in love with someone ineligible," Kincaid said to Felicity as they walked to the door. "I would hate to break your heart by refusing to consent to your marriage."

Felicity's eyes twinkled mischievously. "Perhaps I'll elope to Gretna Green and ask for your permission after the fact."

~

Oliver sat in the dining room of the Maidstone Arms, nursing a glass of ale. His position by the front window gave him an excellent view of the street, and he watched the passersby for a certain blonde young lady. When he left Stonecroft the week before, he hadn't known what he would do next; he had only known he had to get away from Isabelle. So he had gone to Maidstone, intending to hire a post-chaise to take him to London. Since the House of Lords was still in session, he expected his father to be in town, and he knew the time had come to meet with him. If his father still didn't want Oliver to manage one of his estates, Oliver would look for a position elsewhere.

Once he reached Maidstone, however, Oliver had convinced himself that he should conserve his resources and take the mail coach instead of a post-chaise. It wasn't as though his time was valuable, and he could be miserable in a mail coach just as well as in a chaise. Since he had missed the day's mail coach he took a room at the inn, where he decided it would be a shame to leave Kent without exploring the town of Maidstone. After three days of walking up and down the high street, Oliver could confidently say it looked almost identical to the high street of every other English town he had seen.

Oliver sipped his ale and resolved to leave for London the next day. By lingering in Kent, hoping to glimpse a young lady with honey-blonde hair, he was only torturing himself.

"Pardon me," said a voice apologetically. Oliver looked up to see a young lady standing with her hand on the chair opposite his. "I'm sorry to trouble you, but I wonder if I could share your table? All the other tables are taken, and I would rather not eat in the taproom." She paused and blushed. "I'm on my own, you see."

Oliver finished his ale and rose. "You may have the table," he said, smiling politely.

"Oh no," she protested. "I would hate for you to leave because of me. There's plenty of space for both of us."

Oliver nodded and sat back down.

"My name is Mrs. Talbot," she informed him, then paused expectantly, waiting for Oliver to introduce himself.

When it was clear that Oliver wasn't going to oblige her, Mrs. Talbot continued. "It's actually a pleasure to have company. I lost my husband over two years ago, so I've grown accustomed to dining alone."

"My condolences, ma'am." Oliver glanced out the window and saw several carriages drawn up outside the Assembly Rooms across the street. Lord Malthaner alighted from the closest carriage and reached up his hand to help a lady descend. The lady was young and blonde, and Oliver's heart sped up until he recognized Letitia Hunt.

"Truly, I think the worst part of widowhood is the loneliness," Mrs. Talbot continued. The tone of her voice had changed from apologetic to sultry, and Oliver realized that her initial shyness had been feigned.

"Have you no maiden aunts?" Oliver asked blandly.

"I beg your pardon?"

Oliver smiled innocently. "I thought that was the usual solution for a lady in need of companionship. She invites a maiden aunt to live with her."

Mrs. Talbot laughed, as though Oliver had said something particularly witty. "I'm afraid I find maiden aunts dull company."

"Perhaps a cousin then," Oliver suggested.

She trilled a laugh and leaned closer to him. Her

perfume was sweet and cloying, far too heavy for a summer evening.

"I find I prefer male companionship," she confessed. "Are you staying in the inn tonight?"

Oliver finally looked at her properly, and saw that she was about his age, with dark hair and a trim figure. He supposed she was pretty enough, and some men would consider her beautiful, but it made no difference to him. Isabelle had ruined him for other women, and the attractive young widow failed to stir his blood. He realized he would have to marry to father an heir, and the lady he married might look something like this one; beautiful to some, but with the wrong hair, the wrong eyes, and the wrong scent. The thought was depressing.

Oliver had worked himself into a fine state of self-pity when he saw Langley's coach draw up across the street.

"Sir?" Mrs. Talbot said. "Would you like company tonight?"

Oliver's attention was still fixed on Langley's coach. He watched Kincaid alight and offer his hand to Felicity, Miss Flint, and finally, to Isabelle. Something about the situation troubled Oliver. He didn't trust Malthaner, and he dismissed Miss Flint as an ineffective chaperone who would be more interested in the supper buffet than the welfare of the young ladies in her care. Kincaid seemed like a sensible man, but Oliver feared he would be too distracted by Felicity to pay any attention to Isabelle.

"Sir?"

Oliver reluctantly turned back to Mrs. Talbot, who seemed to have raised her voice in an attempt to hold his attention. He noticed that a middle-aged lady at the next table was giving him a disapproving look.

"If you would like company, I can perform any service you desire," Mrs. Talbot said boldly.

"I'm afraid I have a prior engagement," Oliver told her kindly, and he stood to return to his room.

Oliver unearthed his old evening clothes from the bottom of his suitcase and spent half an hour transforming himself into a gentleman of fashion. He couldn't get all the wrinkles out of his cream silk waistcoat and black knee breeches, but he thought he would still pass muster. His shirt points reached his cheeks, his cravat was elaborately tied, and he looked every inch the dandy. His tailcoat gave him some trouble, as he was more muscular across the shoulders than he had been when it was made, but he was eventually able to shrug himself into it. Oliver thought of Mrs. Talbot, who had offered to perform any service he desired, and smiled to himself. She would have been very surprised if he had invited her up to his room to assist him into his coat.

Oliver glanced in the mirror and thought he looked ridiculous, but he hoped he would impress the doorman at the Assembly Rooms. He had observed that most doormen judged a man's worth by the cut of his coat, and took pleasure in denying entry to those they deemed unworthy.

The building that housed the Assembly Rooms was one of the finest examples of neoclassical architecture in Maidstone, but Oliver barely noticed its design as he climbed the steps to the door. The doorman deemed him worthy of entry, and he was ushered in to the main hall.

The dancing had begun, and Oliver spotted Isabelle dancing a cotillion with Lord Malthaner. She was luminous in a gown of pale blue crepe, with her blonde hair in a loose chignon and a strand of pearls around her neck, and the sight of her stole his breath. Oliver supposed he should stand up with one of the hopeful young ladies who were sitting against the wall, waiting for an invitation to dance, but he was lost in the pleasure of watching Isabelle.

Malthaner spotted Oliver before Isabelle did, and squinted at his evening clothes. Before Oliver had arrived, Malthaner's shirt points had been the highest in the room, but Oliver's rivalled them. Malthaner wondered if Oliver was trying to copy his style.

"I say, Miss Fleming," Malthaner remarked. "What is Mr. Oliver doing here?"

"What?" Isabelle asked in confusion. "No. Mr. Oliver left last week."

"It seems he's returned, because he's sitting against the wall, talking to Miss Flint."

Isabelle's first impulse was to turn and look, and it took all her self-control to keep to the pattern of the dance. When she was finally able to turn, she saw that Lord Malthaner was right, and Mr. Oliver was indeed engaged in conversation with Miss Flint. She had never seen him dressed so formally, and if she hadn't known him as well as she did, she might not have recognized him. But there was no mistaking his face, which had occupied her thoughts for the past several weeks.

"I wonder if Langley knows he's here," Malthaner mused.

"Are you afraid that Mr. Oliver will steal your partners?"

Malthaner laughed, as though the idea was ridiculous. "Hardly that, but I'm afraid he'll make a fool of himself, and of the rest of your party by association."

"I see," Isabelle said, deliberately misinterpreting him. "You're worried Mr. Oliver will make a fool of you?"

Malthaner laughed. "He won't make a fool of me, but it may not reflect well on Lord Langley. People may think it odd to have a land agent come to the Assembly Rooms. Does Mr. Oliver even know how to dance?"

"I'm sure he does," Isabelle said, with more confidence than she felt. "He's a former officer and a gentleman's son."

"Yes, but he works as a land agent now."

"I don't see what that has to do with anything."

Malthaner sighed. "My mother says that when people are allowed to rise above their station, the fabric of society starts to fray."

"Perhaps if society's fabric is so delicate, it deserves to be torn," Isabelle remarked. "It might be replaced by something better."

Malthaner laughed. "It's a metaphor, Miss Fleming," he said kindly.

Isabelle shrugged. "I suppose you wouldn't encourage your land agent to attend a county assembly?"

Malthaner laughed. "No more than I would suggest he come with me to Almack's."

The set came to an end. Isabelle curtsied to Malthaner and walked back to Miss Flint, who was still sitting next to Oliver.

"I didn't expect to see you here, Mr. Oliver," Isabelle said.

"I was curious to see the Maidstone Assembly Rooms, Miss Fleming."

Isabelle suddenly felt shy. "Do you dance, Mr. Oliver?"

"I might," he began, and he was about to ask her to dance with him when Isabelle spoke again.

"It's perfectly all right if you don't know how to dance," she reassured him. "Many gentlemen choose not to, and there's a card room next to the ballroom." She realized he probably didn't have money to spend at the card tables and wondered if she had been tactless. "You don't have to play cards, either," she continued. "There will be chairs off to the side, and you can observe the dancing."

"I can be a wallflower, in fact," he said, in a teasing tone.

"I've never heard that term applied to a man," Isabelle said thoughtfully. "But there's nothing wrong with being a wallflower. In any case, some of the country dances are quite simple, and I'm sure you'll pick up the steps easily."

"Will you dance with me?"

"Of course. I'm engaged for the next two sets, but not beyond that. We'll choose one of the straightforward dances, and it won't matter if you miss some of the steps. It will be–"

"Isabelle?" Oliver interrupted, with a smile in his voice.

She realized she had been rambling, and she flushed. "Yes?"

"I know how to dance."

Twenty-One

Isabelle had promised the next dance to the son of a country squire. She found him pleasant, earnest, and very young, although she supposed he was a few years older than she was. She had to force herself to pay attention to him, as her mind was inclined to wander across the room to where Oliver was dancing with Felicity Taylor. Oliver was clearly an accomplished dancer, and he and Felicity made an attractive pair. Isabelle found herself wishing she could trade places with Felicity.

But the time finally came for Isabelle to dance with Oliver, and he led her out to the dance floor as the musicians struck up a waltz.

"I wasn't sure if they would allow the waltz at a county assembly, but I'm glad they did," Isabelle remarked, as she floated around the room in his arms. "To think I was worried that you wouldn't know how to dance! You put the other men to shame, Mr. Oliver."

He smiled. "Would you believe the British military gives dancing lessons?"

"No."

"Then perhaps it's your skill as a partner," he mused. "They say a good partner can make any man look like a good dancer."

She frowned at him skeptically. "I've never heard anyone say that."

Oliver feigned surprise. "No?"

"No, and furthermore, I've danced with a great number of men–"

"A great number, Miss Fleming?" Oliver interrupted.

"During the past Season I've been to more balls than I can remember."

"In that case, I'll concede that you're an expert," he said lightly.

"Thank you," she said, suspicious of the gleam of amusement in his eyes." As I was saying, I've danced with a great number of men, and many of them were horrible dancers. So unless their dancing looked better to others than it did to me, I can't believe that your saying is true."

"Perhaps you weren't a good partner for them," he said.

She frowned again. "What do you mean?"

"I mean, Miss Fleming, that the important thing is not to find someone who's a good dancer, but to find someone who's a good partner for you."

"Oh," she said weakly. "Am I a good partner for you?"

He met her eyes intently. "I can't think of anyone better."

Isabelle understood why the waltz was considered a scandalous dance. Mr. Oliver was only touching her in two places, with one hand on her waist and the other clasping hers, but it felt wonderfully intimate. She supposed it was far less intimate than the kiss Lord Malthaner had given her when he proposed, but while Malthaner's kiss had left her cold, the heat of Mr. Oliver's gaze lit a fire inside her that she barely understood. If she was honest with herself, she knew that her feelings had very little to do with the waltz and everything to do with the man. She was in love with Mr. Oliver; she had been for weeks, but her brain had been slow to catch up to her heart.

The dance ended and the music stopped, but Mr. Oliver kept hold of her hand.

"Are you coming back to Stonecroft?" Isabelle asked. "Hermes was very upset when you left."

He met her eye. "Do you want me to come back to Stonecroft?"

It should have been a simple question, but for Isabelle it was anything but. She wanted to ask him why he had left, why he was considering coming back, and how long he planned to stay.

Before she could answer, there was a hand on her arm. "I think the next dance is promised to me, Miss Fleming."

"Lord Malthaner!" she said in surprise.

"The next set is beginning," Malthaner said persuasively. "We should take our places."

"I don't recall agreeing to dance this set with you," Isabelle said, as he led her back onto the dance floor.

"I could tell you needed rescuing," he said with a teasing smile.

"Thank you, Lord Malthaner, but I didn't need you to rescue me."

His only reply was a knowing smile, and when the

dance began, conversation was difficult. Isabelle knew she should make it clear to Malthaner that she wouldn't marry him, and that her decision had nothing to do with Amelia's delicate condition. She was considering how best to do this when she caught a glimpse of Letitia Hunt. Her friend was standing in an alcove, partially hidden by a floral arrangement, but she appeared to be trying to break free of a man's embrace.

Isabelle broke away from Lord Malthaner and hurried towards Letitia. As she got closer, she could see that Letitia was being held by Lord Braden, who had pinned her arms to her sides and was attempting to kiss her.

Isabelle didn't stop to think about the potential consequences of her intervention. "For shame!" she shouted at Lord Braden. "Release her!"

Braden turned, but he didn't let go of Letitia. "I'll gladly take you in her place," he said insolently. "It's Miss Fleming, isn't it?"

Isabelle drew her right arm back and threw a punch. She wasn't sure whether Lord Braden fell from the strength of the blow or surprise that she hit him, but either way, he went down.

"Isabelle, what have you done?" She turned to see Malthaner standing next to her, looking at her in disbelief.

Braden staggered to his feet and leered at Isabelle. "I'll certainly take you in her place," he said, reaching to grab her arm. She stepped backwards and put up her fists, preparing to hit him again. But suddenly Oliver was there and Braden was on the floor again, dazed by the force of Oliver's hit.

It took Braden longer to get to his feet the second time.

"It's time for you to leave," Oliver told him simply.

"Go to hell," Braden retorted.

"Leave, or I'll send for the magistrate," Oliver said in a voice of authority. "We have a room full of witnesses who can attest to your offensive behaviour."

Braden sneered at him. "She wasn't unwilling, Mr.–" he paused, and studied Oliver curiously.

"Oliver," he supplied.

"I'm not sure I know your family," Braden said contemptuously.

"While I'm sure that's to our credit, it has nothing to do with the matter at hand. I told you to leave. And if I ever hear of you harassing a lady again, I'll make you regret it."

"How will you do that?" Braden scoffed.

"Believe me, Braden, you don't want to find out." Oliver didn't know what he would do to Braden, other than beat him senseless, but fortunately, his vague threat was effective. Braden walked off, holding his handkerchief against his bleeding nose, and Oliver followed to ensure he found the door.

Malthaner rushed to Isabelle and put an arm around her waist.

"Come, Miss Fleming, let me get you to a chair," he said. "You're in shock." He looked at her with concern. "Are you able to walk? Shall I carry you?"

Isabelle highly doubted that he could carry her, and she knew it wasn't necessary. She hadn't had time to think before she hit Lord Braden, and she was a little surprised she had done it, but far from feeling weak, she felt empowered.

"I'm perfectly fine," she insisted.

But Malthaner seemed to doubt it. "Do you need smelling salts? A glass of wine?"

"I'm fine," Isabelle insisted. "But I should find Letitia." Her gaze swept the room until she saw Letitia standing by the wall with Mrs. Hunt, who appeared to be giving her a lecture.

Before Isabelle could move towards Letitia, Malthaner took her hands in his and dropped to his knees in front of her.

"Marry me, Miss Fleming," he said bluntly.

"What?" Isabelle asked in disbelief.

"Miss Fleming, I am humbly requesting the honour of your hand in marriage."

Isabelle didn't think he looked humble at all. In fact, he appeared to be in no doubt of his reception.

"Lord Malthaner, we can't discuss this here," she began. A crowd of interested people had started to form around them.

"I know you wanted to wait, and I respect your concern for your sister, but Isabelle, you have caused a scandal," Malthaner pointed out.

"I didn't cause a scandal," she protested. "Lord Braden caused a scandal by forcing his attentions on Miss Hunt, and I simply came to her aid."

"Isabelle, you hit him," Malthaner said. "There is blood on your glove."

Malthaner was speaking loudly, and Isabelle reflected that anyone who hadn't seen her hit Lord Braden would know of it now. The story would inevitably spread, but she didn't see why Malthaner had to help it along.

"Please get up," she said in a low voice. "Take me back to Miss Flint. We can discuss this later."

"Isabelle, I'm telling you that I still want to marry you, despite the fact that you hit a man," Malthaner continued, as though she hadn't spoken. "People may think you have an undisciplined temper, but I know your actions tonight don't reflect your true character."

Isabelle stared at him in disbelief, and Malthaner mistook her silence for encouragement.

"My mother may object, but I assure you that won't weigh with me," he told her. "Although I don't think she will object, because she knows you are my destiny. In fact, I think I was fated to be here tonight, to save you from ruin."

"If you truly wanted to save me from ruin, you would have hit Lord Braden yourself," Isabelle said scathingly. His comment about destiny jogged a memory, and her eyes widened.

"The Anonymous Admirer," she breathed. "Lord Malthaner, have you been sending me poetry?"

Malthaner nodded. "It was supposed to be a secret," he said petulantly. "I was going to surprise you with the secret on our wedding night."

"Surprise me with *poetry*?" she asked incredulously.

"With the secret, that I am your Anonymous Admirer," he explained. "But there is another poem that I am saving for after we marry."

"No," Isabelle said simply.

"But don't you see, Isabelle?" Malthaner continued, taking hold of her hands. "Marriage is the only way to prevent a scandal. I'm offering you the protection of my name."

"No," Isabelle repeated. "Let go of my hands, please."

Malthaner released her, but he wasn't ready to give in. "But think, Isabelle. I'm afraid that after this unfortunate episode, no other man will wish to marry you."

"Because I hit a man?" Isabelle asked incredulously.

"Yes," Malthaner said with a nod. "And because I put my arm around you in the middle of the Assembly Rooms." Isabelle thought he was speaking even more loudly than before.

"I don't care," she said firmly.

"But Isabelle, consider," Malthaner said. "You'll be plunged into a scandal-broth so hot, you won't escape without a burn."

Isabelle stared at him in disbelief for a moment before giving in to a paroxysm of laughter. Malthaner stared at her in concern, wondering if she was suffering from the same nervous condition that affected her sister.

When Oliver returned from escorting Braden outside, he found Isabelle bent double and shaking, and he rushed to her side.

"Isabelle, are you hurt?" he asked.

"I think Miss Fleming is merely overexcited," Malthaner said. "I have made her an offer of marriage, and she is overwhelmed."

Isabelle collected herself and lifted her face to look at Oliver, and he was relieved to see that she was laughing.

"Oh, Mr. Oliver," Isabelle said. "Lord Malthaner just said I'll be plunged into a scandal-broth so hot, I won't escape without a burn." She chuckled. "Isn't it ridiculous?"

"Ridiculous," Oliver agreed, staring at Malthaner with contempt.

Malthaner raised his quizzing glass and peered at Oliver's shirt-points. "Have you tried to ape my style of dress?"

Oliver sighed. "Malthaner, I can assure you that I haven't tried to ape anything of yours. I had these clothes made before I knew of your existence, and I can blame no one's judgment but my own."

Malthaner laughed. "To think I offered you a position on my estate! I suppose I should thank you for showing me your true character."

Oliver nodded politely. "I could say the same to you."

Malthaner turned back to Isabelle. "Take time to consider, Miss Fleming. I'm sure that when you have had time to reflect, and when you realize how unlikely you are to receive another offer of marriage–"

"I would be honoured to marry her," Oliver said impulsively. "That is, if Miss Fleming will have me."

Malthaner bit out a laugh. "But you're Lord Langley's land agent," he said incredulously. There was a ripple of whispers throughout the crowd.

Oliver almost laughed. There were many reasons why he wasn't good enough for Isabelle, but the fact that he had worked as a land agent wasn't one of them. It was honest work, and he was proud to have done it.

"He is," Isabelle confirmed. She met Oliver's eye shyly. "I would be honoured to marry you, Mr. Oliver."

Malthaner took Isabelle's hands again. "Isabelle, please consider," he began.

"Let go of my hands," she said firmly.

"But Isabelle–"

"She asked you to release her hands," Oliver said.

"This has nothing to do with you," Malthaner said.

Oliver disagreed. He punched Malthaner in the face, and the viscount staggered and fell to his knees. When Malthaner rose to his feet, Isabelle could see blood dripping from his nose onto his snow white cravat. Oliver took advantage of his confusion to grab his arm and escort him out of the Assembly Rooms.

The crisp night air seemed to wake up Lord Malthaner. "Name your second, sir," he told Oliver angrily. "I'll meet you for this."

"No, you won't," Oliver said. He would never fight a duel; his time in the army had given him too great a respect for human life, even if the man in question was a worm like Lord Malthaner.

"I'll tell everyone that you're a coward," Malthaner hissed.

"All right," Oliver said. "While you're at it, you can tell them you're a fool."

Malthaner's look of confusion returned. "Why would I tell them that?"

Oliver didn't reply, for he was already on his way back to the Assembly to search for Isabelle.

"I can't believe the nerve of the man," Malthaner blustered to Lord Braden, who was waiting for his coach to be brought around. "The presumption, to propose marriage to Miss Fleming! Her brother will put a stop to that quickly enough." He shook his head. "There's no way Cliveden will let his sister marry an unknown like Mr. Oliver."

Braden curled his lip and fixed Malthaner with a look

of scorn. "Mr. Oliver? It took me a minute to place him, but I'm damned if he's not a St. Clair."

"A St. Clair?" Malthaner said hoarsely.

"He has Edgeworth's nose," Braden said, enjoying Malthaner's look of shock. "And since the elder son died, I assume he's Edgeworth's heir. I expect Cliveden will be pleased to hear that his sister has received an offer of marriage from the new Marquess of Ashingham."

Twenty-Two

When Oliver re-entered the building, he was pleased to find Isabelle in the entrance hall, but disappointed to see that she was surrounded by a crowd of people. He was longing to take her in his arms, but he hesitated to do so in front of Kincaid, Felicity, Miss Flint, Miss Hunt and Letitia.

He settled for taking Isabelle's hand. "Are you all right?" he asked quietly.

"Yes," Isabelle said, and she realized that she was. While she was concerned for Letitia, and embarrassed to have been the centre of attention, she was proud of the way she had stood up to Lord Braden and Lord Malthaner. Most importantly, though, she was happy. Mr. Oliver had returned and asked her to marry him, and the idea filled her with such joy that everything else seemed insignificant.

"We've sent for the carriage," Isabelle told Oliver. "You'll come back to Stonecroft with us?"

"Of course," Oliver replied.

"I hope you told Lord Malthaner that he's not welcome to return to my house," Mrs. Hunt said to Oliver. "Who ever heard of a man making a marriage proposal in the Maidstone Assembly Rooms? I've never seen such a shameful display."

Oliver correctly deduced that the true reason for Mrs. Hunt's anger was that Malthaner had made his proposal to a lady other than her daughter.

"I'm afraid that with all the excitement, Mrs. Hunt, I wasn't thinking of Malthaner's lodging arrangements," Oliver replied dryly. "But I doubt he will want to remain in Kent."

Mrs. Hunt sniffed. "His valet can take him his things. I'll tell the man to pack as soon as we get home."

A footman announced that the carriages were ready for both the Stonecroft party and the Hunts, so they moved outside. Since Langley's coach was designed to seat four people, the addition of Oliver posed a challenge. Felicity playfully offered to sit on someone's lap, but her suggestion was quickly vetoed by a horrified Mr. Kincaid. Oliver considered renting a horse from the inn so he could follow the coach to Stonecroft, but he was reluctant to let Isabelle out of his sight. In the end, Kincaid ended up next to Miss Flint, with Oliver, Isabelle, and Felicity on the seat opposite.

Isabelle was acutely aware of Oliver's presence next to her, and whenever the coach turned right, she found herself pressed against him. He was solid and comfortable, and she had to resist the temptation to rest her head on his chest. Across from Isabelle, Miss Flint had no reservations about using Kincaid as a pillow, and quickly fell asleep with her head on his shoulder. With the exception of Miss Flint's gentle snoring, the drive back to Stonecroft passed in silence.

If Matthews was surprised to see Mr. Oliver, he hid his emotions admirably, but Hermes showed no such restraint. The little dog rushed at Oliver like a creature possessed, barking loudly enough to rouse the household. He capered around Oliver's legs and managed to express both his joy at Oliver's return and his unhappiness that Oliver had left at all.

"Yes, I was a fool to think I could leave," Oliver said softly, bending down to scratch behind Hermes' ears. "I won't argue the point."

Langley and Amelia emerged from the drawing room, and Oliver was relieved to see that they hadn't retired for the night.

"Mr. Oliver, what an unexpected surprise," Langley said smoothly.

"I need to speak to you, my lord," Oliver said bluntly.

"Certainly," Langley said. "Shall we go to my study?"

Oliver hesitated. Isabelle seemed tired, and Amelia was looking at her with concern. He knew if he went to Langley's study, Amelia would press Isabelle for an explanation, and he didn't want Isabelle to have to face her sister alone.

"I wonder if we could go to the drawing room, so Lady Langley and Miss Fleming can join us," Oliver suggested.

"That's a wonderful idea," Amelia agreed quickly.

Felicity was clearly disappointed to be excluded from the conference, but after a pointed look from Kincaid, she climbed the stairs to her bedchamber. Kincaid gave Oliver a sympathetic look before heading upstairs himself.

When the door to the drawing room had closed, Oliver sat on the sofa next to Isabelle and took her hand in his. Langley raised an eyebrow but said nothing.

Oliver could feel himself sweating, and he loosened his cravat. He supposed he should be grateful that the earl and countess hadn't asked why he was dressed like a London dandy, or why he had been in the Maidstone Assembly Rooms in the first place. He was considering how to ease into the subject of his proposal to Isabelle when she surprised him by speaking first.

"I'm afraid I caused a scandal at the Assembly Rooms tonight," she said simply. "Lord Braden was there, and he took Letitia into a corner and tried to kiss her."

"Oh, poor Letitia," Amelia said, with a look of outrage. "Lord Braden deserves to be shot. Mrs. Hunt does too, for I imagine she stood by and let it happen?"

"Yes," Isabelle said. "That is, I'm not sure she knew exactly what was happening, but I know she encouraged Lord Braden to pursue Letitia."

"Poor Letitia," Amelia said. "But surely someone intervened? Mr. Kincaid, or Mr. Oliver?"

Isabelle took a deep breath. "Mr. Oliver did," she began. "But I actually intervened first. I–er–hit Lord Braden and knocked him down."

Amelia's mouth fell open, and even Langley looked surprised.

"Well done, Isabelle," Langley said.

"I think I took him by surprise," Isabelle confessed.

"I imagine you did," Langley said dryly.

"Did you hurt yourself?" Amelia asked.

Isabelle looked down at her right hand. "No, apart from some soreness of my knuckles where they connected with Lord Braden's nose. Mr. Oliver assisted him out of the Assembly Rooms."

Langley turned to Oliver. "It's fortunate you were there."

"I had some unfinished business in Kent," Oliver explained. To his relief, Langley didn't press the matter.

"Well, that doesn't sound so terrible," Amelia said philosophically. "As scandals go, it could have been much worse. I expect very few people saw it, and the talk will die down quickly."

"It might have done," Isabelle said cautiously. "But unfortunately, Lord Malthaner saw it, and made me an offer of marriage in the middle of the Assembly Rooms. When I turned him down, he made a scene, and everyone saw it."

"Oh, Isabelle," Amelia said sympathetically.

"I'm afraid I laughed at him," Isabelle admitted. "But I couldn't help myself. Amelia, Lord Malthaner admitted to being my Anonymous Admirer! He was planning to surprise me with this secret on our wedding night."

Amelia burst into laughter, and Langley's lips twitched. Oliver sat in stony silence, for he could see nothing humorous in the idea of Isabelle having a wedding night with Malthaner.

"I'm sure no one could blame you for laughing at that," Amelia said, once she had collected herself.

Isabelle shook her head. "Lord Malthaner certainly could. He said I would never get another offer of marriage once it became known that I had an undisciplined temper and an unmaidenly ability to fight."

"I'm sure that's not true," Amelia said stoutly. "Any gentleman of sense would respect a woman who was brave enough to stand up for a friend. If I had been there, I hope I would have had the courage to hit Lord Braden myself." She turned to her husband. "And I'm sure if Robert had been there, he would have wanted me to do it."

"Certainly, my dear, but perhaps not in your current condition," Langley agreed.

Amelia smiled. "You see, Robert is a man of sense. I'm sure when we return to town in the autumn, you will meet a man who will appreciate a woman who will stand up for a friend."

Langley gave Oliver a quizzical look. "I think she may have already met one."

Oliver met Langley's eye and nodded. "After the incident with Malthaner, I had the presumption to make Miss Fleming an offer of marriage, and she accepted."

"It wasn't presumption, it was kindness," Isabelle said quickly. "Malthaner said the scandal would ruin me and I wouldn't get another offer, so Mr. Oliver stepped in to prove him wrong."

"That was certainly very kind," said Langley, with a wry smile.

Amelia appeared to be in shock. "But where will you live?" she asked. "Has Mr. Oliver found another position, or will you live with his family?"

Oliver considered revealing his true identity, but he wanted to tell Isabelle first.

"I need to talk to my father," Oliver said carefully. "He may want me to assist him with the management of his land, and if he doesn't, I'll find another position. I should be able to support Miss Fleming in comfort, although perhaps not in the style to which she is accustomed."

Amelia's brow furrowed. "If your father doesn't want you to work for him, you should come back here and assist Mr. Pettigrew." She turned to Langley. "We could build something similar to the Dower House for Isabelle and Mr. Oliver, couldn't we, Robert?"

"They are certainly welcome at Stonecroft, but Mr. Oliver might have other ideas," Langley said.

Oliver nodded. "If you would allow me, I would like to talk to Isabelle about it."

Amelia nodded. "We'll see you in the morning, then." She held out a hand to her husband, and he helped her to her feet.

"You will?" Oliver asked, surprised by how quickly Amelia had agreed to leave him alone with Isabelle.

"We assumed you would stay here tonight," Langley said. "Unless you're planning to elope?"

"Of course not," Oliver said quickly. "I only meant that I appreciate the chance to talk to Isabelle alone."

Langley gave him a measuring look and seemed satisfied with what he saw. "I'll tell Mrs. Prescott to prepare one of the guest bedchambers for you, Oliver." He and Amelia left, and Isabelle and Oliver were finally alone.

"Isabelle," Oliver began carefully. She looked at him expectantly, and he froze. He supposed he should start by telling her that his name was really Oliver James Montgomery St. Clair, and he was the second son of the Duke of Edgeworth. A son who had been effectively disowned by his father, but through a tragic twist of fate, was now heir to the dukedom. If Isabelle was going to marry him, she needed to know the truth, and she also deserved to know his weaknesses. He should tell her that although he had had the opportunity to save Francis Coates at the

Battle of Waterloo, he had lacked the courage. Most importantly, he should tell Isabelle he loved her, but his tongue was thick in his mouth, and the words wouldn't come.

"There's something I need to tell you, but it's difficult," he began.

Isabelle's face fell. "You've changed your mind about marrying me?"

"No!" exclaimed Oliver. "I want to marry you very much." He paused. "Unless you've changed your mind?"

She met his eye. "No," she whispered.

Oliver turned to face her and took both her hands in his.

"I don't want you to feel forced into anything," he continued. "I know you were a victim of circumstances tonight, and marriage to me wasn't what you wanted."

"It is what I want," Isabelle said shyly.

Oliver met her eye. "I mean, you wouldn't have wanted it if Malthaner hadn't made it necessary."

"I don't understand." Isabelle's bubble of happiness had deflated. Oliver was exactly the man she would have chosen, but she was too embarrassed to say so. She had thought Oliver wanted to marry her because he loved her, but it was becoming increasingly clear that he had simply yielded to a chivalrous impulse.

He sighed. "I mean, Isabelle, I don't want to take advantage of the situation. I'd like to give you the protection of my name, but I would be willing to have a marriage in name only."

"Do you want a marriage in name only?" Isabelle asked, trying to hide her disappointment.

"I want you to be happy," he said. "You may want to wait awhile, to give yourself time to get used to the idea."

Isabelle was quiet for a moment, and Oliver wasn't sure how the conversation had got away from him.

"I don't want to wait," she said resolutely. "I'd like to be married as soon as possible."

Oliver's heart leapt. "I don't want to wait either," he said honestly. "But Isabelle, there's something I have to tell you. You know me as a land agent, but–"

"I was thinking about that," Isabelle interrupted. "I thought you might work for my brother William at Cliveden Manor. He's always complaining that his staff are lazy. I'm sure he would give us one of the nicer cottages."

"You would be happy living in a cottage at Cliveden Manor?" Oliver asked.

"Oh yes," Isabelle assured him. "In fact, I'd prefer it." She smiled at him. "I've never wanted to live in a big house. I don't have the temperament to manage an army of servants."

"I see," Oliver said carefully. "The thing is, Isabelle, I have a confession to make. I haven't been entirely honest about my background. Oliver is my first name, not my last. My real name is Oliver St. Clair." He studied her face but saw no sign that she recognized the name.

"Oh," Isabelle said slowly. She could think of several circumstances in which a man might use a false name, but none of them were good. She remembered the night Oliver had told her he had done an unforgivable thing, and she wondered what he was hiding.

"The truth is, Isabelle–"

"It doesn't matter," she interrupted. "I trust that whatever you did, you did for the right reasons, but it's probably better if I don't know about it."

"I think you need to know," Oliver said firmly.

Isabelle met his eye and decided that even if she hadn't known his real name, she knew his character, and she trusted him.

"Not tonight," she told him. "I don't think I can handle any more surprises tonight. If there's something you need to tell me, I'll listen, but I wish you would wait for another day."

"All right," Oliver agreed. He reflected it was probably wise for him to wait until he had seen his father and learned where he stood. If the duke didn't want to welcome his prodigal son back to the fold, Oliver and Isabelle might be living in a cottage for years to come. Oliver found he liked the idea very much.

"When do you think we might be married?" Isabelle asked shyly.

"As soon as I can arrange things," Oliver told her. "I'll need to talk to your brother and get his consent. Do you know if he's in London, or at Cliveden Manor?"

"William is in London, he rents rooms at a lodging house." Isabelle wondered what William would think about her decision to marry a land agent, and she vowed to write to him as soon as Oliver left. If she was lucky, her letter would reach her brother before Oliver did.

Oliver nodded. "I'll go to London tomorrow to see your brother and get a marriage licence, and when I come back, the vicar can marry us. It won't be a grand wedding, but–"

"I never wanted a grand wedding," Isabelle said truthfully.

She surprised Oliver by leaning in and brushing her lips against his. By the time Oliver realized what was happening, she had already pulled away, and he was left wanting more.

"It's very late, Miss Fleming," he said hoarsely. "You should go to bed." If she didn't move quickly, he wouldn't be able to resist the temptation to follow her there.

Isabelle smiled as she made her way upstairs. She had sensed Oliver's reaction to her kiss, and although her experience of such matters was limited, she was convinced he wasn't completely indifferent to her.

Twenty-Three

As Isabelle was walking along the hall to her bedchamber, her sister's door opened and Amelia stepped out.

"You're still awake?" Isabelle asked in surprise.

"I could hardly go to sleep while you were alone downstairs with Mr. Oliver," Amelia said. "I wanted to listen at the door, but Robert wouldn't let me." She gestured to her bedchamber. "Come and talk to me for a while."

"It's very late," Isabelle protested. "I'm sure you need to sleep."

"I do, but the baby is kicking so much that I won't be able to, so you might as well keep me company."

"All right," Isabelle agreed.

Amelia climbed onto her bed and reclined against the pillows, and after a brief hesitation Isabelle joined her.

"Where is Lord Langley?" Isabelle asked. "I mean . . ."

Amelia smiled at her sister's look of confusion. "Yes,

he usually spends the night here, but I sent him away because I wanted to talk to you. How are you feeling?"

"I hardly know." In the past few hours, Isabelle had experienced too many emotions to analyze. Her heart was still racing from kissing Mr. Oliver, but she wasn't ready to discuss that with her sister. She realized she would have to start thinking of him as Mr. St. Clair, but she wasn't ready to discuss that with Amelia either.

"But you're all right?" Amelia asked.

"I'm all right," Isabelle reassured her. "But I suppose I feel foolish. If I had been firm in my refusal of Lord Malthaner's first proposal, he wouldn't have asked again tonight, and a lot of trouble might have been avoided."

"Malthaner proposed before?"

Isabelle nodded. "The first time was shortly after he came to stay with the Hunts. It took me by surprise, because I felt like I hardly knew him, and I didn't know what to say." She sighed. "You know, Amelia, when I first met Lord Malthaner, I thought he was a romantic hero because he looked like one. He was the most attractive man at the Somertons' ball, so I was flattered when he asked me to dance."

"I don't think that's unusual, Isabelle," Amelia said kindly.

Isabelle shook her head. "But I should have known, even then. All along, I've been frustrated because men judge me for my looks, but I'm really no better than they are."

"It could have been worse," Amelia said carefully. "You could have accepted his proposal."

"I suppose," Isabelle admitted. "I considered accepting him, but when I told him I was concerned that we were barely acquainted, he said he thought he knew me very well. He explained that I was Cliveden's sister, and Langley's sister-in-law, and the beauty of the Season!"

"I see."

"And I didn't want to be defined by my looks and my relations," Isabelle continued. "I tried to turn him down, but he wouldn't believe me. He spoke of going to see William, and I was afraid that Mama would hear of it, so I prevaricated a little."

Amelia looked at her curiously. "How exactly did you prevaricate?"

"I told him I couldn't enter into an engagement until after your confinement, because you were suffering from nervous strain," Isabelle admitted sheepishly. "Too much excitement could precipitate a nervous crisis."

Amelia's mouth fell open. "And Malthaner believed you?"

"I think so," Isabelle said. "I'm sorry, Amelia, I shouldn't have told him that. I don't think he'll spread the rumour around, but I suppose he might if he's feeling vindictive."

Amelia shrugged. "If he does, he'll only make himself look ridiculous. No one will believe I suffer from nerves."

"Well, Malthaner believed it," Isabelle said. "That alone should have convinced me he wasn't a sensible man." She laughed ruefully. "I should have made it clear that I didn't want to marry him when he asked the first time."

"When a man isn't sensible, it can be hard to make things clear to him," Amelia pointed out.

Isabelle shook her head. "It was the same with Dr. Carter. When he didn't believe me, I lied to him."

Amelia's eyes widened. "Dr. Carter proposed to you?" she asked in astonishment.

Isabelle nodded. "Back when Mama and Garland were visiting. I told him I couldn't return his affection, but he didn't believe me. I finally told him I was determined to marry a man with a title."

Amelia chuckled. "Well, Dr. Carter will know you lied when he learns you're going to marry Mr. Oliver."

"I suppose he will," Isabelle agreed. "I shouldn't have lied in the first place, but I didn't have the courage to make him believe the truth."

Amelia smiled. "You seem to have found your courage tonight."

Isabelle shook her head. "I just did what needed to be done, because there was no alternative. I'm not brave like you."

Amelia looked at her in surprise. "What do you mean?"

"I always thought you were fearless."

Amelia laughed. "Oh, no. I've been afraid of so many things. I was terrified when I first met Lord Langley. Gossip made him out to be such an ogre."

"You didn't act like you were afraid," Isabelle remarked.

"Yes, well, I tried to hide it," Amelia confessed. "I pretended to be brave. I did what needed to be done because there was no alternative, but that's what courage is, Isabelle."

"I suppose you're right," Isabelle agreed. "I just wish

I'd found my courage sooner. If I had, Mr. Oliver might not have been drawn into it."

"Do you wish he hadn't been drawn into it?" Amelia asked, looking at her sister intently.

Isabelle considered how to reply. "He doesn't love me, Amelia," she finally confessed. "I think he likes me, and I hope that in time he will grow to love me, but he doesn't find my style of beauty attractive. Shortly after we met, he told me that he prefers ladies who are tall and dark."

"In fact, the exact opposite of you," Amelia said astutely.

"Yes."

"I have some knowledge of marriage, Isabelle," Amelia said, with the confidence of a lady who had been happily married for an entire year. "It's a lifelong commitment, and a man would have to be a fool to offer for a lady without a good reason. Instinct tells me that Mr. Oliver is not a fool, so he must have had a good reason."

"He wanted to save me from a scandal," Isabelle explained.

Amelia looked at her skeptically. "Was he responsible for the scandal?"

"No, but–"

"Perhaps he thought Robert and I would throw you out of our house if the scandal became widely known?"

"No, of course not," Isabelle admitted.

"So there must be another reason Mr. Oliver proposed to you," Amelia said thoughtfully. "I know Robert intends to give you a dowry, but I hardly think the amount would be enough to make you an object of interest to a fortune hunter."

"Mr. Oliver's not a fortune hunter," Isabelle said

defensively. "And I doubt he even knows about the dowry."

"I see," Amelia said with a small smile. "Well, unless someone held a pistol to his head, I can see only one reason for him to propose to you."

"What's that?" Isabelle asked curiously.

"He wants to marry you," Amelia said simply.

Isabelle had hardly dared hope for this.

"We ladies try to make things complicated, but men are simple creatures, Isabelle," Amelia continued.

There was a knock on the door, and seconds later, Amelia's maid entered with a tray that held two slices of sponge cake. She handed the plates to Amelia and Isabelle, bobbed a curtsy, and left as quickly as she had come.

"Lemon sponge cake, with strawberries and cream," Amelia explained happily.

Isabelle smiled weakly. "I see that, but I couldn't, Amelia."

"You've had a long night, Isabelle," Amelia countered. "I'm amazed you had the strength to climb the stairs."

To appease her sister, Isabelle took a bite of cake. The strawberries were sweet, the cream was rich, and the sponge cake had clearly been freshly made. "Where did this come from?"

"Cook made it for me," Amelia said matter-of-factly.

Isabelle looked at her sister with amusement. "Do you regularly eat cake in the evening?"

"Almost every night," Amelia confessed, with a faint blush on her cheeks. "I don't know if you remember, but about a month ago we had this cake with dinner, and when I was hungry at midnight, I sent Robert down to get me another piece. He grumbled a little about crumbs in the bedsheets, but the next evening he brought me cake without being asked." Amelia smiled. "The night after that he brought a slice for himself too, so I think I convinced him of the wisdom of the habit."

Isabelle paused with her fork halfway to her mouth. "Amelia," she asked, "am I eating Lord Langley's cake?"

"It's your cake now," Amelia said. "I think you need it more than he does. Besides, Robert claims he only eats it to keep me company, so it serves him right."

"Where is Lord Langley?" Isabelle asked cautiously, concerned that the earl might appear in search of his wife and his cake.

Amelia laughed at her sister's expression. "Relax, Isabelle," she said. "He won't interrupt us."

Isabelle turned her attention back to the cake. "It's delicious," she said. "I can't believe you eat this every night."

"Not every night," Amelia corrected her. "Sometimes we have custard tarts, but I like this better."

"What do the servants think?"

Amelia laughed. "I never really thought about it. I'm careful not to get crumbs in the bedsheets, so I don't see how it affects them."

"But there's something very decadent about eating cake in bed."

Amelia turned to her sister with a wicked gleam in her eye. "If they knew some of the things we do in the bedroom, they wouldn't be scandalized by the cake."

"Amelia!" Isabelle protested.

"I don't suppose Mama gave you a talk about what to expect in marriage?" Amelia asked.

"No," said Isabelle bashfully.

Amelia laughed. "Probably for the best. It might make you think of her and Mr. Garland, and–" Amelia paused. "Forget I mentioned that. But I suppose I'm the best person to enlighten you."

"That's really not necessary," Isabelle said quickly.

Amelia looked at her sister with amusement and waited for her to elaborate.

Isabelle's cheeks turned an even deeper shade of crimson. "I mean, I trust that Mr. Oliver will tell me what I need to know." She laughed shyly. "I just hope it won't involve bad poetry."

"Well, my wedding night certainly didn't," Amelia said mischievously. "Robert's poetry was very clever."

Isabelle looked at her sister suspiciously.

"All right, there was no poetry involved," Amelia admitted. "But perhaps if you're very fortunate . . ." She let her sentence trail off suggestively.

"Amelia!" Isabelle protested with a laugh. She stood and set her empty plate on the bedside table, then bent to kiss her sister's cheek. "Thank you. I should let you go to sleep."

Amelia smiled. "Good night, Isabelle. Try not to worry too much."

~

"Is it true, Miss?" Daisy asked Isabelle as she drew the curtains open the next morning.

"What's that, Daisy?"

"Is it true that you're going to marry Mr. Oliver?"

Isabelle was asking herself the same question. The

events of the previous evening seemed too extraordinary to be real, and she wondered if it had all been a dream.

"How did you know?" she asked Daisy.

"Everyone's talking about it downstairs, Miss."

Isabelle supposed it wasn't a dream if all the servants knew of it. "Yes, Daisy, but how does everyone know?"

Daisy had the grace to blush. "Mr. Matthews heard Lord and Lady Langley talking about it at breakfast."

Isabelle sat up straight. "What time is it?"

"It's almost midday, Miss. I've never known you to sleep this late."

Isabelle leapt out of bed. "Daisy, I must get dressed," she said briskly.

"Of course, Miss," Daisy said with a giggle. "It would be strange for you to spend the day in your nightgown."

Isabelle thought her maid had chosen an inconvenient time to become a wit. "Please bring me a dress, Daisy," she said impatiently.

"Certainly, Miss Isabelle. I thought the cream muslin walking dress, but if you would rather the blue–"

"It doesn't matter," Isabelle interrupted. "Daisy, have you seen Mr. Oliver this morning?"

"No, Miss," Daisy said. "But Mr. Matthews said he's already left for London."

"I see," Isabelle said, trying to hide her disappointment. She and Mr. Oliver still had a great deal to discuss, and she had hoped to speak to him before he left.

"I could hardly believe it when I heard you were going to marry him," Daisy continued.

Isabelle looked at her maid in surprise. "I thought you liked Mr. Oliver, Daisy."

"Oh, I do, Miss, but at the end of the day, he's only a

land agent. And I heard that Lord Malthaner made you an offer, and he's a viscount! If you married him, you would be a viscountess, and the mistress of an estate instead of a cottage."

"I love Mr. Oliver," Isabelle said, in a tone of voice that Daisy had never heard before. "I'd rather live in a cottage with him than in a palace with anyone else." Speaking the words aloud made her see the truth of them.

Daisy stared at the floor. "But you won't need a lady's maid, Miss," she said quietly.

"Ah," Isabelle said. "Is that why you don't want me to marry Mr. Oliver, Daisy? You're worried you'll lose your position?"

Daisy met Isabelle's eyes and nodded.

"I see. Well, I don't know if I'll be able to keep a lady's maid," Isabelle confessed. "But if I can't, I'll do what I can to help you find another position."

Daisy didn't look cheered by the prospect. "I hate to leave you, Miss," she said with a sniffle. "You've been so kind to me, and I've been so happy here."

This came as a surprise to Isabelle, who hadn't thought that Daisy liked her very much. "Try not to fret, Daisy. I'm sure you'll find a position that you like just as well."

"Thank you, Miss Isabelle," Daisy said. "I must say, it's very romantic. You must love Mr. Oliver very much."

"I do, Daisy." As Daisy helped her dress, Isabelle realized she had been more truthful with her maid than she had been with Mr. Oliver himself. She vowed that the next time she saw her betrothed, she would tell him she loved him.

~

While Isabelle was unburdening her soul to Daisy, Oliver was on the road to London in a post-chaise. Kincaid had driven him to the Maidstone Arms early that morning so he could collect his luggage, pay his shot, and hire the chaise. As he approached London, he was tempted to get a room at Grillon's Hotel and face his father in the morning, but he knew that delaying the meeting would not make it easier. He directed the postilions to a townhouse in Grosvenor Square, where his knock was promptly answered by Wilkinson, the elderly butler who had been in the family's service since Oliver was a boy.

"The duchess is not at home, and the duke is not receiving," Wilkinson said stiffly. He was about to close the door when he recognized Oliver, and his eyes widened.

"Good afternoon, Wilkinson," Oliver said. "Do you think the duke will receive me?"

"Lord Oliver," Wilkinson said, with a tremble in his voice. "I expect he will."

Oliver was led to the study, where he found the Duke of Edgeworth sitting behind his desk. Edgeworth appeared less affected by the sight of his son than his butler had been, but the duke had always been good at hiding his feelings.

"Come in, Oliver," he said, surveying his son through shrewd hazel eyes. "You look well."

"So do you, sir," Oliver said reflexively, although he privately thought his father had aged a great deal. The duke was in his late sixties and still had a commanding presence, but time had rounded his shoulders and hollowed his cheeks.

"Have a seat," Edgeworth invited, before leaning back and looking at Oliver expectantly.

"I was sorry to hear about Rupert," Oliver began. "I heard he died in a riding accident?"

Edgeworth nodded. "He tried to take a fence at Edgeworth Hall and was thrown," he said gruffly. "The doctor said he didn't suffer."

"That's something, at least. How is Mother doing?"

"As well as can be expected. She's in Oxfordshire visiting your aunt, but she'll want to see you. She missed you, Oliver."

"And I missed her."

"I heard you acquitted yourself well in the army," the duke said casually.

Oliver looked at his father in astonishment. "How did you know?"

"I am acquainted with Colonel Selby, and I ran into him in London about a year after you left. He told me he had met a young officer who bore a strong resemblance to me, and asked if I was related to a man named Mr. Oliver. He didn't know, of course, that I had a son named Oliver."

"What did you tell him?"

Edgeworth smiled. "The truth. I wasn't acquainted with anyone named Mr. Oliver. But I suspected it was you, of course, since my inquiries in London had found no trace of you."

Oliver stared at his father. "You looked for me?"

Edgeworth raised an eyebrow. "Of course. You are my

son. And once I knew what you were calling yourself, it was easy enough to follow your career."

"I see," Oliver said, struggling to come to terms with the fact that his father had cared enough to keep track of him. "You didn't try to communicate with me?"

"You changed your name and didn't inform me you were going to war," Edgeworth said dryly. "I assumed you didn't want to communicate with me. My name and address, however, have not changed."

Oliver flushed and looked at the floor, unable to meet his father's eyes. He hadn't considered the possibility that the duke had been waiting for Oliver to contact him.

"I understand you sold out several months ago," Edgeworth continued. "I confess I lost track of you then. Did you return to London?"

"I've been working as a land agent at Stonecroft. Lord Langley's estate." Oliver thought he saw a flicker of hurt in his father's eyes.

"Managing another man's estate," Edgeworth remarked.

"If you recall, sir, you didn't want me to manage yours," Oliver said defensively. "But I like the work, and I think I do it well."

"I don't doubt it. Why do you think I didn't want you to manage Edgeworth Hall?"

Oliver looked at his father in confusion. "You wanted me to join the army."

Edgeworth sighed. "I didn't want you to manage Edgeworth, Oliver, because I knew you were more capable than Rupert. And while that might not have mattered while I was alive, after I died you would have had to take orders from him."

"I knew that," Oliver protested.

"You might have thought you did," Edgeworth said. "But if you thought Rupert's ideas would harm the estate, you would have found it very hard to go along with them."

"I could have left when Rupert inherited," Oliver pointed out.

Edgeworth nodded. "You could have. But the land is in your blood, and I think it would have been difficult."

Oliver nodded. Much as he hated to admit it, he could see his father's point. "What did you think I would do when you cut off my allowance?"

Edgeworth shrugged. "I thought you would run out of money and be back on my doorstep within a month. You would learn a lesson, and I would resume your allowance."

Oliver's cheeks reddened. "I'm not here to beg for an allowance."

"I didn't think you were," Edgeworth said. "But I intend to give you the same allowance I gave Rupert, as well as Ashingham Court."

Oliver was silent for a moment as he thought about it. Ashingham Court in Sussex was one of the duke's secondary estates, and was traditionally given to the heir apparent. His father had given it to Rupert when he turned twenty-one.

"The thing is, sir, that I'm engaged to be married," Oliver said.

"Congratulations. And you don't think your prospective wife would want to live at Ashingham?"

Oliver smiled. "She did tell me she would rather live in a cottage than on a large estate," he remarked.

"She sounds like an interesting girl. What's her name?"

"Miss Isabelle Fleming."

"Cliveden's sister? I've heard she's beautiful."

Oliver frowned. "She is, but she's much more than that. And I don't want to move her into Ashingham when we might be forced to leave if I quarrel with you. It wouldn't be fair to Isabelle. I would rather look for another position as a land agent."

The duke met his eyes. "Ashingham's entailed, of course, so I can't make it over to you legally, but I promise I won't take it away from you."

Oliver still hesitated, and his father sighed. "I know you think I'm a harsh parent, Oliver, and perhaps I should have done things differently. I can't change the past, but you have my word that I won't interfere with Ashingham."

Oliver knew it was the closest his father would come to an apology.

"All right," he said. "Thank you, sir."

Edgeworth nodded. "Rupert was to be married this fall," he remarked. "Your mother was looking forward to the wedding."

"His betrothed must be devastated," Oliver remarked.

Edgeworth shrugged. "It was Fairclough's eldest girl. Fairclough paid me a call shortly after Rupert died to tell me exactly how devastated his daughter was. She was expecting to marry the heir to a dukedom, and now she's forced to try her luck on the marriage mart again."

"I see." Baron Fairclough owned an estate close to Edgeworth Hall in Derbyshire, so the Ffaircloughs were well acquainted with Oliver's family. Oliver remembered the baron as a good-natured gentleman with an unpleasant wife and three equally unpleasant daughters.

"Yes. Fairclough even suggested that since his daughter had been betrothed to the Marquess of Ashingham, and you are now the Marquess of Ashingham, she could marry you instead."

"But that's ridiculous!" Oliver spluttered. He stood and paced the room. "Sir, you must see that. Even if I wasn't promised to Isabelle, you couldn't expect me to marry a young lady simply because she was betrothed to my brother."

"I don't," the duke said calmly. "I told Fairclough you wouldn't tolerate my interference in your affairs."

"Oh," said Oliver.

"But I know your mother will want to attend your wedding," Edgeworth continued. "Have you set a date?"

"We don't want a big wedding, sir, or a lot of fuss. Isabelle is the Countess of Langley's sister, and we hope to get married at Stonecroft next week."

Edgeworth smiled. "Then it seems your mother and I will have to travel to Kent."

Twenty-Four

Oliver spent the night in his parents' house and breakfasted with his father before setting off in search of Isabelle's brother William, Viscount Cliveden. Since William had lost his Mayfair townhouse at play the previous year, he was renting rooms in a lodging house on the outer fringes of London's fashionable quarter. Hard work and economy had significantly improved his financial situation, but he was still very careful not to overextend himself.

When Oliver knocked on the door of William's lodging house, he was met with the disappointing intelligence that Lord Cliveden was not at home.

"When do you expect him to return?" Oliver asked the landlady.

"I couldn't say."

"I see," Oliver said politely. "Tell him the Marquess of Ashingham called, and will return tomorrow." It was the first time he had used his title, and the words felt strange on his tongue.

The landlady's mouth fell open. "The Marquess of Ashingham?" She glanced behind Oliver, as though expecting to see a marquess hiding behind him. The only marquess she had seen before had been elderly and afflicted with arthritis, with golden rings on his fingers and a fob dangling from his waistcoat. Although Oliver spoke with the right accent, his youth, vigour, and lack of ornamentation seemed unbefitting of a marquess.

"Hard to believe, isn't it?" Oliver said wryly.

"Yes," the landlady admitted. She had been overjoyed when William moved into her lodging house, and had expected him to lead other noblemen to her doorstep, but after a year of disappointment she had almost ceased to hope. She remembered her manners and dropped a curtsy. "Beggin' your pardon, my lord, but I didn't expect to see a marquess today."

Oliver's eyes twinkled. "That's perfectly understandable."

"I understand Lord Cliveden's sister is married to an earl, and I've been hoping he would honour us with a visit, but so far, I haven't seen any earls. I don't suppose you're related to Lord Cliveden?" she asked hopefully.

Oliver smiled. "Not yet."

"Very nice," she said vaguely, and curtsied again. "Would you care to leave a card?"

"I'm afraid I don't have one," Oliver confessed. "I only recently inherited the title, you see."

"I see." The landlady studied Oliver through narrowed eyes, clearly suspicious of a man who claimed to be a marquess but carried no calling cards. "Well, Lord Cliveden isn't home, and I don't know when he'll return."

William did not return to his rooms that day, but

spent a pleasant afternoon with his friend Freddie Micklebury. The young men found their way to Micklebury's club, where Lord Malthaner was ranting about the new Marquess of Ashingham to anyone who would listen. Malthaner claimed Ashingham had gone mad and knocked him down in an unprovoked attack at a county assembly.

"I haven't met the new marquess, but he has my sympathy," Micklebury said, after Malthaner had moved on in search of a fresh audience. "Malthaner was probably talking too much. I've been tempted to knock him down myself." He paused and looked at William. "Heard he's been dangling after your sister. She's not going to marry him, is she?"

"Not if I have anything to say to it." William couldn't put a finger on why, but he had never liked Malthaner, and didn't think he would be right for Isabelle.

"Fellow's a bit of a scoundrel, you know," Micklebury said. "You know that tale that went around, that he saved a child from being trampled by a mail coach?"

"What about it?"

"I heard it wasn't Malthaner who saved the child, it was his sister. He only watched it happen, then took the credit for it."

William agreed that it was a rotten thing to do, then promptly forgot about Lord Malthaner. The young men went from the club to the opera, in search of a dancer who had caught Micklebury's interest. Unfortunately, the dancer had no interest in Micklebury, and their attempt to go backstage after the show was unsuccessful. They returned to Micklebury's rooms to share a drink, and

William finally fell asleep on his friend's sofa at three in the morning.

When Oliver called at William's lodgings the next morning, he was met with another suspicious look from the landlady, who appeared pleased to tell him that Lord Cliveden had still not returned.

"I'll wait for him," Oliver announced. He was impatient to meet with William so he could get a marriage licence and return to Stonecroft. He had told Isabelle he hoped to return the day after he left, but as things were going, he would be lucky to make it back within a week.

"Beggin' your pardon, but I have no way of knowing if you are, in fact, acquainted with Lord Cliveden," the landlady said haughtily.

"I am not," Oliver admitted.

"Right," the landlady said, clearly satisfied to have wrung this admission from him. "And I have no way of knowing who you are."

"I have explained to you, I am the Marquess of Ashingham."

"That's right," the landlady said with a smirk. "A marquess who doesn't have a calling card, and dresses so plain? I wasn't born yesterday, *my lord*." Her last words were delivered with sarcasm as she closed the door in his face.

On the following day, Oliver came prepared to argue with the landlady, but the woman simply sniffed and showed him to a set of modest rooms. William was seated behind a desk, reading a letter that had been delivered the day before. Oliver would have found the letter very interesting had he been permitted to see the contents.

Dear William,

I expect Mr. Oliver will reach you before this letter will, and if I had been thinking more clearly, I would have sent it with him instead of through the post. So you may already know that he has made me an offer of marriage. What you won't know is that I want to marry him very much, and I hope you will give your consent to the match. Mr. Oliver may not tell you of the circumstances that led to our betrothal, but he proposed to save me from a scandalous situation in the Maidstone Assembly Rooms. Lord Braden was pestering Letitia Hunt, so I knocked him down, and I'm afraid it caused a bit of a fuss. Fortunately, Mr. Oliver didn't hesitate to sacrifice himself to save my reputation.

Your loving sister,
Isabelle

William set down the letter and stood to greet Oliver. His landlady had told him of Oliver's earlier visits, but William hadn't been able to guess the reason for them. Unlike the landlady, William didn't doubt his visitor's identity. He had never met Oliver, but he had been acquainted with his brother Rupert, and the family resemblance was clear.

"My lord," William said respectfully. "My condolences for the loss of your brother."

Oliver nodded. "Thank you."

William gestured to a chair, but his guest declined it and paced the room instead. "I don't suppose you know why I have come," Oliver said nervously. He still felt unworthy of Isabelle, and now that he was facing her brother, he didn't know how to begin.

"I'm honoured by your visit," said William cautiously. He remembered Malthaner's story about being attacked at an assembly, and he hoped that Oliver wasn't celebrating his new title with a spree of random attacks on his fellow nobles.

Oliver continued to pace. "Thank you."

"Can I offer you a drink?" William asked politely. Although Oliver appeared anxious, he didn't have the look of a man who was mentally unhinged, and William wondered if it was possible to judge a man's sanity by his outward appearance.

"No. Look, Cliveden," Oliver began. "I'm here because I want to marry your sister."

William's jaw dropped. "Marry Isabelle?"

"Yes."

"I didn't even know you were acquainted with her."

"I met her at Stonecroft," Oliver explained.

"I see," William remarked.

Nerves prompted Oliver to emphasize his wealth rather than his love for Isabelle. "My father means to give me an estate, Ashingham Court, so I will be able to give Isabelle every advantage."

William's face flushed, and he looked at Oliver with embarrassment. "I'm sure you are very eligible, but I'm afraid it's impossible."

Oliver's heart sank. He had refused to consider the possibility that William would say no. "May I ask why?"

"Isabelle is already engaged," William said apologetically.

Oliver's face fell. "Is it Malthaner?" he asked hoarsely, regretting his decision to let the man off with nothing worse than a bloody nose.

"Who?" William looked surprised. "No. Between you and me, I've never cared for the fellow."

"Then who is it?" Oliver demanded. He didn't understand how Isabelle could have failed to tell him she was already engaged, and he wondered if her brother had arranged a match without her knowledge.

William paused, wary of the look in Oliver's eyes. "I received a letter from Isabelle yesterday," he said carefully. "She wishes to marry a Mr. Oliver. He's the land agent at Stonecroft."

"I see," Oliver said slowly. "And you intend to allow her to marry a land agent?"

William shrugged. "I don't see how I can refuse. I won't deny that I hoped she would make a better match, but the most important thing is that she's happy. From everything she's written, this Mr. Oliver is a hard-working, upstanding man. Langley's an excellent judge of character, and I'm sure he wouldn't have hired him without looking into his background."

"Hard to say," Oliver hedged.

"Yes, well. Regardless of his background, I'd have a hard time saying no, because Isabelle loves him."

"Did she say so?" Oliver asked, trying to keep his emotions from showing.

"Not in so many words, but every letter she wrote to me was so full of Mr. Oliver that even a fool could see how she felt! I'm lucky that Langley franked her letters, otherwise I'd have had to pay a fortune to read about the way the man's hair curls, and how the corners of his eyes crinkle when he smiles." William shook his head in disgust. "She even told me what he thinks about novels. I mean, what kind of man reads novels?"

"It does seem unusual," Oliver agreed.

"But although reading novels is a bit eccentric, I don't think it's a reason to refuse the match," William explained.

"Probably not," Oliver said. "What else did she write?"

William laughed. "Well, Isabelle would never admit she was jealous, but she certainly didn't like it when other ladies spoke to Mr. Oliver. She wrote that a young lady named Miss Taylor flirted with him shamelessly."

"I see." Oliver tried to keep his tone casual. "Did she tell you how the betrothal came about?"

"Apparently Lord Braden was pestering one of her friends at a county assembly, and Isabelle knocked him down! I thought that was the most surprising part of the story, because I can't imagine Isabelle hitting anyone! My sister Amelia might, of course, but Isabelle has always been rather delicate."

"It seems you underestimated Isabelle."

"What?" asked William, surprised by the steel in Oliver's tone. "You know, I suppose I did. In any case, after she struck Lord Braden, there was a lot of fuss about a scandal, so Mr. Oliver offered her marriage. Isabelle wrote that he sacrificed himself to save her reputation, but the story sounds fishy to me. I suspect he actually wants to marry her and used the scandal as an excuse to make her an offer."

"Very likely," Oliver agreed.

"It's awkward for me to say, being her brother, but I don't think many men would consider marriage to Isabelle a sacrifice," William said. "Do you?"

"Definitely not," Oliver choked out, before losing control of himself and doubling over with laughter.

William stared at him in concern. He couldn't understand why the marquess seemed deliriously happy to learn that the woman he wanted to marry was in love with another man. He wondered if there was some truth to the rumours that Malthaner was spreading.

"My lord?" William asked nervously.

Oliver made a heroic effort to collect himself. "Since I'm going to marry your sister, you should call me Oliver."

Although Isabelle had vowed to tell Mr. Oliver she loved him as soon as he returned, her resolve was tested when nearly a week passed with no sign of him. London was only a day's journey from Stonecroft, so she couldn't imagine what was taking him so long. She worried that William had refused to consent, or that Oliver had been unable to obtain a marriage licence. She also remembered the secret Oliver had been about to confess, and she wondered why he had been forced to change his name. During her worst moments, she worried that he was regretting his impulsive decision to offer her marriage.

Felicity, Miss Flint, and Mr. Kincaid left to return to London the day after Oliver did. Adrian returned to Stonecroft the day after, and was disappointed to learn he had missed the excitement at the Assembly Rooms.

"Mr. Oliver played a deep game," he remarked to Langley. "I never took him for the sort of man who would swoop in and steal Miss Fleming as soon as I left. But despite that, I like him, Robert. Are you planning to give them the dowry you promised?"

"I suspect the dowry is the least of Mr. Oliver's concerns," Langley said cryptically.

"Spoken like a man who has more money than he knows what to do with," Adrian grumbled. "I don't suppose Mr. Oliver's family can have much of it, though. I've never heard of a family named Oliver. Why, he may not even have any family!"

"Some might consider that an enviable situation," Langley remarked, smiling indulgently at his brother.

"But don't you think Mr. Oliver's behaviour was odd? Why would he say he was leaving and then show up at the Maidstone Assembly Rooms?"

"Decidedly odd," Langley agreed. "However, after hearing about what transpired at the Assembly, I can only be glad that he did."

Mrs. Hunt and Letitia came to visit, and Mrs. Hunt managed to imply that Isabelle's engagement to Mr. Oliver was cause for condolences rather than congratulations. Isabelle struggled to give a civil reply, and Letitia was clearly embarrassed by her mother's behaviour. Amelia sensed the tension and suggested that Isabelle and Letitia might enjoy a walk in the rose garden while she and Mrs. Hunt had tea.

"I'm sorry about Mama," Letitia said, once she and Isabelle were outside. "I don't think she can help herself. But Isabelle, I'll always be grateful for what you did at the Assembly Rooms."

"I really didn't do very much," Isabelle said awkwardly.

"Yes, you did," Letitia insisted. "I could hardly believe my eyes when you hit Lord Braden!"

"I could hardly believe it either," Isabelle admitted. "I

acted before I had time to think about what I was doing." She paused as she remembered the way that Braden had mistreated her friend. "How are you, Letitia?"

Letitia smiled. "I'm well."

Isabelle met her eye, and was surprised to find that she believed her. Letitia's look of anxiety had been replaced by one of confidence. She was dressed differently, too, in a faded blue walking dress that flattered her blonde hair and fair complexion. Isabelle suspected the dress was old, but it suited Letitia better than the styles she usually wore. Either Letitia had rebelled against her mother's fashion choices, or Mrs. Hunt had simply given up on her disobedient daughter.

"Is your mother very angry with you?" Isabelle asked.

"Oh, yes," Letitia replied with a laugh. "Mother has declared that she won't take me back to London when they go in the autumn. She means to bring my sister Sybil out next year, and she doesn't want Sybil tainted by her association with me."

"I'm sorry, Letitia," Isabelle said sympathetically.

"I'm not," Letitia said firmly. "I'm going to live with my grandmother in Tunbridge Wells. When we were there last month, she invited me to live with her as her companion, and I told her I would think about it. After the incident at the Assembly Rooms, I decided that I'm going to do it."

"I see," Isabelle said slowly. Her first thought was that it was a horrible waste. Letitia was both pretty and good-natured, and if a man could see past her shyness and her overbearing mother, she would make him an excellent wife. As a companion, she would be at the mercy of her grandmother's whims, and her agreeable nature meant that people would likely take advantage of her. "Perhaps you'll meet a young man in Tunbridge Wells," Isabelle said optimistically.

"I might," Letitia said philosophically. "But I know it's unlikely, and I accept that. My grandmother still enjoys good health, so my duties will be those of a companion, not a nurse. Life in Tunbridge Wells will be easier than life with my mother, and it will certainly be preferable to marriage with Lord Braden."

Isabelle realized her first reaction had been hypocritical, and if she had spoken her thoughts aloud, she would have sounded a great deal like her own mother. Letitia was right, and in her place, Isabelle would likely have made the same choice. After all, Isabelle had turned down Lord Malthaner's offer of marriage when there was no guarantee she would ever receive another proposal.

"It sounds like an excellent idea," Isabelle said warmly. "I'm pleased for you, Letitia."

"I only hope I haven't caused trouble for you," Letitia said. "That scene with Lord Malthaner, and then your engagement to Mr. Oliver–"

"You haven't caused trouble, Letitia," Isabelle said honestly. "I want to marry Mr. Oliver."

Letitia gave her a searching look. "You care for him?"

Isabelle nodded. "I love him," she said simply.

"I thought you might," Letitia said with a wry smile. "That night we came to dinner with Lord Malthaner, and he insulted Mr. Oliver–Isabelle, did you spill your wine on Lord Malthaner deliberately?"

"I might have," Isabelle admitted.

Letitia laughed. "He deserved it."

"He certainly did," Isabelle said. "I can't believe I was

so deceived by his looks, Letitia. I was so pleased when he asked me to dance at the Somertons' ball."

"I think any young lady would have been flattered by his attention," Letitia said kindly. "And you realized his true character in time, so it seems everything has ended happily."

"I suppose it has," Isabelle agreed. If she could only be confident that she could make Mr. Oliver love her, her joy would be complete.

~

On the fifth day of Oliver's absence, Isabelle received a letter:

Dear Miss Fleming,
  I have been unexpectedly delayed in London, but I hope to return to Stonecroft within the next few days.

Yours faithfully,
Oliver St. Clair

"Is the letter fit for my eyes?" Amelia asked, in a teasing tone. Isabelle knew her sister was asking if she had received a love letter that was so effusive she was embarrassed to share it. The truth was that Isabelle was upset by how far from lover-like the letter was. Oliver didn't say that he missed her or looked forward to seeing her, and there was certainly nothing to suggest that he cared for her. The most promising phrase was 'yours faithfully,' but that seemed like a fragile thing on which to pin her hopes.

"There's nothing scandalous," Isabelle assured her sister, but she made no move to show Amelia the letter. The fact that it was signed Oliver St. Clair would understandably baffle her sister; Isabelle was still getting used to it herself. She realized she had referred to her betrothed as Mr. Oliver in her letter to William, and wondered if her brother had been confused when a man named St. Clair called to ask for her hand.

Amelia noticed her sister's disappointment. "What does Mr. Oliver write?" she asked.

"He has been unexpectedly delayed in London, but he hopes to return to Stonecroft soon."

"I see," Amelia said carefully. "That's not so bad. It's not surprising that it's taking him time to get a marriage licence, and he may have other affairs to set in order before his marriage. I understand you're impatient–"

"Yes, I am," Isabelle agreed, because it was a convenient explanation for her disappointment. The real problem, though, was that Oliver's letter gave her no sign that he was impatient to see her.

Twenty-Five

Amelia's labour pains began before dawn the following day. The physician from London, Dr. Overholt, was roused from sleep, and the midwife was summoned from the village. Dr. Carter presented himself several hours later and was shown to the drawing room, where Adrian and Isabelle were playing picquet.

"Good morning, Mr. Stone," Dr. Carter said to Adrian, carefully avoiding Isabelle's eyes. "I heard the midwife had been summoned for Lady Langley, and I wanted to make myself available in case assistance was needed."

"How are you at picquet?" Adrian asked. "You may take my place; I've had the devil's own luck today."

To Isabelle's relief, Dr. Carter declined the invitation to play cards and announced his intention to go upstairs to see how the countess was faring.

"If you think you should," Adrian said doubtfully.

Dr. Carter thought he should, so he climbed the stairs and spent several minutes skulking in the hallway outside Amelia's bedchamber. When he finally mustered the courage to knock, Amelia's maid came to the door.

"My name is Dr. Carter," he said politely. "I came to ask if I could be of assistance."

"We don't want him, Betsy," Amelia called. "Tell him that if he tries to enter this room, I'll knock him down!"

Langley's voice came next, calm and amused. "I thought you didn't approve of violence, my darling?"

"This is an exceptional circumstance," she huffed. "I think it would be quite satisfying to hit someone, and I think it would be justified. I've told Dr. Carter I don't want him here."

"I won't argue with your logic," Langley said calmly. "But I don't think you should try to get up. If you're determined to hit someone, you can hit me."

"But I have no wish to hit you," Amelia said in surprise. "I think the best solution would be for you to hit Dr. Carter if he tries to come in."

"I'll tell him to wait downstairs," Langley said diplomatically.

Dr. Carter decided he had heard enough and retreated towards the stairs, reflecting that he would never understand the nobility. When he returned to the drawing room, he was met with a knowing smile from Adrian.

"Your services were not needed?" Adrian asked. "You needn't feel obligated to stay to entertain us." Dr. Carter walked to the sofa without replying.

Two hours later, Matthews announced the arrival of Mrs. Hunt and her daughter.

"Letitia and I came to call on Lady Langley, and were surprised to see the doctor's gig outside," Mrs. Hunt began. "I wondered if Lady Langley's time had come, but if Dr. Carter is down here playing cards, I suppose she must not be in childbed."

"Lady Langley preferred a midwife, at least for the initial stages." Dr. Carter explained loftily, as though this was a perfectly understandable preference. "Lord Langley wanted me to wait downstairs."

"There's a physician from London up there too," Adrian put in. "My brother wanted to be sure the countess received the best care." Dr. Carter glowered at him.

"I'll ring for tea," Isabelle suggested.

Ten minutes later, Matthews approached Adrian with a nervous look on his face. "I'm sorry, Mr. Stone, but there are two ladies here demanding to see the earl. I'm afraid one of them is most insistent."

"We're not at home to visitors, Matthews," Adrian said in frustration. "Tell them to come back another time."

"I've already tried that. They don't want to come back another time," Matthews said apologetically.

"Well, if they don't want to come back, they can stay away," Adrian said. "It's all the same to me. In fact, it might be better if they stay away." He glanced around the room. "We're rarely short of company at Stonecroft."

Matthews cleared his throat. "The problem, Mr. Stone, is that the ladies are refusing to leave."

"I suppose they could wait on the doorstep, but I think it would be deuced uncomfortable."

Matthews cleared his throat. "One of them claims to be a baroness, Mr. Stone."

Adrian brightened. "In that case, I expect she has her

own home, and the means to go back to it. There's no reason for her to stay here."

"I have no wish to stay here," came a haughty voice from the doorway. Isabelle turned to see a middle-aged lady dressed in an elegant gown of black bombazine, closely followed by a young lady who was also wearing black.

"Lady Fairclough and Miss Fairclough," Matthews said nervously from the doorway.

Adrian stood and bowed. "I'm afraid this is not a good time for a visit, ma'am. The countess is in childbed, and–"

"My business is not with the countess," Lady Fairclough interrupted, with the air of one accustomed to command. "I wish to see the earl."

Adrian looked at her as though she were deficient in understanding. "I have just explained that the countess is in childbed."

"Yes, but where is the earl?"

"The earl is with the countess," Adrian said.

Lady Fairclough looked appalled. "Surely he's not with her during her *confinement?*"

Adrian snorted. "I'd like to see someone try to keep him away."

"Perhaps you can help us," Lady Fairclough said. "We are looking for the Marquess of Ashingham. We heard he was at Stonecroft."

Adrian made a show of looking around the room. "I don't see him here. We're not hiding any marquesses under the sofa cushions, I promise you. Have you considered the possibility that your marquess might not want to be found?"

Lady Fairclough gave Adrian a look of acute dislike.

"My daughter is betrothed to the Marquess of Ashingham," she explained.

Adrian gave an understanding nod. "Well, if he's about to be married, he's probably sowing his wild oats before the ceremony. He won't thank you for chasing after him, believe me."

"I can assure you, ma'am, that there are no marquesses in the neighbourhood," Mrs. Hunt put it.

At that moment, Hermes decided he wished to make Miss Fairclough's acquaintance, and he trotted over to sniff at her skirts. She recoiled in alarm, which Hermes interpreted as a sign that she wanted to play, and he nipped at her ankles.

"Hermes, no!" Isabelle said firmly, chasing after the dog. "I'm sorry, Miss Fairclough. He's only a puppy, and he wants to play with you."

Unfortunately, Miss Fairclough had no wish to play with Hermes. She sank on to a chair and drew her knees up to her chest, hoping that if she kept her feet off the floor they would be out of the dog's reach.

Lady Fairclough sighed. "I suppose we should leave," she said, with a suspicious look at Hermes. "I can't imagine what Lord Ashingham would be doing in this madhouse."

"We won't try to stop you," Adrian said in an encouraging tone.

"But Lord Malthaner seemed so certain," Lady Fairclough said. "He's told everyone in London that Lord Ashingham was at Stonecroft, pretending to work as a land agent."

Adrian shook his head. "Our land agent's name is Mr. Oliver."

Lady Fairclough frowned. "Yes, that's what Lord Malthaner said, but it didn't make sense. Why would Ashingham work as a land agent here? I can understand why he might want to conceal his identity if he were having a tryst with a local girl, but Lord Malthaner said he was actually working on the estate."

"Perhaps Lord Malthaner was playing a joke," Adrian suggested. "I heard he and Mr. Oliver had a bit of a skirmish at the Assembly rooms, and Malthaner may have sought retribution by sending you after Mr. Oliver."

Isabelle had refused to believe it at first, but there were too many coincidences to ignore. "What is the marquess's name, Lady Fairclough?" she asked.

Lady Fairclough seemed to notice Isabelle for the first time. "Oliver St. Clair," she replied.

As absurd as it seemed, there was no other explanation: the ladies were looking for her Mr. Oliver. She wondered if Mr. Oliver was truly hers, since Lady Fairclough claimed he was engaged to her daughter. Since Oliver had lied to them all about his name and his background, she couldn't dismiss the possibility that he had lied about being free to marry her. Tears stung her eyes, and she ran blindly out of the room.

Oliver spent the drive back to Stonecroft engaged in the pleasant contemplation of what Isabelle might have written about him in her letters to her brother. He fully intended to tease her about them, and he arrived at Stonecroft feeling happier than he had in months. He was so impatient to see Isabelle that he decided to seek her out before changing out of his travelling clothes.

When Oliver entered the drawing room he found a chaotic scene, but he didn't find Isabelle. Lady Fairclough and her daughter stood cowering in fear of Hermes, who was gambolling around their ankles as though it was some sort of game. Mrs. Hunt sat on the sofa with her legs tucked underneath her, in case Hermes took an interest in her next. Letitia Hunt was nobly trying to distract the puppy by offering it a feather she had pulled from her mother's turban, and Dr. Carter was watching with disapproval. Adrian stood with a drink in his hand, and appeared to be enjoying himself immensely.

Hermes was the first to notice Oliver, and rushed to give him a joyful greeting.

"I'm pleased to see you too, Hermes, but I must insist that you behave," Oliver said firmly. Hermes sat at attention and wagged his tail, giving every appearance of a perfectly behaved dog, and Oliver bent to pick him up.

"Ah, Mr. Oliver," Adrian said, with a gleam of mischief in his eyes. "Allow me to introduce Lady Fairclough and her daughter, who are eager to make your acquaintance. Apparently, Lord Malthaner has convinced them that you are a marquess in disguise."

"I see," Oliver said warily.

Lady Fairclough surveyed Oliver appraisingly before dropping a curtsy.

"Lord Ashingham," she said obsequiously. "It is a pleasure to see you again. I trust you remember my daughter Mary."

Oliver nodded. "Miss Fairclough," he murmured politely.

"Are you acquainted with these people?" Adrian asked Oliver. The tone of his voice made it clear that he didn't think the acquaintances did Oliver credit.

"Yes," Oliver admitted.

"*He* is the Marquess of Ashingham," Miss Fairclough blurted in frustration.

Adrian gave Oliver a questioning look.

"It's true," Oliver confessed.

For the first time in her life, Mrs. Hunt was shocked into silence. Her mouth fell open, and she gaped at Oliver in disbelief.

Lady Fairclough addressed Oliver again. "Lord Ashingham, you may have heard that Mary was betrothed to your unfortunate brother."

"Ah," Oliver said warily. "My condolences on your loss, Miss Fairclough. My brother's death must have been a great shock to you."

Miss Fairclough nodded sadly.

"You must understand, Lord Ashingham, that Mary has suffered a great disappointment," Lady Fairclough told him. "She expected to marry the Marquess of Ashingham, heir to the Duke of Edgeworth." She gave Oliver a meaningful look.

Oliver feigned ignorance and devoted himself to the task of scratching Hermes' ears.

"So Fairclough and I thought that perhaps you might consider . . ." Lady Fairclough let her thought trail off, and looked at Oliver expectantly.

"Ah, I see," Oliver said. He turned to Miss Fairclough. "Don't worry, Miss Fairclough," he said gently. "Regardless of what your parents think, I would never go along with such an arrangement. I'm sure the notion of marrying me in place of my brother is repugnant to you."

Miss Fairclough's expression made it clear that she didn't consider the idea of marriage to Oliver wholly repugnant. He was far more attractive than she remembered; really, the only thing she found offensive was his dog, and she was confident she could persuade him to give Hermes away. "Perhaps if we got to know each other, we would find we would suit," she suggested.

"If circumstances were different, that might have been true," Oliver said kindly. "But as it turns out, I'm about to be married very soon."

Lady Fairclough frowned. "But there has been no announcement in the papers," she protested. "I think that given the situation with your brother, it is your duty to consider my daughter–"

"No," he said simply. "I'm sorry, Lady Fairclough, Miss Fairclough, but I'm afraid it's impossible." He turned to Adrian. "Where is Isabelle?"

Adrian narrowed his eyes. "You know, Oliver, I'm not sure I should tell you."

"Not tell me?" Oliver was reaching the limit of his patience. "What do you mean?"

"You see, Oliver," Adrian began, then paused. "Can I still call you Oliver, or would you prefer Ashingham? Or my lord?"

"You can call me whatever you damned well please, if you'll only tell me where I can find Isabelle."

"There is no need for such vulgar language," Miss Fairclough said primly. "Remember, you are in the presence of ladies."

THE MYSTERIOUS MR. OLIVER

"You can leave if you don't like it," Oliver said unrepentantly.

"That's exactly what I told them!" Adrian exclaimed. "Not quite in those words, but that was the gist. I don't understand why so many people want to visit us."

"Where is Isabelle?" Oliver asked again.

"I wanted to talk to you about that," Adrian said. "I see myself as a brother to Isabelle, and this whole business seems too smoky by half. First you told us you were leaving the county, then you showed up at the Assembly Rooms and assaulted Lord Braden and Lord Malthaner! I suppose I can't I blame you for that, because I hope I would have done the same if I'd been there. But then it took you almost a week to get a marriage licence, and now a lady has appeared, claiming you're a marquess. You must admit it looks suspicious."

Oliver sighed and raked a hand through his hair, causing a tuft to stand on end. "I didn't know I was a marquess until recently."

"Yes, but you might have told us about it when you learned of it," Adrian pointed out reasonably. "And as though that wasn't enough, Lady Fairclough says her daughter has some claim to you."

"I have explained that she does not," Oliver said impatiently.

"Yes, you did," Adrian acknowledged. "But how are we to know if that's true? Perhaps there was an arrangement, but you decided to cast her off when you met Isabelle. If that were the case, one might question your character."

"Miss Fairclough was betrothed to my brother, but she has no claim on me."

307

Adrian eyed him skeptically. "So you say. But how do we know you won't say the same of Isabelle, if you meet a lady you like better?"

Oliver stared at Adrian in disbelief. "I will never meet a lady I like better," he said simply. "I love Isabelle. I've loved her for weeks. And if you won't tell me where she is, Adrian, I won't answer for the consequences."

Adrian's brow cleared. "Well, if you love her, that's all right then."

Oliver took a step towards him. "Where is she, Adrian?"

Adrian sighed. "The truth is, Oliver, I don't know. She left after the Faircloughs showed up, and she didn't say where she was going."

Twenty-Six

Isabelle walked across the grounds without thinking about where she was headed. Her thoughts were full of Mr. Oliver; how kind he had been when she hurt her ankle, and how his eyes gleamed when he teased her. After she had walked in circles for half an hour, she found herself by the Old Cottage, and she was reminded of how patiently Mr. Oliver had taught her to box. She decided he wasn't the sort of man who would trifle with a lady's affections, and he wouldn't have offered her marriage if he was already committed elsewhere.

She started back to the main house, prepared to confront the Faircloughs and stake her claim to Mr. Oliver, or the Marquess of Ashingham, or whatever he chose to call himself. Matthews barely recognized her as she swept through the entrance hall towards the drawing room; her cheeks were flushed, her hair had come loose from its pins, and her expression was one of steely determination.

Isabelle never made it to the drawing room, for she

met Oliver coming out of it. He was still in his travelling clothes, his hair was dishevelled, and she thought she had never seen him look more attractive. Before she knew what was happening, he pulled her into an embrace and kissed her.

"Isabelle," he said roughly.

"Mr. Oliver?" she asked, surprised by the violence of his emotions. "Or should I call you my lord?"

"You should call me Oliver." He relaxed his hold and took a step back so he could look into her eyes. "I missed you, Isabelle." He kissed her again, and didn't release her until they were interrupted by the sound of footsteps on the stairs.

"I hate to interrupt," Langley said, with a gleam of amusement in his dark eyes. "But I came to inform you that Amelia has safely delivered a son, and they are both well."

"Oh, that's wonderful!" Isabelle exclaimed.

"Congratulations, sir," Oliver said.

"Thank you," Langley said. He glanced towards the drawing room and saw Lady Fairclough, Mrs. Hunt, Dr. Carter, and Adrian clustered near the doorway. "I wasn't aware you were entertaining, Adrian," Langley said. "If you'll excuse me, I'm going to return to my wife and son."

Oliver's kiss had distracted Isabelle from the question of his identity, but the sight of Lady Fairclough reminded her of it. "Is it true that you're a marquess?" she asked him.

"Yes," he admitted. "But Isabelle–"

"And are you engaged to Miss Fairclough?" she interrupted.

"No!" he said vehemently. "I can explain it all." He

glanced at the knot of people who were still watching them from the doorway of the drawing room. "But not, I think, in front of this audience." He swept Isabelle into his arms and carried her past an astonished Matthews and out the door. Hermes followed closely at his heels, determined not to be left behind again.

"Where are we going?" Isabelle asked.

"My cottage, so we can be private," Oliver said.

"Do you still want to marry me?" Isabelle asked nervously.

"Of course I still want to marry you," Oliver exclaimed. "And I certainly hope you're not going to cry off after kissing me so thoroughly in front of that crowd."

"I'm not going to cry off," Isabelle told him. She was enjoying the feeling of being held against his chest, and amazed by how easily he was carrying her. "Do you know, Oliver, when I turned my ankle and you threatened to carry me back to the house, I wasn't sure you could do it."

"You should have had faith, my darling," said Oliver, who was secretly relieved that the cottage wasn't farther away.

They made it to the cottage at last, and Oliver set Isabelle down. When he tried the door, he realized the cottage was locked and he no longer had the key.

"I'm sorry, Isabelle," he apologized, feeling foolish. "We can go back to the house, or–"

Isabelle sat on the cottage step, unwilling to wait any longer. "We can talk here. Why didn't you tell me you were a marquess?"

Oliver sat down beside her, and Hermes arranged himself at his feet. "I wasn't a marquess when I met you," he explained. "And it's only a courtesy title. I don't have a seat in the Lords or anything."

This explanation failed to pacify Isabelle. "But if the Marquess of Ashingham is a courtesy title, that must mean–" she paused and stared at him. "Oliver, is your father a duke?"

Oliver nodded. "He is the Duke of Edgeworth. We were estranged, but I met with him when I went to London last week, and we had a reconciliation of sorts."

Isabelle was desperate to know why he had kept his background a secret, but there was a more pressing question to be addressed first. "Why did Lady Fairclough say you were betrothed to her daughter?"

"I'm not engaged to Miss Fairclough," he said firmly. "She was betrothed to my brother Rupert, who was the marquess until his death two months ago. That night at dinner, when Mrs. Hunt mentioned a nobleman who died, she was talking about my brother."

"Oh, Oliver, I'm sorry," Isabelle said, reaching out to take his hand. "Was that how you learned of it?"

He nodded.

"No wonder you were devastated," Isabelle said sympathetically. "But why would Lady Fairclough say that you were betrothed to her daughter?"

"She hoped to convince me that Miss Fairclough had been betrothed to the title of the Marquess of Ashingham, and not to the man."

"But that's ridiculous!" Isabelle exclaimed.

"That's what I told her," Oliver said. "And I explained that I was already betrothed, to a young lady who saw me as a man, not a marquess."

"But I don't understand why you didn't tell me, especially after you asked me to marry you." Isabelle met his eye. "Was it a test, to see if I would marry you when I thought you were only a land agent?"

"No!" Oliver said emphatically. "I tried to tell you before I went to London, but you said you didn't want to know."

"I did?" Isabelle tried to recall the conversation.

Oliver nodded. "I told you I had something to confess, and you told me you didn't want to hear it. You said you trusted me."

Isabelle's memory of the conversation came flooding back. "I didn't think you were going to confess to being the son of a duke. Most people wouldn't consider that a shameful secret."

"It's not shameful in itself," Oliver said quietly. "But I thought my father was ashamed of me. After I finished at Cambridge, he wanted me to join the army, and I refused."

"But you did join the army," Isabelle said, looking at him in confusion.

"Yes. I fought with my father, and he cut off my allowance. A week later, I won some money at cards and bought a commission. I didn't tell my father, and I didn't use my real name. I was determined to succeed or fail on my own merit."

Isabelle nodded slowly. "When you told me your real name was St. Clair, I thought you had changed your name because you had done something nefarious, like robbery or treason."

Oliver gaped at her. "Something nefarious?" he asked incredulously. "*Treason?* And you wanted to marry me in spite of it?"

"I thought you must have had a good reason for whatever you had done," Isabelle explained. "I know that sometimes things are more complicated than they seem."

"I don't deserve you, Isabelle," Oliver said with a chuckle. He put an arm around her shoulders and pressed her to him. "I can't believe you thought I was involved in something criminal."

"You never wanted to talk about your time in the army, and you told me you had done unforgivable things," she said defensively.

Oliver's expression changed. "I have done unforgivable things, Isabelle." He proceeded to tell her about his time in the war. It was the first time Oliver had talked about the horrible things he had seen, and Isabelle listened in silence. He ended by telling her how he had watched his friend Major Coates get shot off his horse at Waterloo. Oliver hadn't stopped to help him, and he would carry the weight of that decision for the rest of his life.

"But Oliver, you were at war," Isabelle pointed out. "You were forced to do things you would never have done under ordinary circumstances. And from everything you've said, if you had stopped to help Major Coates, you would both have died."

"We likely would have," Oliver admitted. "But I still wish I had tried."

Isabelle shook her head. "I'm glad you didn't," she told him. "Risking your life is noble when you have a chance to save someone, but when there's almost no chance, it's just foolish. You had a duty to the army, Oliver. If our soldiers routinely took foolish risks, we would have lost far more men, and we might not have won the war."

"You make a good argument, Isabelle," he said quietly. His expression lightened, and he smiled. "It's one of the reasons I love you so much."

Isabelle's eyes widened. "You love me?" she asked, hardly daring to hope.

"Of course I love you!" Oliver exclaimed. "I've been in love with you for weeks. What did you think was going on between us?"

"I enjoyed talking to you, and I thought you enjoyed talking to me," she said carefully. "As time went on, I thought you found me attractive, even though I don't have the style of beauty you admire."

Oliver laughed, and Isabelle didn't know whether to be flattered or insulted.

"You really have no idea, do you?" he asked, when he finally collected himself.

"No idea of what?"

"You're beautiful, Isabelle," he said. "Calling you attractive is like saying Michelangelo had some talent with paint."

Isabelle looked at the ground, afraid to meet his eyes.

"And your beauty is definitely the style I admire," Oliver continued. "I lied because I didn't want to shock you with the truth of exactly how much I admired it."

"Oh," Isabelle said inarticulately.

"But before long it wasn't just about your beauty. I admired *you*, Isabelle. I've met many beautiful women, and none of them light up a room the way you do. I could talk to you all day, and it wouldn't be long enough. And it got to the point that whenever you weren't nearby, I was thinking about where you were, what you were doing, and when I could see you again."

"So when you offered for me," Isabelle said slowly. "It was because you truly wanted to marry me, not simply to save me from a scandal?"

Oliver laughed. "Isabelle, I've wanted to marry you for weeks."

"Why didn't you tell me this before?" she asked. "The night when I came to your cottage, after Lord Malthaner and the Hunts came to dinner–you kept trying to send me away! I thought we were friends, but that night you acted as though I was a child in the nursery."

Oliver sighed. "I didn't think I was good enough for you, but as long as I had no prospects, I knew I wouldn't succumb to the temptation to offer for you. But when I heard Rupert had died, and I knew I was the heir, I thought it was dangerous. I wanted to court you, but I loved you too much to marry you when I didn't think I deserved you."

"So what changed your mind?"

"I believe it was the thought of you marrying Lord Malthaner," Oliver said lightly. "I may not deserve you, but I think I'll be a far better husband to you than he would be. The man's an idiot, Isabelle."

"Be serious, Oliver," Isabelle protested.

He sighed. "When we drove to Maidstone with your mother and Mr. Garland, I ran into Major Coates' widow in the Maidstone Arms," he began.

"That's who she was!" Isabelle exclaimed.

"You noticed?"

Isabelle nodded. "You looked so distressed to see her," she explained. "And I remembered you telling me it was cruel to raise a man's expectations when you didn't intend to fulfill them. I thought she might have broken your heart."

"No," he said quickly. "But the sight of her made me think of Coates, and I was surprised to learn she had remarried, only two years after his death. She said that if their positions were reversed and she had died, she would have wanted Coates to be happy. At the time, I thought it was a poor excuse, but I've come to think that she was right. If I had been shot and Coates had decided he couldn't save me, I wouldn't have wanted him to waste his life torturing himself."

"Of course you wouldn't," Isabelle agreed.

"It helped to look at it that way," Oliver continued. "I also thought about the things you said when you came to my cottage on the night I learned of Rupert's death. You told me there was nothing to be gained from dwelling on the mistakes of the past."

"I didn't think you took me seriously that night," she said, surprised that her words had such an effect on him.

"Oh, I took you very seriously, Isabelle. I always have." He pulled her into his arms and kissed her fiercely.

When Oliver finally relinquished her mouth, Isabelle realized she was sitting on his lap. "Why didn't you tell me you loved me after the dance at the Assembly Rooms?" she asked. "When you didn't return from London right away, I wondered if you were regretting your decision to offer for me. And then you sent me that *awful* letter–"

"What was wrong with the letter?" Oliver asked, bewildered. "I explained I was delayed in London, and that I would return as soon as I could."

"It was only twenty-six words long, and that's if you include the greeting and signature," she told him. "Twenty-seven, if you count St. Clair as two words. I'm sure you were busy in town, but I thought you could have found the time to write more than twenty-six words!"

"Twenty-seven," Oliver corrected, with a gleam in his eye. "I always count St. Clair as two words."

"But there was nothing to say that you missed me, or that you were impatient to see me. Nothing at all to suggest that you cared about me."

"You know, Shakespeare said that brevity is the soul of wit," Oliver tried. "I think it was in *Hamlet*."

"You're comparing that letter to *Shakespeare?*" Isabelle asked incredulously.

"No," Oliver said quickly. "Certainly not. The next time I write you a letter, I'll do better. But as a wise person once said, there's nothing to be gained from dwelling on the mistakes of the past." He paused to admire the blush on her cheeks. "You're beautiful when you're angry. I mean, you're beautiful all the time, but the emotion does something to your eyes–"

"Now you're trying to distract me," Isabelle protested.

"Unsuccessfully, it seems," he remarked. "The thing is, I thought Lord and Lady Langley might read the letter, and I didn't want to embarrass you."

"I would rather be embarrassed by too much affection than too little from the man I love."

Oliver kissed her roughly. "You love me?"

"Of course, I do."

"Well, in fairness, sweetheart, you could have told me that before. I had to learn it from your brother."

Isabelle's eyes widened. "William told you that?"

Oliver smiled. "I made the mistake of introducing myself to William as the Marquess of Ashingham, and he wasn't terribly impressed. For some reason, he was convinced you were in love with the land agent."

Isabelle blushed. "Why would he think that?"

"Well, he got your most recent letter, in which you explained you had accepted my proposal to avoid a scandal," he explained.

"I don't think I phrased it quite like that."

"Perhaps not. But it seems I featured prominently in some of your earlier letters to your brother."

"Yes, but I wasn't always complimentary," Isabelle said, without thinking.

Oliver's lips twitched. "Now I really must read the letters. I wonder if William would sell them to me? Since you would prefer to live in a cottage, perhaps I should sell Ashingham Court and use the proceeds to buy your letters."

"Now you're being ridiculous. What is Ashingham Court?"

"One of my father's estates in Sussex. It is traditionally given to the heir apparent, so he's giving it to me. Strictly speaking, though, it still belongs to him, so I won't be able to sell it. But we certainly don't have to live in the main house. If you would rather live in a cottage, sweetheart, I'm sure we could find a vacant one on the estate."

"People would think we were mad!" Isabelle exclaimed with a laugh.

"They probably think so already," Oliver said wryly. "Your brother told me that Malthaner is spreading a rumour that I attacked him without provocation at the Assembly Rooms."

"He is a lying scoundrel," Isabelle said indignantly. "Malthaner, I mean, not William."

"He is, but we shouldn't let him trouble us," Oliver said. "Coming back to the subject of Ashingham Court, I think I would prefer to live in the main house. But if you want to live in a cottage, my darling, I'll happily join you there."

"I suppose I could tolerate the main house," Isabelle mused. "Is it terribly large and impossibly grand? Will I get lost trying to find the dining room?"

"Impossibly large," Oliver teased. "But don't worry, you won't starve. I'll draw you a map of the place."

Isabelle laughed. "Will we bring Hermes with us to Ashingham?"

"Of course." Oliver reached down to pat the dog, who was still sitting next to his feet. "You don't think we would leave him behind?"

"You left him at Stonecroft when you went away the first time," Isabelle pointed out.

"He reminded me of you," Oliver explained simply. "I thought he would be a constant reminder of someone I loved deeply but could never have." He bent down to kiss her again. "But now that I have you, my darling, I'd like to be reminded of you as often as possible."

Twenty-Seven

Isabelle and Oliver were married in the Stonecroft parish church a week later. The Duke and Duchess of Edgeworth travelled from London for the ceremony, as did Isabelle's brother William. Lady Marguerite and Mr. Garland did not attend; they were believed to be in Yorkshire, supervising the construction of Garland Castle. Isabelle had sent them an invitation, but she doubted that it was received before the wedding took place.

Amelia insisted that she had fully recovered from her confinement, and left her son in the care of his nurse while she went to the wedding. The vicar was advised to keep the sermon short, since Amelia was anxious to return to her baby, and Adrian declared it was the finest wedding he had ever attended.

Oliver was in full agreement with Adrian on that point; in fact, as he walked out of the church with his bride, he told her it was the happiest day of his life.

"This is the happiest day of my life too," Isabelle said, smiling up at her husband. At Oliver's request, she had been married in her yellow satin dress. He had never seen her look more beautiful, and he could hardly believe she was his.

"I don't deserve you, my darling," he murmured, as he wrapped an arm around his wife's shoulders.

Isabelle leaned over to whisper in his ear. "I think you do, Oliver."

"I can't believe that Isabelle was spending so much time with Mr. Oliver, and I didn't know it," Amelia remarked to Langley. The newlyweds had left for a trip to the seaside, and the Langleys were in the nursery watching their son, Lord Julian Stone, sleep in his bassinet.

"You had a lot on your mind," Langley pointed out.

"Yes, Robert, but I always have a lot on my mind. I should have known what was going on with Isabelle."

"I think Isabelle has shown that she can look after herself."

"I suppose she can," Amelia reflected. "And I think it's worked out for the best. I think she'll be happy with Mr. Oliver." She paused. "I suppose I should call him Ashingham now."

"I expect he'll let you call him Oliver," Langley remarked. "He doesn't strike me as the pretentious type."

"Certainly not," Amelia said with a laugh. "Why, he worked so hard, I never guessed he was a nobleman."

"Noblemen, of course, are notoriously lazy," her husband remarked.

Amelia blushed. "You know I wasn't referring to you, Robert. I just meant that I had no notion–" she broke off and stared at her husband suspiciously. "Did you know who he was?"

"I had a strong suspicion," Langley admitted. "I met him once, before he entered the army. He looked different then."

"And you still hired him to be your land agent?" Amelia asked in disbelief.

"Temporary land agent," Langley corrected. "Don't forget, my love, that when I hired him he was the second son of the Duke of Edgeworth, and he had no expectation that he would inherit. He had served his country in the war, and had a very complimentary letter of recommendation from his superior officer. He seemed qualified for the post; would you have wanted me to deny him employment simply because he was the son of a duke?"

"You could have asked him."

"Yes, but can you imagine if people knew we had a duke's son working here? We would never have been free of Mrs. Hunt."

"Poor Mrs. Hunt," Amelia said. "And to think of how she treated Oliver when he was kind to Letitia. I wish I'd seen her face when she learned he was a marquess!"

"Perhaps it will teach her to be kinder to our staff," Langley mused. "She'll wonder if we are employing a marchioness to empty the chamber-pots."

"I still think you could have told me who Oliver was," Amelia said reproachfully.

"I wasn't certain, Amelia."

Amelia looked at him skeptically. "But I'm your wife, Robert. You could have told me of your suspicions."

Langley smiled. "My love, I promise you that the next

time I suspect that I'm employing the son of a duke, I'll let you know immediately."

Amelia sighed. "I suppose I'll have to be satisfied with that." She looked down at her son and smiled. "I expect you'll teach Julian all your ways."

"I hope to do so," he said unrepentantly.

Amelia chuckled. "Robert, imagine what Mama and Mr. Garland will say when they learn that Isabelle has married the Marquess of Ashingham. They'll boast of it to everyone they know."

"You're right, my love," Langley agreed. "I'm afraid the Garlands will visit the Ashinghams in preference to us."

Amelia's laugh woke Baby Julian, who blinked at his parents before falling back asleep.

"Look, Robert, he's smiling at me," Amelia whispered in awe. "I think he recognizes me already."

"He's a remarkably intelligent child." Langley doubted that a sleeping newborn could recognize anyone, but he knew better than to say so to his wife.

"I had planned to play matchmaker for Isabelle, you know," Amelia mused. "I think I would have been good at it, although I don't think I could have chosen better than she did herself."

"It's probably for the best," Langley remarked. "I'm not sure I would have enjoyed hearing you sing the praises of other men." He smiled down at his son. "With the exception of Julian, of course."

"I suppose I could play matchmaker for William," Amelia said thoughtfully. "Or your friend Mr. Kincaid. When Miss Taylor has her Season, she'll need a chaperone, and I don't think Miss Flint is the ideal lady to do it.

But if Mr. Kincaid married, his wife could chaperone Felicity."

"That would certainly be interesting," Langley remarked.

"There's no reason to look so skeptical, Robert. I'm sure Mr. Kincaid won't have any trouble finding a suitable wife. He's reasonably attractive, and he seems like an honourable man."

"I suspect that's part of his problem," Langley said dryly.

"Oh, no, Robert," Amelia said seriously. "It's only the very foolish young ladies who think they want a rake or a rogue. Any young lady with sense wants a man with a good heart and an honourable character." She smiled at him. "Why do you think I fell in love with you?"

"My love, this flattery is overwhelming," Langley said. He drew her onto his lap, and Lucas Kincaid's concerns were forgotten.

Epilogue

The Marquess of Ashingham's Townhouse
Mayfair, London
March, 1818

My dearest Isabelle,
    I love you. I will spend the time that we're apart counting the minutes until I see you again, and dreaming of the things I'll do to you when we're reunited.

Love,
Oliver

P. S. I understand you prefer your letters to be more than twenty-seven words long, so I have added this post-script.

P. P. S. I love you.

Isabelle set the letter on her dressing table with a smile.

"If you could keep your head still, Miss, I could get these pins in your hair," Daisy admonished her.

"I'm sorry, Daisy," Isabelle said contritely. Daisy had been in awe of Isabelle's status as a marchioness for about a week, after which she had seemed to forget Isabelle's exalted position.

Oliver strode into the room with Hermes at his heels, and his face lit up at the sight of his wife.

"I've missed you, Isabelle," he said, leaning down to kiss her cheek. His gaze lingered on her face before dropping down to the neckline of her gown. She was wearing a new dress of Pomona green silk, and the wolfish gleam in Oliver's eyes told her he approved of her choice.

He finally noticed Daisy, who was staring at him as though petrified. "Good evening, Daisy," he said absently. The maid blushed, bobbed a curtsy, and scurried out of the room. Although Daisy seemed to have forgotten that Isabelle was a marchioness, she never forgot that Oliver was a marquess.

"I hope she finished styling your hair," Oliver remarked. "Although if she didn't, we would have a good excuse to stay home tonight."

"We can't stay home, I promised Amelia we would be there," Isabelle told him. Amelia was hosting a ball in honour of Felicity Taylor, who had turned twenty-one and was finally making her *ton* debut.

"We could send her a note," Oliver suggested. "The Marquess and Marchioness of Ashingham regret that they are unable to attend. Lady Ashingham's maid was indisposed, so her hair could not be dressed, and she couldn't leave her bedchamber."

Isabelle laughed. "My hair will do well enough, Oliver," she told him. "I told Amelia you would dance with Felicity. You know that dancing with you will raise her credit in the *ton*."

"I don't want to dance with Miss Taylor."

"You sound like a schoolboy, Oliver," Isabelle chided.

"I don't see how anyone could fault me for wanting to spend an evening with my wife after such a prolonged separation."

Isabelle rolled her eyes. "Oliver, we were only apart for one night." He had written his love letter the previous morning, before travelling to Ashingham Court to ensure all was in order there. They had come to London for the winter, but since Oliver believed there was nothing worse for an estate than an absent landlord, he visited Ashingham every few weeks. Fortunately, the estate was only forty-five miles from London, so he could make the journey in the morning and return the following afternoon.

"The nights are longer in the winter, Isabelle, and it passed very slowly without you." He brightened. "Langley can dance with Miss Taylor. He's far more impressive than I am."

"I think you underrate yourself," Isabelle said.

The Marquess and Marchioness of Ashingham were society's most sought-after guests. When Malthaner first spread the rumour that Oliver had worked as a land agent at Stonecroft, it was seen as a good joke, but when it became known that Oliver had quietly married the beauty of the Season, Miss Isabelle Fleming, he was seen as either very fortunate or exceptionally clever. Many people believed that Oliver had taken the position at

Stonecroft to give himself the opportunity to court Isabelle. Malthaner's remarks had been accurately attributed to jealousy, and he had gone to the Continent to nurse his resentment.

"If you really think we're that noteworthy, we might be a distraction," Oliver mused. "This should be Miss Taylor's night, after all. And don't forget, Kincaid can dance with her too."

"Do you think that will be awkward, since he's her guardian?"

Oliver smiled. "Perhaps, but I expect he'll find a way to dance with her all the same. Between him and Langley, they won't need me."

"Perhaps not," Isabelle agreed. "But it will be an opportunity to see your parents. Your mother told me they plan to attend."

"Much as that's an inducement, Isabelle, I think I would still prefer to spend the evening with you." Oliver's parents were making an effort to build a relationship with him and Isabelle. Time seemed to have softened the duke, and it had also given Oliver a better understanding of him.

"But your parents hardly ever go to balls," Isabelle said. "They're only going tonight because the Langleys are your friends, and they expect you to be there."

"I suspect they're really going to see you," Oliver teased. His parents had liked Isabelle from the moment they met her. "You know they prefer your company to mine."

Isabelle shrugged. "I suppose I could go by myself."

As Isabelle had expected, Oliver decided that if his wife was going to the ball, he would go too. He rang for his valet, and half an hour later he was elegantly dressed in black pantaloons, an ivory waistcoat, and a navy blue tailcoat. His neckcloth was simply tied, and he wore no jewellery apart from a signet ring. Oliver's valet, Knowles, had quickly learned that the new Marquess of Ashingham favoured a plain style, and did not want to spend any more time getting dressed than was strictly necessary. Knowles had initially been disappointed that he couldn't showcase the full scope of his artistic talents, but he had to admit that Oliver's style suited him.

When he returned to Isabelle's bedchamber, he found her staring out the window, apparently lost in thought.

"Plotting your next novel?" he asked her.

"Something like that," Isabelle said with a smile. She had finished her first novel the previous autumn, with a significant change to the plot; the hazel-eyed butler was the new hero of the tale. Oliver had been concerned that readers would find the story unbelievable, but Isabelle thought people faced enough realism in their everyday lives, and many people seemed to agree with her. She had found a publisher for her work, and the novel had been released the month before to generally favourable reviews. At Isabelle's insistence, the book had been published anonymously; she wanted it to succeed or fail on its own merit.

But that night, Isabelle wasn't thinking about her writing. She was thinking about her own story, and how lucky she was to have found a husband who made her as happy as Oliver did. She thought Oliver was happy too; she knew the memories of the war hadn't left him, and she doubted they ever would, but they troubled him less frequently.

Oliver led his wife down the stairs to the entrance hall, where a chagrined footman advised him that the carriage wasn't ready yet. On impulse, Oliver turned down the hall to their own darkened ballroom and stuck his candle into a sconce on the wall. "I'm afraid I've forgotten how to dance," he teased Isabelle. "Since we have a ballroom, perhaps we should practise."

"We don't have any music," Isabelle pointed out.

"We don't need music."

Isabelle allowed Oliver to draw her into his arms, and he pressed her to him. The only light came from the single candle and the weak winter moonlight that streamed through the windows, but despite the darkness, Oliver knew every curve of her face.

"This is unlike any dance I've ever done," Isabelle said, resting her head on his shoulder.

"I told you I'd forgotten how." Oliver turned his head to whisper in her ear. "Do you remember the Maidstone Assembly, when you were concerned that I might not know how to dance?"

Isabelle laughed. "I felt very foolish when I saw you dancing with Felicity, and I realized that you dance better than I do."

"I didn't think you were foolish, Isabelle," he said seriously. "By then, I had loved you for a long time, but I hadn't wanted to admit it. That night, when you promised to dance with me, even if I barely knew the steps, I couldn't deny it any longer."

There was a noise in the doorway, and Isabelle saw their butler, Gilbert, turn and walk away.

"I think Gilbert saw us, Oliver," she said with a nervous laugh. "The servants will think it's odd that we're dancing in the dark."

"If you can believe it, Isabelle, I rarely think about the servants when I have you in my arms. But since you've brought it to mind, I expect they think it's natural for a man to want to dance with his wife after such a long time apart."

That brought a smile to her face. "Oliver, it was one night."

"As I said, a long time." He lifted her off the floor and spun her around before setting her gently back on her feet. "By now, I imagine the servants know that I'm in love with you. So long as it doesn't interfere with the payment of their wages, I doubt it's a matter of great concern to them."

"Perhaps not," Isabelle conceded. "You know, Oliver, I imagine the carriage is ready, and the sooner we leave for the ball, the sooner we can return."

Oliver saw the wisdom of his wife's argument, and led her out to the waiting carriage.

Acknowledgments

This book wouldn't have been possible without the support of my mother, who encouraged me to write, and my husband, who took over the parenting duties while I was doing so. I am grateful to Mary Matthews for her help with editing.